THE
GUILTY
PATIENT

BOOKS BY LUANA LEWIS

The Perfect Patient

THE
GUILTY
PATIENT

LUANA LEWIS

bookouture

Published by Bookouture in 2024

An imprint of Storyfire Ltd.
Carmelite House
50 Victoria Embankment
London EC4Y 0DZ

www.bookouture.com

Storyfire Ltd's authorised representative in the EEA is Hachette Ireland
8 Castlecourt Centre
Castleknock Road
Castleknock
Dublin 15 D15 YF6A
Ireland

ISBN: 978-1-83790-445-7
eBook ISBN: 978-1-83790-444-0

For Sam, Leor, Ella and Robbie

PROLOGUE

Appeal for Witnesses After Body Found in River Sheen

Oxfordshire Live

Officers and emergency services were called out on the morning of 2 March to a report of a body in the River Sheen outside Taybury Village. The deceased has been identified as Alice Kelly, 25, of London.

Investigating officer, Detective Constable Nina Ayola of Thames Valley Police, said: 'We would like to speak to any witnesses who may have seen Ms Kelly in the early hours of Sunday morning and who may be able to help police gather further information about what happened to her.'

The body was discovered by a local dogwalker who alerted emergency services. Gary Weaver of Sedgwick Road described the shock of finding Ms Kelly's body. 'I was walking my Labrador along the riverbank when she started behaving funny; she was very excited and wouldn't stop barking. I couldn't get her to come back to me so I went over to see what was going on, and that's when I saw the body. I couldn't believe what I was looking at. The water isn't too deep there, so I went in to get a closer look. The poor girl was floating face down and I tried to turn her over to check if she was still breathing, but I could tell it was too late.'

'Our thoughts are with Ms Kelly's family, who are being supported and kept up to date regarding the progress of our investigation,' Det Constable Ayola said.

Anyone with information has been urged to contact the police by calling 101 or making a report online.

ONE

'I'm scared I've killed someone.'

Mia Phillips spoke in a calm, flat voice as she sat in the armchair opposite Dr Tara Black.

Tara took a moment to regroup, blinking away her surprise. That was not what she had been expecting to hear her new client say. 'But you're not sure?'

'That's why I'm here.' Mia picked up the glass of water Tara had placed on the table beside her and drank half of it down. 'I want to know the truth.'

She was a petite, spiky-looking creature. Her hair was cropped short, emphasizing her lovely bone structure and large, dark eyes. Her black shirt and trousers were loose and asymmetric and paired with chunky boots so that the outfit hung together with a sense of edgy style. And, under that baggy clothing, Mia was heavily pregnant.

Tara cracked open the spine of her fresh notebook with its bright red cover. She smoothed down the first page with her palm and then wrote Mia's name and the date on the first two lines. Something about all those blank pages ahead, waiting to be filled with the intricate details of a life, always brought her a sense of anticipation. Of fresh hope.

Tara had more than twenty years' experience as a psychologist, but one of the things she loved most about her job was that whenever a new client sat down in the armchair opposite hers, she had no way of predicting what was about to happen.

'Who do you think you may have killed?' Tara asked.

'Her name was Alice Kelly,' Mia said, 'and she was my best friend. My only friend, really. Three years ago, we went away together for the weekend, to a cottage near Oxford. Alice went out for a walk the first night we were there, and she never came back. Her body was found in the river the next day. She had bruises everywhere.'

Mia spoke without much feeling, as though she was describing events from a television show she'd seen, rather than the violent death of her closest friend.

'So the police must have investigated Alice's death?'

Mia nodded. 'But they could never say for sure how she died. The coroner said that the bruises could have been caused by her body being in the water, and he couldn't rule out an accident. No one was ever charged or arrested.'

'And I assume you were interviewed by the police?'

'A few times.' Mia was looking somewhere past Tara's shoulder, as though she was lost in thought.

'Was there ever any suggestion that you were involved in Alice's death?'

'No.' Mia lapsed into silence. Then she stood up, pushing her hands into her back and stretching, before walking over to stand in front of the painting Tara had put up only recently. It was an abstract piece in blues and greens, with a yellow circle and two silvery shapes in the top left corner. Tara had picked it up at an art fair she'd gone to with Olivia; it reminded her of a happy place, of somewhere sunny and warm.

'Doctor Edwards told me that you're an artist?' Tara said.

Mia stayed staring at the painting, her back to Tara. 'No. I mean, I used to be interested in photography. Now I just work in an art gallery. For my mother-in-law.'

'I see.'

Mia had been referred to Tara's clinic by her colleague, forensic psychologist Anthony Edwards, who practised in Oxford. They had met while Tara had been working with Jade Jameson, a teenager accused of a murder she claimed to have no memory of committing.

'*The client wants to be seen urgently,*' he'd said on the phone, '*and I can't fit her in. If you have space, I think you might find this case interesting. It involves a recovered memory. A traumatic one.*'

Mia turned around, her eyes taking in everything around her. 'I like your office. It's calm in here.'

After so many years working in utilitarian, shared National Health Service hospital offices, Tara had put some of her soul into furnishing her consulting room, wanting to create an atmosphere that was as much welcoming as professional. She'd picked out mid-century modern-style vintage furniture: a simple desk and two upright grey-linen armchairs.

Her prized possession was the pale blue Persian rug that used to belong to her mentor, Neil. He had given Tara her first job and the two of them had gone on to work together in public hospitals for over a decade. When he'd retired, the rug had been a goodbye gift.

Having finished examining the room, Mia came to sit down again. She was staring down at her hands. Her nails were so badly bitten that raw skin was exposed underneath each one.

'If Alice died three years ago,' Tara said, breaking the silence, 'why have you decided to come forward now?'

'Because I only remembered what I did two days ago.' Mia paused, choosing her words more carefully. 'Well, that's not completely true. I saw some... things... before. But two days ago

I remembered everything and I haven't been able to think about anything else since. That's when I called Doctor Edwards. I researched psychologists who work with these kinds of cases, and I thought he'd be a good choice because he was in Oxford, which is near where Alice died. But he said you'd be the best person to help me. I really hope you can. Because I have to know if what I remember is real.'

For a few moments, Mia's eyes were desperate. Seconds later though, the blank expression was back.

Tara felt a small shiver. An unexpected jolt. It took her a moment to recognise the feeling as excitement. A sensation she hadn't felt in such a long while. For many months now, since Daniel had died, she'd felt little of anything.

'Let's start with Alice,' Tara said. 'How did the two of you meet?'

TWO

TEN YEARS EARLIER

Mia is in another box. She has spent most of her life in these boxes, these dismal rooms with small windows. She's lying on her back, on a bed with no linen, looking up at the ceiling. Even that is ugly: white pockmarked squares and a fluorescent strip light.

The room is narrow, maybe three metres by two and a half metres, and the walls are bare. The carpet is worn away in places and Mia suspects that the navy colour hides the dirt. There are bars on the window. She's heard there have been robberies on campus.

Her suitcase stands in front of the empty cupboard. She can't bring herself to unpack yet; the only thing she's taken out of it is her camera, which sits in the middle of the built-in desk

The other students in the shared flat are all in the living area and she can hear them laughing. Mia hasn't met them yet. She'd arrived as late as possible, at the end of freshers' week. She hadn't wanted to see everyone else arriving with their parents, kissing their families goodbye.

She feels a deep, deep sense of despair. She's sinking. Her

limbs are heavy as concrete, pinning her to the mattress. She doesn't know if she can do it, this time.

It will get better, she tries to convince herself, *when there is a routine, a class schedule, places I have to be, books I have to read, essays I have to write. This bad feeling inside me will fade. The bad thoughts will be pushed out.*

Someone taps on the door. Mia ignores the sound and carries on staring up at the square panels that all join together to make up the ceiling. Her head is filling up with fog. The white squares above her become blurry.

She hears the door opening and then a cheerful voice rings out. 'Hi, I'm Alice.'

There is a silence. 'Are you okay?'

It takes a huge effort, but Mia manages to turn her head. The girl, Alice, is wearing dramatic black eyeliner, and a tiny gold stud sparkles in her nose. Her thick auburn hair hangs to her waist.

'A couple of us are in the kitchen making dinner. Are you hungry?' Alice is looking around the bleak room and her eyes linger on Mia's still zipped up suitcase. She keeps talking, though Mia hasn't said a word. 'There's plenty of food, if you want to come and hang out. I'm a veggie, but the others aren't.'

'Thanks for asking, but I'm not hungry.'

'Are you Fine Arts too?' Alice says. 'All the others here are as well. I think they put us all together. The building we'll be in is a trek across the city but apparently there's a bus.'

Alice doesn't seem bothered by Mia's silence. She walks over to the desk and reaches out as if to pick up the Leica.

'Don't!' Mia sits up. 'Sorry, but please don't touch that.'

'It looks really expensive. Is it?'

Mia nods.

'Wow, I love it.' Alice pivots around and pouts. 'Will you photograph me?'

Mia sits up. 'Look, I don't do the whole friends thing. I prefer to be on my own.'

'Really?' Alice doesn't seem put off at all; she's more... intrigued. 'I admire that. I'm like a people addict; I can't spend two minutes on my own. I'll bet I can change your mind though, because I think we're going to have so much fun. You'll see. It's going to be amazing.'

The constant chatter is a relief and Mia feels herself relaxing. Her arms and legs don't feel so heavy, so pinned down anymore. Alice, in her mini-skirt and with all that wild hair, has brought an energy to the room that is hard to resist.

THREE

'From that first day, it was so easy to be Alice's friend,' Mia said, 'and that had never happened to me before. Most people find me awkward to be around, because I'm quiet and I get tongue-tied. But Alice was the opposite, she loved meeting new people and she was genuinely interested in everyone. It was true what she said, she didn't like being alone. And she never minded me being quiet.'

Tara was taking notes as Mia spoke. The first few pages of the fresh red notebook were already filling up with her scrawl, which included abbreviations that only she would be able to decipher and stars where she needed to go deeper into what Mia had said.

'You said that you and Alice were living together, at the time she died?'

Mia nodded. 'After first year of uni, Alice and I shared a flat for two more years in Bath, then we moved to London together and found a flat share in Clapham. I was taking a photography diploma and Alice was doing a management course. She was always more interested in the business side of things. We were both working part-time as well, trying to get experience at different art galleries—'

Mia was interrupted by the sound of her phone ringing. She took her mobile out of her bag, which was on the floor next to her chair, looked at the screen, then disconnected the call and tucked it back in again. When she sat back in her chair, she sighed and looked down fleetingly at her belly before looking up at Tara.

'When is your baby due?' Tara asked.

'In four weeks.' Absently, Mia began biting her thumbnail. She did not look down at her belly again. 'Alice wanted to open her own gallery one day. She was incredibly ambitious. She would have done it too.'

So far, everything Mia had said about her friend was positive and affectionate, which begged the obvious question: What would drive Mia to violence, whether real or imagined? What had happened in those years between the girls first meeting and Alice's death?

'Mia, why would you want to hurt someone you loved?'

'I don't know.'

For the first time in the interview, Tara sensed that her client wasn't being fully honest. 'You must have thought about that, though, now you've had this memory?'

Mia bit down on her thumbnail so hard that Tara flinched. 'I haven't thought about anything else.'

'But you haven't come up with an answer?'

'I don't want to believe I would hurt her on purpose.'

Mia had not yet told Tara exactly what she had remembered doing to Alice. Tara glanced at the clock and decided there wasn't enough time left in the appointment to go there; she wanted to get some more background information first, to get some idea of Mia's personality. She would delve into Mia's memory of Alice's death in detail in their next session, which was scheduled for the following day.

For the rest of their meeting, Tara focused on Mia's life history. Mia was twenty-eight years old. She was an only child, born in Leicester, but her family had moved around frequently during her childhood. Her father was an engineer working on mining contracts and they'd lived all over Europe and the Middle East. Her mother had died of cancer when she was seven. Again, Mia had told Tara this without emotion, claiming she couldn't remember much about her mother. She'd then been looked after by a series of nannies, none of whom seemed to have been significant in her life. Mia had attended international schools before returning to England, to an all-girls boarding school when she was fourteen. She said she'd been fine academically but struggled socially and had always felt isolated.

Mia's father now lived in St Albans, with his second wife and their two children. She described their relationship as 'fine' but 'distant'. They apparently didn't see each other often.

Mia had been married to her husband, mathematics teacher Tom Phillips, for two years. She seemed positive when she spoke about him, and proud when she told Tara he had recently been promoted to deputy head at the comprehensive secondary school where he worked. Mia herself was employed full-time at an art gallery in Hampstead that was owned by Tom's mother, Julia Leonard.

She reported no significant illnesses and no mental health diagnoses, and she was not taking any medication. She had no criminal record.

So, other than some difficulty with forming friendships, there weren't any real clues as to why Mia feared she may be a killer.

'Have you ever been violent before?' Tara asked her.

Mia shook her head. Her phone began ringing again and this time when she retrieved it from her bag, she looked down at the screen a little longer. 'I'm sorry, I have to take this call.'

'Go ahead.'

Mia heaved herself out of the chair with some effort, her body off balance from her swollen belly. She went over to the window, speaking with her back to Tara, sounding both apologetic and somewhat submissive.

'I'm sorry. I forgot... I will, yes... I said I will. I promise. I'm so sorry, I'll have to call you back. I can't speak now, I'm in the middle of something at work.'

Mia disconnected the call and came to sit down again, still clasping the phone in her hand.

'Is everything all right?' Tara asked.

'I had an appointment at the hospital and I completely forgot about it. My husband's been waiting for me.' Mia glanced up at the clock on the wall. 'I haven't told Tom I'm seeing you. I haven't told him anything about... this. I don't want him to know, until I'm sure. One way or the other.'

Tara closed her notebook with the pen propped inside. 'There is one thing I need to tell you before we go any further. If we do discover that this memory is real, and that you are responsible in some way for Alice's death, then the police will need to be informed. I can help you with that, but it would need to happen. With or without your permission. Do you understand?'

Mia nodded. Her arms and shoulders tensed up as her hands gripped the armrests, her fingertips digging into the fabric. 'I understand. Whatever happens, I need to know what I did. And if I need to be punished.'

FOUR

The office was getting stuffy with the heating on and Tara opened the windows to let in some air before her afternoon session. From where she stood, she had a calming view over a small garden square opposite her building.

Tara's clinic was in a two-storey mews house, tucked away on one of the streets behind Marylebone Station. She had bought the small building two years earlier, when she'd started a private practice after working in public hospitals for almost two decades. The mortgage had been eye-watering and she had managed it only with the help of a significant loan from her partner, Daniel. The plan had been to share the running costs with her colleague and friend Olivia, a psychiatrist, but that plan had to be put on hold when Olivia had fallen pregnant by mistake and taken a year's maternity leave.

And then, in a sick twist of fate, the insurance money from Daniel's death had saved the clinic. He had insisted that Tara take out a policy that would cover the mortgage in full. A policy that neither of them ever thought they would need because neither of them could have imagined that Daniel would not live to see his fiftieth birthday.

When she'd started the clinic, Tara had wanted to work with complex therapy cases, but that too had changed after Daniel died. For the past year, she'd only taken on assessment reports for high level managerial positions while she dealt with her own emotional fallout. That type of work paid well but it didn't exactly have the adrenaline factor. Which was perhaps why Tara had agreed to see Mia at such short notice when Anthony had explained that the case involved a traumatic, previously buried memory.

Tara also had to admit that she was drawn to the darker cases, the ones that resonated with her own ghosts. Her parents had been murdered when she was sixteen and their case too remained unsolved.

After standing at the window a while, letting the soothing view wash over her, Tara went back to her desk to go over her notes. In many ways, Mia's case was unlike anything she had worked on before. For a start, criminal cases were usually referred to her through solicitors, not by the clients themselves. This was also the first time anyone in Tara's office had actually wanted to confess to murder.

Mia was full of contradictions. On the one hand, she was shy and soft spoken, and she seemed sad and lost, and all of that evoked a feeling of empathy and protectiveness in Tara. But there was a different side to her too. Mia had told her story with so little emotion and she had been guarded about telling Tara why she might want to hurt her best friend. It was hard to believe that she did not at least have some idea about why she might commit the ultimate act of violence.

If Mia was responsible for Alice's death, perhaps in some kind of dissociative episode where she'd blanked out, could she be dangerous? Tara had not felt at risk while sitting opposite her new client, but then they had not touched on the killing itself in the first interview.

Tempting as it was to open her browser and scour the

internet for more information on Mia Phillips and Alice Kelly, Tara held back. She tried not to research clients too early in the process, because she needed to form her own first impressions without being influenced by media reports or whatever else might be found in cyberspace.

After Tara had reviewed her notes and typed them up, she made herself a coffee and sat down to check her email while waiting for her next client to arrive. A couple of new enquiries had come through. And there was another one of those emails she had been avoiding.

Pierre Henry. Tara sat and stared at his name a while without touching the keyboard.

In his first message, Henry had explained that he was a senior partner in a law firm in Switzerland and that he needed to meet with her regarding a financial matter. Tara had initially assumed it was a scam, but when she looked up the company, it seemed legitimate. The website showed a picture of Pierre Henry, a refined-looking older man who was a named partner.

Instinct told her that this was not a coincidence. Daniel had often travelled to Switzerland, among other places, for work. That was partly how he had managed to spend nights with Tara while his wife Sabine believed he was away on business. The last work trip he'd ever taken had been to Geneva. As far as she could remember, there had been nothing out of the ordinary about it; two construction companies merging into one, or something to that effect. Daniel had never really talked much about his work. He'd always said that while his role in mergers and acquisitions was lucrative, it wasn't particularly exciting.

Tara did remember that Daniel had come straight to her place after landing at Heathrow.

She felt the usual flickers of guilt and shame as the thoughts lurking at the back of her mind pushed forwards. *If it wasn't for you, Daniel would still be alive. He should not have been walking beside you that night. You insisted he take you out for*

*dinner. You were the one who wanted to stop hiding. But he had
a family. If it wasn't for you, Daniel's children would still have
their father.*

Tara had been lucky. Her injuries in the hit-and-run were
mild, a fractured clavicle and a concussion. Daniel had lost his
life.

She couldn't bring herself to open that email.

She was relieved when the doorbell rang. Her client was
right on time.

Later that evening, back home at her cottage in the Garden
Suburb in London, Tara dropped her gym bag down inside the
front door. Her shoulders were already aching after the kettle
bells class.

She'd forgotten to turn any lights on before leaving that
morning and the house was dark, inside and out. And terribly
quiet. She closed her eyes a moment, listening for the sound of
Daniel's voice.

It's so good to be back. He'd let himself in and set his suitcase down in the hallway. Then he'd hang up his coat, always
on the same peg, the one right on the end. He'd take off his tie.
Then he would come over to where Tara was waiting at the
kitchen door and hold her.

Those small, comforting routines that she'd taken for
granted and that she could not bear to forget.

Tara wandered through to the kitchen and found herself
standing in front of the open, mostly empty fridge. She
supposed she should eat something, but she couldn't be
bothered.

With coffee brewing on the stove, Tara sat down at her
kitchen table intending to finally open Pierre Henry's latest
message, but she was distracted by an email from Mia at the top
of her inbox. The subject line read: *Important.*

Mia explained that she'd had gone to her rescheduled ante-natal check-up late that afternoon and that the consultant was concerned about her blood pressure, which was higher than it should be. Apparently, she'd also been experiencing headaches and blurred vision. Mia had been advised to take a few days off work and to rest as much as possible. She was concerned about driving or using public transport to travel to Tara's office in central London. Mia said that although she was very keen to see Tara, she had to delay their next meeting until she got the all-clear from her doctor.

Tara was reluctant to leave the gap between sessions too long, given Mia's impending due date. Plus, there was always the possibility the baby could be born early, especially if Mia was having complications. Ideally, she wanted to complete the assessment within ten days.

Tara made her decision quickly and sent a reply offering to go and see Mia at home. Besides the other practicalities, it would give her a chance to get a glimpse inside Mia's life.

Within minutes, Mia had responded, gratefully accepting Tara's suggestion.

Tara took a sip of her strong coffee. Right. Pierre's email. She opened it.

This one was pretty much the same as the previous message he'd sent her. He wanted to set up a meeting about a time-sensitive financial matter. Tara pressed the reply button and began typing. *Thank you for your email.* She asked for more details before agreeing to a meeting. She clicked send, still hoping she was wrong about the link to Daniel.

FIVE

Mia and Tom Phillips lived in Wembley, a large suburb north-west of London which was in the catchment area of the school where Tom worked. The neighbourhood was diverse and buzzing, with a good selection of shops, restaurants and bars, and some lovely green spaces. Tara could see Mia feeling at home there; it matched her edgy vibe.

The couple's apartment was on the third floor of a stylish new development not far from the station. Mia looked quite well when she opened the front door. She was casually dressed in a close-fitting top, pulled over her bump, and velvet tracksuit trousers. Her face was make-up free but glowing, and she was barefoot.

Tara was relieved but surprised to see her so at ease, given the concerns about possible pre-eclampsia symptoms of headache and blurred vision she'd mentioned in her email.

The apartment was compact, but well-appointed and modern. As Tara stepped through the front door into the entrance hall, she could see through into a small room, which looked like it would become the nursery. A crib was pushed up against the far wall, still completely covered in plastic. Beside

that were several shopping bags stacked on the floor, presumably full of equipment they would need for the baby, and all of
them unopened. There was nothing else in there, nothing on
the walls and no curtains. The room had a hollow feel about it.

Tara paused, staring in. 'It looks like you're starting to get
the nursery ready.'

'My mother-in-law has done most of the shopping.' Mia's
tone was rather dismissive.

Tara was beginning to notice that Mia tended to avoid any
discussion of the fact that she was soon to become a mother.
And while pregnant women often touched their bellies, Mia
barely even looked at hers.

'How are you feeling about the baby?'

Mia shrugged. Then her eyes welled up and it looked as
though her sadness was about to break through. But the tears
did not come; she blinked them back. 'I'm not excited. I know
I'm not supposed to admit that, but it's true.'

'And your husband?'

'Tom is thrilled. He can't wait.' Abruptly, Mia turned away
and walked through to the living room.

Unlike the nursery, this space was cosy and furnished with
attention to detail. It was open plan, not large but bright and
airy. A sleek kitchen took up one wall while the living area was
on the other side with an L-shaped sofa and a large, happy-
looking Yucca plant dominating the space. A set of French
doors led out onto a tiny balcony.

Black and white photographs of the London skyline lined
the walls, but Tara's eyes were immediately drawn to the large,
framed photograph of a woman that was propped up on the
desk in the corner.

Mia walked over to where the picture had been placed and
adjusted the frame, checking it was securely balanced against
the wall. 'This is Alice.'

Tara moved closer so she could get a good look at the photograph. It was a close-up of Alice Kelly's head and shoulders as she faced the camera head on. Alice had a strong face, not classically beautiful, but compelling, with a powerful sensuality captured in the black and white tones. Her almond-shaped eyes were emphasised with a sweep of black eyeliner, and they burned out of the photograph with the intensity and beauty of youth. A heart-shaped pendant around her neck lay close to her throat.

It was terrible to think that the young woman in that photograph had lost her life at only twenty-five years old.

'Yesterday, you asked me why I would want to hurt her,' Mia said.

'Yes. And you didn't give me an answer.'

Mia ran her fingers over the glass covering Alice's face. Tara felt a small shiver down her back as she watched her.

'I was jealous.' Mia turned her back to Tara as she said this, as though she was ashamed. 'Because of Tom.'

'Your husband?'

'Yes. He loved Alice first.'

SIX

THREE MONTHS BEFORE ALICE'S DEATH

Three portraits of Alice hang on the back wall of the art gallery, dominating the white-washed room. The photograph in the centre, a close-up of Alice's face, is Mia's favourite. It captures her friend's soul and her fierce spirit. Alice's eyes burn into the people who look at her.

In the other two photographs, Alice is nude. In a tasteful way, though. In one of them, stripes from the window blinds fall across Alice's torso, enticing the viewer to want to look deeper, to see what's underneath. The third photo, Mia has to admit, is a copycat of her hero, Bill Brandt, but she doesn't care because she's still only a student and he is her inspiration. In that one, only Alice's crossed legs are visible, and behind them, there is a view out of the window of their shared flat. The angle of Alice's legs frames the tower block opposite.

Right now, Alice is across the room, standing arm in arm with her mother, who has come down for the evening to see the exhibition. The two of them are laughing, their heads close together, and Mia feels very alone. Her father couldn't make it. Instead, he sent flowers with a predictably impersonal printed message. *Well done! Dad.*

Julia has come to stand beside Mia. She brings with her the floral scent of her favourite perfume as she hands Mia a glass of white wine. 'You should be proud.'

'Thank you,' Mia says, 'and I'm so grateful. Really. I can't thank you enough.'

As part of their final assignment, the students on Mia's diploma in photography had to put on an exhibition of their work and Julia had offered them her art gallery to host the show. This was a huge coup as the diploma was through a community college, and hardly a prestigious enough course for a display at Julia's place in Hampstead.

The doorbell jingles and when Mia looks across the room, her heart swells and gallops. Julia's two sons have arrived. First there's Freddie, and then right behind him, Tom.

Tom.

An older man follows the two brothers into the gallery. Mia doesn't recognise him, but given the way Julia's expression changes and her body stiffens, she suspects it must be Julia's ex-husband, David – the boys' father. He keeps his distance while the two boys come straight over to say hello to their mother.

'Our very own Ian Rankin.' Freddie gives Mia a playful punch on the arm.

Mia feels her cheeks go bright red. Freddie had helped all the students hang their paintings. On permanent sick leave from the army, he's always around doing odd jobs at the gallery. She's too shy to get a single word out.

Tom isn't looking at her, though; he's staring at the portraits of Alice.

Julia and her boys are laughing now, chatting about something or other, but Mia zones out. She slips away into the small kitchen at the back of the gallery where she busies herself refilling jugs of water and opening another box of cheap white wine. She washes up a few glasses that have collected in the sink. None of this really needs doing, but Mia needs a break.

Being with other people is so exhausting; she would feel much happier if she was behind the lens of her camera.

She wishes she had her Leica with her now, so she could capture the angles of Tom's face. She rearranges the clean wine glasses into neat lines on the paper towel, picturing his eyes. Green or blue, depending on the day and the colour of his clothing.

Mia delays a couple more minutes, drying the glasses, until she decides she had better go back out, or it will seem weird. When she returns to the gallery, the exhibition is buzzing. More and more people are arriving, crowding the space. All the other students have family and friends there, supporting them.

Alice is standing in front of her portraits and Mia goes to join her.

Alice takes hold of Mia's hand and gives her a brief squeeze. 'You make me look so beautiful.'

And now Tom comes over to join them. He stands in front of those portraits, gazing at Alice in wonder.

Alice is right, she is more luminous in those photographs than she is in real life. This is the first time that Tom really sees her. It's the way he will always see her.

Mia's hands tighten into fists as she digs what is left of her fingernails deep into her palms.

SEVEN

Mia was standing at the desk, staring at the close-up of Alice's face as she described the night of the exhibition, and the first moment she had realised that Tom was falling for Alice.

'I know it sounds ridiculous, but I loved Tom the moment I laid eyes on him. He came into the gallery to see Julia one day, and that was it. I've loved him ever since.'

'It doesn't sound ridiculous.'

Tara had felt the same way about Daniel. He had been her brother's best friend and the first time Matthew had brought him home from school, Tara had taken one look at him and she had known. She had only been nine years old then, but her feelings had never changed. There was such a thing as love – or at least chemistry – at first sight. Something powerful and primitive and real.

Tara had gone over to the kitchen counter, where she was balancing her notebook as she wrote. 'Were Tom and Alice seeing each other at the time she died?'

'They'd been inseparable for about three months.'

'It must have been difficult, living with Alice and seeing the two of them together.'

Mia nodded. 'I hated myself, because of this kind of... greed for what they had. I literally felt sick with envy, sometimes. My headaches were really bad those few months.'

'Did Alice know how you felt about Tom?'

'I think she guessed I had a crush on him, but I don't think she knew... how much it hurt. I never told her. And it didn't matter how I felt because Tom wanted Alice. He didn't see me.'

'Until after Alice died?'

Mia swallowed. 'Tom and I... I guess we were both in shock. It's all such a blur now, but after Alice died we spent so much time together, and then, on the day of her funeral, we...' Mia sighed, then tailed off. 'It sounds terrible. But it wasn't like that. We both just missed her so much.'

Tara noted how choppy Mia's speech was when she talked about Alice and Tom's relationship. Even now, she struggled with what it brought up inside her.

Mia pressed her fingertips into her temples and closed her eyes a moment. 'I stole her life, didn't I?'

Mia picked up the portrait of Alice, took a long last look at it, then opened the desk drawer and tucked the photograph inside, before closing it firmly.

'Are you ready to tell me what you remember doing to Alice?' Tara asked.

Mia nodded. But she wasn't saying anything.

'You said that this memory came back to you two days ago. Could you start by telling me where you were and what you were doing when this happened?'

Mia paced up and down between the desk and the balcony door as she spoke. 'I remember I had one of my headaches when I woke up that day. I get them a lot, but this was a really bad one. There was this sharp pain behind my eyes and all the way down my neck and I couldn't take painkillers because...'

Mia stopped short of saying that it was because she was pregnant. There was a brief pause before she continued. 'So I'd been awake since three in the morning, and by the time I got to Carolyn's office for my appointment, it was like my head was full of fog.'

Tara interrupted. 'Who is Carolyn?'

'Carolyn Goring. My psychotherapist. I'd been seeing her for almost two months.'

Tara took a moment to absorb this new piece of information. 'Are you saying that this memory came back to you in a therapy session?'

'Yes. That's right.' Mia went over to the balcony doors and opened them wide, letting in a rush of cold air. 'Carolyn knew that a close friend of mine had died. I told her I didn't want to talk about it, but she kept asking about Alice. She wanted to know everything about her. About us. Carolyn was convinced that Alice's death was connected to some of the problems I'd been having.'

'What sort of problems?'

Mia glanced down at her belly, but her eyes didn't stay there long. 'Since I found out I was pregnant, I haven't been sleeping properly. The headaches are getting worse too, and they come more often. I'm so tired that some days I don't want to get out of bed. If Julia didn't need me at the gallery, I'd just stay under my duvet. I don't feel happy about anything, even though I have so much to be happy about.'

Tara went over to sit down on the sofa. Mia was still pacing.

'Okay. Tell me more about the session where this memory came back.'

'Like I said, I felt foggy... strange, all over the place. I didn't speak much at first. I remember lying on my back, looking up at the chandelier, and all I could think about was the pain. It felt like my head was full of nails and it was going to explode from the pressure. But then... I was seeing all these shimmering crystal drops, shaped like tears, and I could hear Carolyn's voice, saying *"Tell me about the night Alice died."* Over and over and over. And at first the crystals were empty, but then I started to see colours inside them. Red, yellow, blue. And then I started really looking and inside each bead of glass, I could see things.'

So far what Mia was describing sounded more like a hallucination than a memory, as if she had been in some kind of dissociated state of mind. Surely Mia's therapist would have picked that up?

Tara waited, but Mia said nothing more and so she prompted her a little. 'So you started to see things inside the beads of the chandelier. What exactly did you see?'

Mia sighed. She wiped something away under each of her eyes, but there were no tears. 'I'm sorry. I thought I was ready for this, but I can't go through it again. Not yet.'

Tara suppressed a flicker of frustration. She was acutely aware of time passing. Mia was thirty-six weeks pregnant and there wasn't any time to lose.

Still though, this was a balancing act. Pushing Mia too far too soon wouldn't help her blood pressure and high levels of stress could distort her memories further.

'So, to be clear,' Tara said, 'before this therapy session, you had no memory at all of hurting Alice?'

'Nothing. I've never—I've always thought I was asleep in bed when she went out that night.' Mia was staring down at her hands, pressing the pad of her thumb against each of her ragged fingernails in turn.

'And in that session, did you describe what you were seeing to Carolyn?'

Mia nodded.

'Did she ask you any questions to try and understand whether it was something that had really happened, as opposed to your imagination?'

Mia shook her head. 'I wanted Carolyn to tell me that what

I saw wasn't real. But she didn't, she just kept pushing me. She made me go over that night, again and again and again, every-thing, every single second until I couldn't take it anymore. I got up and left and I never went back to that office after that session.'

'Would you feel comfortable giving me permission to see Carolyn's case notes about your treatment?'

'Sure, if that will help.' Mia had answered without hesita-tion. She seemed about to say something else but was inter-rupted by the sound of the front door opening and a voice calling out hello.

Seconds later, a man walked into the living room. He was classically good looking, square-jawed and broad shouldered. He also took care with his appearance. Tara observed that he was clean shaven, with neatly cut dark hair and dressed in a well-fitting suit.

'What are you doing home?' Mia looked embarrassed, as though she'd been caught doing something she shouldn't be.

Tara assumed this must be Tom, Mia's husband.

'I was worried about you. You haven't been picking up your phone.' Tom looked at Tara, clearly surprised to see her sitting in his living room. 'What's going on?'

'I... I had this appointment with Doctor—' Mia looked at Tara as her words faded. She was so flustered that she was blanking out and could barely remember Tara's name.

Tara stood up to introduce herself. 'I'm Tara Black.'

Tom shook Tara's hand in a distracted way, still looking at his wife. 'What kind of appointment?'

'She's a psychologist,' Mia said.

'A psychologist?' As Tom approached Mia, bending down to kiss her cheek, Mia subtly moved away from him.

'How's the headache?' he asked her.

'Much better.'

'Have you eaten today?'

'Tom, please. Stop.' Mia began biting down hard on her thumbnail.

The couple were facing each other, close, but not touching, and the strain between them was obvious. Mia was uncomfortable that Tom had walked in on them; she had not expected him to come home.

'I think I need to lie down,' Mia said. 'Is it okay if we finish for today?'

EIGHT

After she'd left Mia and Tom's flat, Tara looked up Carolyn Goring's website. Much like Tara's own, it was brief and to the point, providing only the basic details about Carolyn's practice on Harley Street. Carolyn was a psychoanalytic psychotherapist with over twenty years' experience. Her photograph, which looked like a professional headshot, showed a confident, warm-looking woman somewhere in her late fifties. The site also had a note saying that Carolyn was currently fully booked and had a waiting list of several months.

When she got back to her office, Tara sent an email to Carolyn, introducing herself and explaining that she had Mia's permission to see her case notes. She included a scan of a consent form that Mia had signed.

In the meantime, a response to her email from Pierre Henry had arrived. He confirmed that the matter he wanted to discuss was related to the estate of Daniel Franks. Even though Tara had sensed this was coming, she still felt a dull thud of shock in her core. She read on. The solicitor was in London for a series of client meetings and he suggested they meet in person to have a discussion. That evening, if possible. Despite the strong urge to avoid whatever this was, Tara sent an email straight back, saying she'd be there.

That done, Tara headed into the kitchenette to make a strong pot of coffee. As she opened the cupboard and reached up for the coffee pods, the scent of Olivia's cranberry teabags, tart and energising, rushed out at her.

She missed the distant murmuring of Olivia's voice, the sound of her footsteps as she let her clients in and out of the building, and most of all, their frequent check-ins about their lives and cases in this tiny kitchen. She couldn't get used to the solitude of private practice since Olivia had been on maternity leave. Like Tara's home, the clinic was too quiet.

While she waited for the coffee to drip through, Tara's mind was pulled back to the impending meeting with the Swiss solicitor. Her heart beat faster at the thought of it.

To distract herself, she opened WhatsApp, scrolling through a new set of photos of Jonah which Olivia had sent through the day before. Tara messaged her friend back, confirming their lunch date. She wasn't yet ready to tell anyone about the Swiss solicitor.

The rest of the day was spent with Donna Allders, a young woman who was being considered for a position as a financial analyst in an investment firm where she would have access to highly sensitive and confidential client information. Donna was barely out of her twenties and Tara was surprised both at how young she looked and how casually she was dressed. She arrived for her interview in jeans and trainers and with wet hair, as though she'd just stepped out of the shower.

This was interesting because the company she was applying to was conservative and strait-laced. Tara wondered whether Donna was showing her rebellious side, or if maybe part of her didn't really want the constraints of this job?

The major part of this first interview consisted of psychometric questionnaires, which would take Donna around ninety minutes to complete on a tablet. While her client was focused on that task, Tara felt a growing apprehension about her meeting about Daniel's estate.

She distracted herself by checking her schedule for the following day. Her next appointment with Mia Phillips was scheduled for late morning, at her home. There hadn't been any response yet from Mia's psychotherapist about the case notes, but then it had only been a couple of hours since Tara had contacted her.

Tara glanced up at Donna, who sat opposite her across the desk, frowning as she concentrated on the questionnaire. The afternoon passed in a relaxed silence that felt like the calm before the storm.

Once Donna had left, Tara still had half an hour to kill before the meeting with Pierre Henry. Restless now, with nervous energy flowing through her entire body, Tara tidied her office. She changed the angle of her two armchairs, so they were facing each other perfectly square on. She fluffed up the cushions, checked that the tissue boxes were full and dusted the side tables. Next, she vacuumed, taking special care over Neil's rug. Tara went over to her desk and sent her old colleague an email, asking how he was enjoying his retirement. She suggested they find a time to grab a coffee.

After that, she vacuumed the stairs.

Finally, it was time to leave.

Pierre Henry had asked Tara to meet him at a private members' club in Mayfair. The place had the luxurious feel of old money: all charcoal-painted walls and antique furniture. A fire crackled inside the hearth of a limestone fireplace, and solid walls and doors ensured privacy.

They sat with cups of coffee in front of them, served in white bone china. For once though, Tara had no desire for caffeine. There was enough adrenaline pumping through her veins already.

Pierre, silver haired with wire-rimmed glasses, had greeted her with an elegant foreign accent and a brief handshake. He explained that he was an executor of Daniel Franks' estate.

'Did you know Daniel well?' she asked.

'Actually, not at all. Mister Franks dealt with one of my colleagues at the firm, who has since moved on. I took over after the very sad circumstances of his death.' Pierre had kind eyes.

Tara did not want to feel the sadness that was always there, pushing up under the surface. It had only been a year since Daniel had died, but it felt like a decade. She felt as though the last shreds of her youth had died with him.

'So, as I mentioned, with my colleague leaving, and the inevitable bureaucracy, it has taken time to unravel various matters. But I can now inform you that you have been named as a beneficiary in Daniel Franks' will.'

Tara nodded, feeling sick at the thought. People close to her had a habit of dying too young. Unexpectedly. Violently.

The road is slick after the rain. Empty. A string of coloured lights sways in the night-time breeze. Daniel's arm is heavy across her shoulders.

'We're both unhappy,' he says. 'I'm going to ask Sabine for a divorce.'

'Please don't leave your family because of me.'

A hum at the edges of her awareness. A car in the distance. The sound of an engine picking up speed.

Tara blinked herself back to the room as Pierre opened the leather folder he held on his lap. 'There is a Swiss bank account containing funds that are ready to be transferred to you once the relevant documents are completed. I can also make provision for you to open an account in your name, similar to the one that Daniel held.'

This information came as a complete shock. Why would she want or need a Swiss bank account?

Tara shifted in her chair. Her shoulder was aching. That happened sometimes, a reminder of her injuries after the accident. It always hurt more when she was tense.

Daniel had wanted to provide for her and to make sure she was secure, and Tara tried to take comfort in that. But there was no way she could accept this money.

'I would like the funds to be returned to Daniel's family. Can you help me to arrange that?'

'Before you decide, there are other considerations you should be aware of.' Pierre lifted his coffee cup and took a sip. She noticed the faint grey hairs on his wrist and the sound of the ticking of the grandfather clock in the corner. 'I would like to go through these with you if I may?'

She nodded.

'The account currently contains a sum of one million euros. An amount of money has regularly been transferred out of this account, on a monthly basis, to a different account.'

'A different account?' There was silence as Tara absorbed this, trying to work out what was really being said.

Pierre nodded. 'Yes.'

'Who owns this account?'

'If you agree to accept this bequest, and once we have all the documentation in order, you will have all the details of the bank account and the transfers that were made. It will be up to you to decide whether to continue making these transactions. You would of course be free to use this money however you choose; you're under no obligation. But Mister Franks wanted you to have all of this information.'

'Is Daniel's wife aware of this inheritance?'

The solicitor cleared his throat. 'Mister Franks' instruction was that this was to remain a strictly private matter.'

NINE

Tara had left the meeting with Pierre Henry and walked, with no sense of where she was going – the world around her a swarm of people and a blur of oncoming headlights. There were tremors in the pavements beneath her feet as the walls around her heart cracked open.

By eleven o'clock that night she was still wired up and she found herself at the front door of her cottage, pulling on her trainers and slipping outside.

She had promised herself she would stop going back to the old house. She shouldn't risk it, not after the last time, when people living on Wildway Close had reported her strange behaviour, and a police car had arrived to drive her home.

For over a year, she'd kept her word, but tonight her legs had a momentum of their own and she could no longer resist the pull. She walked the route she had not taken in almost a year,

There must be a reason that Daniel had wanted her to have the money in that bank account.

There was only one person Tara could think of whom Daniel could have been supporting all this time. A person closely connected to her. A person who needed to remain in hiding.

Her head was spinning too fast to know if she was thinking straight. But she could not come up with any other explanation for this strange and secretive inheritance.

Matthew. *My brother could be alive.*

Why else would Daniel set up this elaborate inheritance?

Within minutes, Tara was back at her childhood home, sitting on the grass verge, concealed in the shadows. A four-bed, golden brick and ivy house on a cul-de-sac right next to Hampstead Heath. A place for families. A house of pain.

I didn't hear anything. I was asleep.

Tara could still see the look in the police officers' eyes. Suspicion. Disbelief. No one believed her story that she did not remember. No one but Daniel.

I don't know where my brother is.

Tara was sweating in the cold.

For decades, she had tried to feel her way around the dark corners of her memory but there was never anything more to find. All that remained were flashes of a bloodstained pillow and blood spatter against a white wall.

A year earlier, after she'd lost Daniel, she had decided to accept the not knowing. Life was short and precious, and she had to make the most of what she had left and move forwards. But it had been far easier to make that decision when she didn't actually have any way of finding the answers she had craved for so many years. Now that might have changed.

It was suddenly obvious to Tara what she was going to do. What she needed to do. She could not let this opportunity go because it might be a chance to stop living in limbo. She would accept Daniel's inheritance and she would find out where he had been sending that money all these years. She could leave yet another question in her life unanswered. She needed the truth.

TEN

First thing the next morning, Tara parked outside her own office and then took a walk across to Harley Street. Carolyn Goring, Mia's ex-psychotherapist, had sent an email late the night before to say that Tara could pick up a copy of Mia's case notes, and that Carolyn would be free to hand these over at eight o'clock.

The day was chilly but sunny and Tara's pace was brisk. The movement helped to settle her mind, which was still swirling after the meeting with the Swiss solicitor and her late-night visit to Wildway Close.

There is a Swiss bank account containing funds that are ready to be transferred to you once the relevant documents are completed.

Mister Franks' instruction was that this was to remain a strictly private matter.

On Harley Street she passed a series of imposing buildings, with name plaques listing different clinics and medical services. Just before she reached Wigmore Street, she found the building she was looking for, the Horizon Clinic. The place had a grand feel, with high ceilings and polished parquet floors.

After giving her name at the desk in the lobby, one of the receptionists led her up a wide, curved staircase to an office on the first floor.

There was a solid, matronly feel about Carolyn Goring, with her soft curves, flowing cream top and sensible shoes. Her office had the same tranquil, slightly old-fashioned feel as Carolyn herself, with sunshine-yellow silk curtains and heavy antique furniture. Like Tara, Carolyn had two wingback armchairs, but she also had a therapy couch. That was where Mia would have been lying down when she'd seen herself hurting Alice.

Tara glanced up at the ceiling. The chandelier was exactly as Mia had described it, with rows of cascading crystal teardrops.

'Please, take a seat,' Carolyn said.

The two of them faced each other across the uncluttered desk with its worn, green leather top. On its surface were a square clock and two small wooden figurines, which looked like African fertility dolls.

An A4 envelope with Tara's name on it lay in front of Carolyn. She placed a hand protectively down on top of it. 'I've made a photocopy of Mia's file for you.'

Carolyn didn't sound too thrilled about that, and Tara didn't blame her. The confidentiality of the therapy relationship was sacred, and breaking it always felt wrong.

'Thank you. I appreciate you coming back to me so quickly.'

'I understand you're a clinical psychologist?' Carolyn kept her hand firmly on top of that envelope. She was in no rush to hand over Mia's notes.

'Yes, that's right, I run a private practice in Marylebone.'

'Have you been there long?'

'Almost two years now.'

'And before that?' Carolyn wore a pair of reading glasses on a chain around her neck and she put these on as she looked at Tara more closely.

'I was in the NHS,' Tara said, 'in the Neurology Service at the Royal University Hospital.'

'What sort of cases do you take on in your clinic?'

'Psychological assessments, mainly. Profiling for managerial roles as well as family and criminal cases. I also have an interest in memory disorders.'

'Do you offer psychotherapy?'

'No. Not at the moment.' Tara was surprised to find herself under scrutiny. Carolyn's gaze was intense and she felt her cheeks heating up.

'Why is that?' Carolyn removed her reading glasses, letting them hang down again on the chain. Her eyes lit up with curiosity.

'Personal reasons,' Tara said.

Because Daniel's death was the last straw and I can't carry other people's pain anymore.

'I see.'

Carolyn had hit on a sensitive topic and Tara was sure that her flushed cheeks were a giveaway that she was uncomfortable. She had the feeling that Carolyn Goring was looking for the chinks in her armour. But then, Tara knew she had a tendency to be suspicious when the conversation turned personal. She was on much more solid ground when focusing on the lives of others.

'So Mia isn't seeing you to continue her psychotherapy?' Carolyn had relaxed back in her chair now, with her hands resting loosely on the armrests. There were no rings on her fingers, but she wore a chunky gold bracelet on her right arm, decorated with various charms.

'No.'

'What is this all about then?'

'I'm sorry, I can't go into the details.' The consent form Mia had signed gave Tara permission to see Carolyn's notes and to discuss Mia's case with her, but Tara's own interactions with Mia remained confidential.

The silence between them grew increasingly awkward. Perhaps Carolyn felt insulted that Mia had chosen to see another clinician.

Tara cleared her throat. Looking away from Carolyn's gaze, her eyes were drawn back across the room to that therapy couch. It was covered in green linen, with a single white pillow.

'I leave it to my patients to choose whether they would like to lie down,' Carolyn said, still watching her closely. 'Some people find that it frees them up and helps them talk more easily about what's inside.'

Lying down was such a vulnerable position to be in, though. Tara could not imagine anything less appealing than letting her guard down.

Carolyn stood up and held the envelope out to Tara. 'Mia is a complex young woman. I hope you can help her.'

ELEVEN

TWO MONTHS BEFORE ALICE'S DEATH

Carolyn sits alone at her table with a glass of sparkling water fizzing in front of her. He is late. Again.

People run late all the time. It doesn't mean anything.

Her gut tells her something different though.

He's late because he doesn't care.

He had left a message on her mobile, while she'd been in sessions. He said he'd been delayed at work and she should go ahead to the restaurant. He'd meet her there as soon as he could.

He's late. That's all. Nothing has gone wrong.

So why does she carry this feeling of dread in the pit of her stomach?

Things between them feel different, lately. His mind is always somewhere else. He is less affectionate and often too busy to talk on the phone. Or to talk at all. Carolyn is always telling her clients not to ignore their instincts, but now she very much wants to ignore her own. The small things add up and she has to admit that she is afraid he has lost interest.

When she'd first arrived at the restaurant, most of the tables had been empty. Now they are filling up and she feels conspicuous, sitting alone. The couple at the next table are young and sun kissed.

She wonders how long he'll keep her waiting. When she checks her phone there are no new messages. Carolyn shifts in her chair, crossing her legs the other way, pulling the top of her dress up a little higher and the hem down a little lower. Her leg kicks back and forth. She loathes the red wrap-around dress she's wearing. She doesn't like the colour or the style; it's too flashy and too exposing. She hates high heels, too. She's wearing all of this because she is trying to please him. She suspects he finds her frumpy because she has always chosen comfort over style and clothes don't particularly interest her.

It shouldn't be this way. He holds too much power.

Something is wrong.

But then he walks through the door and she breathes a sigh of relief as he catches her eye and waves. She drinks him in as he comes closer. Navy blazer and tie, in great shape for his age. Silver-rimmed glasses. He is so sure of himself. That, most of all, is what compels her.

He stops to say something to the waitress, his hand, briefly but heavily, placed on the young woman's upper arm as they share a joke.

Carolyn feels a spike of jealousy. She smiles to hide it.

TWELVE

The air was icy as Tara walked the few blocks back to her office huddled up inside her puffy coat. She was glad to be enveloped in the cosy warmth of her clinic as soon as she stepped through the door. Once she'd taken off her coat, she headed straight up to her office, sat down at her own desk, and opened the sealed envelope Carolyn had given her.

Inside was a slim cardboard folder with *MIA PHILLIPS – CLOSED* printed on a white label stuck across the front. Carolyn's notes consisted of eight typed pages, double-spaced. The dates of the sessions indicated that the treatment period had been relatively brief, taking place over two months, with sessions scheduled twice a week.

Initial session. Low mood and sleeping difficulties experienced for a period of approximately six months. Symptoms began in early pregnancy. Psychotherapy treatment plan agreed. History taking.

The first couple of pages gave details of Mia's history, and the information lined up with what Mia had told Tara herself. Carolyn had commented: *Mother depressed? Father distant and uninvolved.*

Alice's death was dealt with only briefly: *Traumatic death of friend and flatmate Alice Kelly. During period of mourning, Mia developed a relationship with Alice's boyfriend Tom Phillips. Survivor guilt?*

The rest of the pages contained brief descriptions of sessions that were so general they could pretty much have been applied to any client.

Discussed symptoms. Attends sessions regularly. Motivated for treatment. Explored feelings towards husband. Marriage stable. Ambivalent about pregnancy.

There was nothing about the techniques Carolyn had used and no details about any information that had emerged during treatment.

The final note, about the session where Mia's memory of killing Alice had supposedly returned, simply read: *Final session. Free association about Alice Kelly's death. Mia terminated session early and decided not to continue with treatment.*

According to Mia, in that final session she had remembered killing her best friend, and she had talked about that in detail, repeatedly. Had Carolyn not thought that information was important to include in her notes?

Tara let out a sigh. She had hoped that understanding more about Mia's therapy sessions might have given her clues as to what was going on in Mia's mind when she confessed to killing Alice, but the emptiness of these case notes was striking. It was as though anything of value had been left out.

To give Carolyn the benefit of the doubt, perhaps she had been careful about what she'd included in her notes. Perhaps she didn't want to include anything that might give the impression Mia was actually guilty if Carolyn believed the memory was pure fantasy.

Tara flipped back through her notes to re-read the way Mia had described that last therapy session.

I wanted Carolyn to tell me that what I saw wasn't real. But

*she didn't, she just kept pushing me. She made me go over that
night, again and again and again, everything, every single second
until I couldn't take it anymore.*

Carolyn was an experienced therapist and her instinct that
Mia needed to talk about Alice was probably correct. Whether
Mia realised it or not, she was still struggling to process the
trauma of her best friend's death. But the way Mia described
that final therapy session did raise red flags. Enforced repetition
was one of the ways in which false memories could be created
in someone who was vulnerable and depressed, and a good therapist should know that.

Mia is a complex young woman.

That was an odd thing to say. As if Carolyn was trying to
warn Tara about something, or to give the impression that Mia
could not be trusted.

Tara had begun to wonder whether those case notes were
the originals, or if they had been retyped and strategically
edited. And if so, what exactly had been changed or left out?

There was more frustration to follow in Mia's case. Tara had
been due to go back to the flat in Wembley later that morning
for their next session, but instead Mia had sent her an email
saying she had to cancel. Mia claimed she had to go in to work
at the gallery and that she would be in touch to reschedule.

Tara questioned whether this was true. It seemed strange
that Mia was suddenly well enough to travel into work, despite
being advised to rest due to potential pregnancy complications
only the day before.

Despite Mia's apparent desperation to know the truth, she
also seemed ambivalent about coming back to Tara's office, and
this was the second appointment she'd changed at short notice.
It was starting to seem significant that Mia had not yet explicitly
told Tara exactly what it was she remembered doing to Alice.

The envelope containing Carolyn's case notes was still on Tara's desk. Tara took the eight pages out and read through them once again, to see if she may have missed anything. She hadn't. The notes were as brief and unhelpful as they had been the first time she'd gone through them.

One thing Carolyn's therapy notes did confirm was that Mia's pregnancy was the catalyst for her depression. Maybe the pregnancy was also in some way linked to Mia's confession? Mia clearly felt guilty because she had been envious of Alice at the time she'd been killed, and because she had 'benefited' from Alice's death. With Alice out of the way, Mia had been able to get Tom's attention.

Tara spent time downloading a few more recent research papers about False Memory Syndrome. There was one in particular that caught her interest. The researchers had found that people with a history of trauma or depression were more at risk for producing false memories when they were asked to talk about feelings related to their difficult experiences.

Which was exactly what Carolyn had asked Mia to do. But because Carolyn had not made detailed notes, it wasn't possible to pinpoint precisely what had happened in that session.

With the cancelled appointment leaving her with too much time to think, Tara's mind kept wandering back to Pierre Henry and the information he had promised to send her about Daniel's bank account. She wondered how long it would be before she received the documentation which could open Pandora's Box.

She went over to her filing cabinet and flipped through her various questionnaires. There were a few brief ones covering symptoms of anxiety and depression that would be useful to have Mia to fill out. She also had a test that looked at a person's tendency towards deception when answering, which could provide some interesting information too. Tara decided that since Mia couldn't get into the office, she would deliver these to her in person.

It wouldn't hurt to get a look at Mia's persona in her workplace, either.

THIRTEEN

The Leonard Gallery was tucked away on a pedestrian alley in the heart of Hampstead Village, in between a café and a hairdresser. The window was dominated by an enormous abstract painting in varying shades of red. Tara found the piece quite unsettling. Like gazing into a pool of blood. But maybe that said more about her state of mind after that walk to Wildway Close the night before.

An old-fashioned bell tinkled as Tara opened the door and entered a minimalist space with white-washed walls and white-painted floorboards. For a moment, she had the sensation that she was floating, with no boundary between walls, floor and ceiling.

Tara had been expecting to find Mia, but instead an older woman was behind the sleek white desk frowning at an iPad screen. She looked up as Tara walked in. 'Morning. Please feel free to have a look around, I'm here if you need anything.'

'Is Mia Phillips here?'

'Mia's not in today. Can I help with something?' The woman stepped out from behind the desk. She was striking, tall and elegant, wearing a black velvet blazer over skinny trousers.

Her silver blonde hair was arranged in a casual bun at the nape of her neck. 'I'm Julia Leonard, the owner of the gallery.'

So this was Mia's employer and mother-in-law.

'I'm Tara Black. I have some documents to drop off for Mia.' Tara was caught slightly off balance as she'd not anticipated that she'd be introducing herself to Mia's mother-in-law. She was hesitant to say she was a psychologist because that was Mia's private business.

'The name rings a bell,' Julia said, appraising her with keen eyes. 'My son mentioned he'd met you. You're Mia's new psychologist?'

Tara nodded.

'Is everything all right?' Understandably, Julia found it somewhat unusual that Mia's psychologist had turned up at her place of work.

'Yes, I wanted to drop off a few questionnaires. What time is Mia due in?'

'She won't be in today. She's taken a few days off, she's not feeling very well.'

'Right.' Tara's intuition seemed to have been correct. Mia had made an excuse to miss their appointment.

'Do you want to leave the documents with me?'

'Thank you but I'll wait and give them to Mia in person.'

'Of course. Let me give her a call and tell her you're here.'

While Julia went back behind her desk to use her phone, Tara walked around the small gallery space. Several paintings of different sizes were hung around the walls, all of them painted in varying shades of red, with thick and textured oil paint. The pieces were labelled with numbers instead of names and most of them had yellow dots on the wall next to them, presumably indicating they were sold.

Tara stopped to look more closely at one of them. *Fifteen*. It was small, only about ten centimetres by ten centimetres, and an intense, crimson red.

Where had Daniel been sending that money?

'I can't seem to get hold of her.' Julia's polite smile was tinged with worry. 'Mia's not picking up. I'll give it a few minutes and I'll try again.'

Tara nodded.

'I can always tell when a piece of art connects to someone's soul,' Julia said, pointing at the small red canvas. 'This one speaks to you,'

'You're right, it does.'

'Mia brought this artist to me. Her name is Olga Frisk, and her pieces are selling like hotcakes. My daughter-in-law has impeccable taste.' Julia reached out to straighten the small painting, which as far as Tara could see was already straight. 'The truth is, I don't know what I'd do without Mia now. She deals with everything – the technology side of things, the mailing list, the accounts. But honestly, it's such a waste.'

'What do you mean?'

'Mia has a rare talent. She could have such an interesting future ahead of her in the world of photography. But she hasn't touched her camera in years. Not since—'

'Since Alice died?'

Julia nodded. 'Mia should be doing so much more than working with me. But her camera is sitting in a cupboard in my back office, gathering dust. She won't even take it home.'

Tara was still struggling to get a sense of who Mia really was. She wondered if Julia had picked up anything about Mia's potential difficulties or risk factors, either to herself or to other people. 'How long has Mia worked for you?' she asked.

'It's been almost ten years now. Mia and Alice turned up at my gallery, carrying their portfolios, all bushy-tailed and bright-eyed, and desperate to get a foothold in the art world. I gave them some part-time work in the gallery. Mainly on weekends, or if I had an exhibition on. They'd help with setting up, serving drinks and so on. Never hurts to have a couple of pretty faces around, does it?'

'It sounds like Alice and Mia were close?'

'Very,' Julia said. 'Exceptionally close. Mia has barely any family of her own, and Alice was like a sister. They had so much in common. Both of them had such a passion for art and design, but Mia was always the tastemaker. She has such an eye for quality. In art, clothes, everything. Always. Mia is a true artist and I think Alice envied that.'

It was surprising to hear Julia put it that way. When Tara had interviewed Mia, it had seemed that Mia was the one with the envy problem.

'I understand that your son and Alice were a couple at the time she died. It must have been difficult for him too. For all of you?'

'Difficult is an understatement. Tom was absolutely devastated. But frankly, that relationship was never going to last. It would have burned out sooner or later, even if Alice had lived.'

'What makes you say that?'

'Well, Alice was a bit of a magpie, always attracted to anything shiny. Mia's talent. Tom's goodness. And money. Alice was attracted to money most of all and Tom was never going to make enough money for her tastes as a schoolteacher.' From her disapproving tone, it was clear that Julia had not exactly been a fan of Alice Kelly.

Julia had her phone in her hand and she tried Mia's number again. Then she shook her head. 'Still no answer.'

Tara could see that she was unnerved about not getting hold of Mia.

'I really hope you can help Mia,' Julia said. 'I've been worried about her ever since she's been pregnant.'

'May I ask what you've noticed that worries you?'

'Well, Mia's always been quiet; she's shy and she's never been much of a people person. But since she's been pregnant, she's been terribly withdrawn. It's obvious she's feeling low. I suppose she wasn't quite ready for a baby, but I've tried to convince her that children are a blessing, always, even if their arrival comes as a surprise. I couldn't live without my boys.'

'Is there anything about Mia's behaviour that's been a concern?' Tara was hesitant to come out and ask Julia specifically about aggressive behaviour. Her question was as close as she could get without compromising Mia's privacy too much.

'Absolutely not. Mia has always been an absolute pleasure to have around, and a real support—' Julia tailed off as if her mind had drifted elsewhere. She hovered next to the now extra-straight painting, one hand resting lightly on the wall, looking preoccupied.

'You look worried,' Tara said.

'It's not like Mia to turn her phone off.' Julia dialled another number. 'Freddie darling, listen to me, I need a favour. Could you to go over and check on Mia—'

Julia was interrupted and Tara could hear a man's voice, but she couldn't make out the words. As she listened to him, Julia's smile dropped and the blood drained from her face.

FOURTEEN

The cottage close to where Alice Kelly had died was a couple of miles outside the city of Oxford. According to Tara's navigator, the drive out there was supposed to take around an hour and fifteen minutes. Tara set out from Hampstead, straight after leaving Julia's gallery, and after some initial frustration at the clogged London roads, by some miracle she had a clear run from the time she reached the motorway.

Freddie, who was Mia's brother-in-law and Julia's younger son, had told his mother that Mia had asked him to drive her out to the cottage that morning. The place belonged to David Phillips, Tom and Freddie's father, and had apparently been standing empty ever since Alice's death.

After leaving the main roads, Tara had to negotiate a series of narrow lanes that wound through a wooded area. These were a challenge in her SUV and she had to pull over tight to the side every time a car came towards her in the opposite direction, which thankfully wasn't too often. Finally, after a last sharp left turn, a set of open wooden gates appeared in a gap between tall hedges and the navigator announced that she had reached her destination.

Tara pulled up on the empty driveway. On the face of it, the traditional cottage in front of her should have been charming. Painted white, it had a steeply pitched roof, leaded windows and a pale-green front door. Wisteria branches, bare for the winter, wound their way across the lintel and around the windows.

Obviously, the knowledge that a young woman had died violently here was colouring her response. But still. The tall trees and hedges on all sides seemed to block out any light and behind the leaded windows the house was unnaturally dark. The front door was ajar, but otherwise the place was silent and appeared deserted.

Tara's first impression was of an overwhelming sense of gloom.

She pulled her briefcase across from the passenger seat onto her lap and reached into it for her phone. There was no reception. When she stepped out of the car and looked around, there were no other houses visible from where she stood. She hadn't realised the cottage was so isolated. Given the problems Mia was having in her pregnancy, it seemed reckless to have come out there. It could be a sign that Mia's emotional turmoil was growing more intense.

Tara pushed aside a rising sense of apprehension as she walked towards the house. She hadn't given much thought to rushing out here alone to check on Mia. But now she was acutely aware that Mia was a woman she barely knew, who was potentially unstable and possibly even dangerous.

Tara called out hello before pushing open the front door and entering the cottage. She stepped straight into a bare living room. The ceilings were low and criss-crossed with thick wooden beams; barely any light straggled through the grimy windows. There was no furniture, only the dust-covered floorboards.

On the opposite side of the room, Mia stood rooted to the

spot in front of the fireplace. Her arms were stiff at her sides as she stared into the middle distance. Behind her, the photograph of Alice was propped up on the stone mantelpiece.

'Mia, are you all right?'

'Freddie came over to my place this morning because Julia wanted him to sort out the nursery furniture and hang the curtains. I asked him to drive me out here. It's not his fault. I begged him.'

Instinct made Tara stop just inside the door and she didn't try to go any closer. 'Where is Freddie? I didn't see a car outside.'

'I asked him to go to the services to pick up some food. I wanted to be alone for a while.'

Wide-eyed and tense from head to toe, Mia reminded Tara of a nervous deer who sensed a hunter with a gun nearby. Tara found herself gripping the top handle of her briefcase with both hands and her chest felt tight, so that it was harder to breathe. As though her own body was channelling Mia's nerves.

'Tom keeps a key in the safe at home,' Mia was saying, 'and I used it to let myself in. He doesn't know I took it. I suppose Julia will tell him I'm here.'

'You could have asked me to come out here with you,' Tara said.

'You would have said no.'

She was right. There was no heating in the cottage and it felt colder inside than outside. Tara was picking up a whiff of damp. This was about the last place Mia should be.

In her head, Tara was calculating the distance to the nearest hospital, which was the John Radcliffe. That would probably be at least half an hour's drive, maybe longer taking into account the country lanes.

Being out at this isolated cottage was bringing back strong memories of the Jameson case. That time, it had been Tara's suggestion that Jade Jameson go back to the murder scene for a reconstruction. And that night at The Onyx Hotel in Soho had almost ended in extreme violence.

While the facts in Mia's case were very different, the feeling Tara had when she was with Mia was similar. That prickle of danger at the back of her neck.

'Nobody else ever comes here anymore.' Mia stared down at the thick floorboards. 'My father-in-law cleared everything out. Every stick of furniture. I suppose he'll sell the place, once enough time has passed, and everyone's forgotten about Alice. But I don't want to forget.'

'Why did you want to come out here so badly today?' Tara asked.

'This morning, when I woke up, I kept seeing everything I went through with Carolyn in that last session. I couldn't think about anything else. This feeling of guilt inside me is getting so bad. I thought if I came out here, if I forced myself to go through it all again, then I'd know for sure... if what I can see is real.'

Maybe she was right. Maybe being back at the place where Alice died would help to clarify everything. Tara wouldn't have suggested it in Mia's advanced state of pregnancy, but now they were both there, they may as well make the most of it.

'Shall we go through it together?' Tara said.

Mia looked Tara in the eyes for the first time since she'd arrived. She nodded. Then she turned around to face the photograph. There were a few moments of silence before she began speaking again. 'It was Alice's idea to come out here. She loved this place. I'd been working on my portfolio for ages, trying to get an agent, and Alice said we should come to the cottage and take some photographs out by the river. Tom's always had a key, and he knew it was empty that weekend because his dad was away with his new partner so he said we could use it.'

Mia paused again. Again, her fists clenched and

unclenched and she looked down at the floor. 'I knew it was a mistake. I had such a bad feeling on the drive out here. We should never have come out here together after what happened the night before.'

FIFTEEN

ONE DAY BEFORE ALICE'S DEATH

Alice is alone in the gallery.

The exhibition had gone well and almost all of the pieces had sold, so Julia had been in a good mood when she'd left. Now Alice was supposed to be clearing away the empty wine glasses and canape trays and packing them back in their boxes, ready for the caterers to collect. Then she was supposed to vacuum and straighten the place out. But she's not doing any of that.

Instead, she paces up and down for a few minutes because she wants to be sure that Julia is not coming back. Then she double checks the front door is locked, turns out the lights and goes into the back office. She opens the top drawer of Julia's desk and takes out her boss's leather-bound address book. Julia is old-fashioned and not exactly security conscious; she keeps all her passwords written down on the back page.

Alice feels a small stirring of guilt as she holds the address book in her hands. It's worn with use. Some of the ink on the older entries has faded with age and a few pages are coming loose. She reminds herself that this is what people do to get ahead. It happens all the time. It's not a crime. She doesn't think it's a crime, anyway. She's not entirely sure.

The password for Julia's computer is *Freddie* of course, Julia's favourite son.

Alice plugs a memory stick into the desktop and begins to download everything that's on there. A message pops up: it will take eight minutes.

Eight minutes is an eternity.

While she's waiting, she puts the address book back in its place in the drawer. *Damn*. She forgot to look exactly at where it had been positioned. And the drawer is very neat. She must not leave any trace. Oh well, there's nothing that can be done now; she'll have to hope for the best.

Alice's heart is racing and she's sweating. She paces up and down behind the desk.

'What are you doing?'

Alice nearly jumps out of her skin. Mia has crept in so quietly. Floating around the place like a ghost.

'What are *you* doing here?' Alice says.

'Julia called me. She felt bad that she'd left you to clear up on your own and she asked if I could I help out. She's happy to pay both of us.' Mia comes closer. She sees Alice's thumb drive, the blue light flashing. 'What are you doing in here?'

'I'm copying Julia's hard drive,' Alice says calmly.

'Did she ask you to back it up?'

Alice shakes her head. She can't lie to Mia. She just can't.

Mia looks at her, realisation dawning.

'It's nothing,' Alice says. 'Everyone does it.'

'Everyone does what exactly?'

Alice looks away, at the screen. There are still five long minutes remaining.

'You're stealing.' Mia looks as if she's about to faint. She's so sensitive about these things. She has a concrete sense of right and wrong, as if God was constantly looking over her shoulder. 'You can't do this.'

Alice concentrates on the blue flashing light on her memory

stick. Thankfully the computer is speeding up and time is going faster. Three minutes remaining.

Come on, come on, come on.

When she looks up, Mia is still staring at her with those eyes of hers. Wide, frightened eyes that accuse her. 'Please, Alice. There is a ton of sensitive data on there – client lists, invoices, personal stuff. Why would you want any of that?'

'I didn't want to tell you like this, but I'm leaving the gallery.'

'What?' Mia looks confused for a minute. Like she's gone blank.

'I have a new job. I'm sorry, this isn't how I wanted you to find out. It's full time, at the Sharp Gallery. Someone made an introduction for me. I'll get commission on top of the basic salary. James has galleries all over Europe, and in New York. I can maybe get you in there too—'

'You're giving him Julia's data? Is that what this is about?'

Mia takes a step towards her.

Alice takes a step back, her eyes still on the memory stick. 'It's insurance, that's all. I might need it one day. You never know.'

'Insurance for what?'

'I wish you wouldn't be so naïve,' Alice says. 'We can't even afford to keep living in London. We're illegally subletting an apartment in a shitty, dangerous council block. No fairy godmother is going to come along with her magic wand and wave it over us and suddenly make our lives okay. We have to create our own opportunities.'

Mia looks like she's about to lunge forwards and rip the memory stick out of that port.

This is a disaster. Julia has taken Mia under her wing and Mia adores her. Mia doesn't have a mother of her own, or any family really, so she is fiercely loyal to Julia. Which is exactly why Alice did not want her friend to know what she was doing.

'Julia's gallery is really small,' Mia says. 'She can't afford to lose any business. You can't steal from Julia to give to James Sharp—'

'It's not stealing! You don't understand.'

Mia takes another step forward. '*What is it then?* What is going on?'

She's red in the face. Alice has never seen her so upset. Mia is usually so meek and mild.

Alice is getting nervous, but she holds her ground. 'I am doing this and I'm not changing my mind so there's nothing you can do about it. Forget you saw me in here.'

It's done. The download is complete. Calmly, Alice ejects her memory stick and slips it into the pocket of her trousers. She turns off the desktop.

'I need to get this place straightened up,' Alice says. 'Are you going to calm down and help me?'

SIXTEEN

Mia had been walking around the room as she spoke, sometimes pressing her hands into her lower back or rolling her shoulders. As she spoke about the events leading up to Alice's death, some of the tension dropped from her body and her movements became more fluid, which seemed a good sign.

Tara was finding herself breathing easier too as Mia relaxed. 'So you and Alice had been arguing that weekend because Alice had copied some data from Julia's computer?'

'It all seems so unimportant now,' Mia said, 'but at the time, I was really freaked out. It felt as though everything was coming at me at once. First seeing Alice and Tom together all the time, and then Alice getting this new job she was so thrilled about. Like I said, the envy was overwhelming, and I hated myself for it but I couldn't stop feeling that way.'

Tara was scrawling some notes, which was challenging given that there was no furniture, so nowhere to sit down and nowhere to balance her notebook.

'I think that maybe Alice was nervous about her new job. She was going to be working on commission so maybe she wanted Julia's list of buyers to set herself up.' Mia turned to look at Alice's portrait and gave a deep sigh. 'It wasn't the first time she'd done something like that.'

'You mean, stealing?'

'We used to waitress at the same restaurant when we were at uni, and sometimes Alice would skim off a bit of money. She didn't see anything wrong with it. Her family had a really hard time with money when she was growing up, after her dad left them, and she always had this thing about not having enough. She always needed extra. It was like a kind of fear she had. I'm not even sure she would have done anything with Julia's data, she probably just wanted it for a sense of security, before she left.'

'If you were so angry at Alice for what she'd done, did you still think it was a good idea to go away together for the weekend?'

Mia shook her head. 'I don't know. We'd already arranged everything for the trip, and the truth is I really needed those photos for my final assignment. Maybe I thought I could change Alice's mind about using Julia's data, and get her to delete it all. Like I said, everything is such a blur, because of what happened afterwards. It's hard to remember what I was thinking.'

Mia was staring at Alice's photograph now, as though she was talking directly to her, rather than Tara. 'Alice was trying to make things right between us. The whole way out here, she was talking to me as though nothing was wrong but I didn't say a word. I don't remember a single thing she said either. All I remember was that my head was starting to hurt.'

'When you arrived here, how were things between you and Alice, that first day?'

'We were kind of okay. Alice had brought bags of food and some wine. We unpacked and then we went down to the river and took some photos. But the headache was getting worse and I was anxious because I'd forgotten to bring my meds – I have these strong painkillers I take for migraines. I went up to bed early.'

Mia yawned. Tara could see that she was growing tired, and the yawning could be a sign of overwhelm, of her body trying to shut down. She should be convincing Mia to leave this damp, freezing cottage. But Tara wanted to push her just a little further. She needed to know what Mia had seen in Carolyn Goring's office.

'So you went up to bed early, and then Alice decided to go out for a walk in the middle of the night. Did that seem strange to you?'

'I'm not sure. I mean, not really. Sometimes in London she'd pop out to the corner shop if she had a craving for sweets or chocolate or the odd cigarette. And she used to love that we had a 24-hour Tesco round the corner from us. She found that comforting, she'd go and walk around in there if she couldn't sleep. We'd never been out to the cottage together before, so I don't know if she did the same thing here. Alice had been out to this cottage a few times with Tom, so she knew the place much better than I did.'

'Was Tom at the cottage at all that weekend?'

'No, he had a bachelor party to go to.'

There was a pause as Mia turned away from the portrait. 'Alice said she needed air. I understood that. This cottage has always had this horrible musty smell. It's still there now.'

Mia reached out to hold on to the mantelpiece with her ravaged fingernails. She seemed a little unsteady.

'Do you need to sit down?' Tara was concerned Mia might be dizzy.

'I let her leave. I wouldn't speak to her and I didn't even try to stop her.'

. . .

Mia seemed to find her balance. She let go of the mantelpiece, and then abruptly, she walked out of the living room. Tara followed behind her as she climbed the creaking stairs to the first floor. Upstairs there were two bedrooms and a small bathroom. Like the ground floor, the ceilings were low with wooden beams, and all the rooms had been stripped bare.

Mia entered one of the rooms. 'This was where I slept when we were here. Or tried to sleep.'

She walked over to the window, pulled her sleeve over her hand, and wiped away the dirt. Tara went over to stand beside her. From up there they had a clear view across the narrow strip of garden. The space was neatly kept, with the hedges trimmed and the edges of the flower beds clearly defined. Someone had been tending to it.

A path down the centre of the grass led to a wooden gate. Beyond that Tara could see the river. The water was murky and still. Thick foliage and crooked trees grew along the banks.

'The last time I ever saw Alice I was cruel,' Mia said. 'She wanted to make things right between us and I wanted to hurt her. Maybe if I had been different, if I'd been kinder, she wouldn't have gone out that night.'

The smell of damp was stronger upstairs. The atmosphere was feeling more and more oppressive, and Tara's instinct to get out of the cottage was getting stronger too.

Mia's gaze was fixed on the brown, swirling water.

'We were alone down there,' she said, pointing. 'The two of us, alone down there, beside the river.'

'Tell me what you see.'

SEVENTEEN

THE NIGHT OF ALICE'S DEATH

Mia lies in bed on her back. She is cold and in pain. All she wants is to sleep, but sleep will not come.

The voice is back. Tormenting her. The voice that comes with the headaches.

I know who you are.

I know what you do.

I see everything that's inside you.

The others don't see, but I do. I know you.

Her head is full to bursting with poison and there is no escape.

The house creaks around her and she is afraid, lying there, frozen under the too thin sheet. She could get up and go look for a blanket but she can't move. She lies still, trying to ignore the voices and the spikes of pain surging behind her left eye.

When the door of her room opens, she feels a burst of fear.

It's only Alice.

'Are you awake?'

Mia doesn't speak. Alice comes closer and climbs into bed next to her.

'Have you ever been hungry?' Alice says. 'I mean really hungry?'

Pressure is building up in Mia's head, and it's so cold and her vocal chords have frozen solid.

'That hunger never really goes away,' Alice says. 'If you feel it when you're a child, it's always there. I remember all those times when we got to the supermarket checkout and my mum would get nervous. I can still smell her nerves. That awful, sweaty, scared smell. We'd never have enough money and we'd always have to put stuff back. Sometimes her card wouldn't work at all and we'd have to leave everything behind.'

Mia can hear Alice's voice, but there is the other voice too.

I know what you did. You need to be punished.

'I'm not going to live my mother's life, battling from month to month, afraid of not having enough money for food before the next payday. I'm going to be different. And I'm going to take you with me.'

Alice's voice is like honey, thick and sweet. Alice wants to corrupt her. Alice wants to convince her to let the evil inside.

'I hate it when you're angry with me,' Alice says, 'I can't bear it when we fight. In the morning I'm going to make you my special cinnamon toast and you'll forgive me. I know you will.'

Mia is so confused; the two voices are blending together, Alice and the other one, both speaking at the same time and the spike behind her eye twisting further into her brain until she is sure she is losing her mind.

Alice sits up and looks at her. 'Mia, are you listening? Say something, please.'

Mia cannot speak. She closes her eyes tight, the pain and the voices taking her over.

'Okay, I give up,' Alice says. 'I'm going for a walk. I need some air.'

. . .

When Mia steps out of the back door, she can't see a thing. There is a different kind of dark, out at the cottage. The kind you don't get in the city. Thick and heavy and black.

Soon though, her eyes adjust. The gate at the bottom of the garden is wide open and she walks quickly and silently towards it. The night wraps itself around her and swallows her up.

She is invisible.

On the other side of the gate there is a path that runs along the river. Mia's footsteps are muffled against the soft, slippery earth and the only sound is the rushing of water.

There is movement ahead of her. A familiar silhouette, tall and graceful, with a scarf around her shoulders. Alice. Mia speeds up. The green-eyed monster is awake and it claws at her chest with sharp talons.

Her whole life, this ugly beast has been inside her.

Alice is so easy to love.

No one will ever love you.

Mia's right hand feels heavy; something is weighing her down. She looks down and sees she is carrying her camera. The thin black strap hangs down, trailing on the ground.

Where did that come from?

She doesn't remember taking it with her when she left the house.

Mia is so close now that she can smell Alice's jasmine-scented perfume. It mingles with the earthy, metallic smell of the riverbank. Suddenly, all of her pain is gone and her head is clear. She feels so peaceful.

Mia grips the strap of her camera with both hands, lifts it high above her head and slips it down around Alice's throat.

EIGHTEEN

Mia was still standing at the window, looking down towards the river. On the outside, she seemed quite calm. Unnaturally so.

'How do you feel?' Tara asked her.

'I'm fine.' The flat, emotionless eyes and voice were back.

'Were those the same images you saw in Carolyn's office?'

'Exactly the same.' Mia looked down at her hands, frowning at her ragged nails, as if shocked at the state of them. 'Alice was struggling, trying to get her fingers under the strap. But I was pulling it so tight around her throat. And then, after a while, I felt her go limp. That's where it ends. But I can see it and hear it and smell it all so clearly. It feels real.'

Tara could not be sure if there was any truth to what Mia had just described doing to Alice. The memory had an unreal, dreamlike quality. Tara also found it hard to believe that Mia could so easily have overpowered Alice. Mia had always described Alice as being tall, and Mia herself was so petite.

Maybe Tara didn't want to believe it. The images had also been gruesome, and graphic.

Slowly, Mia slid down the wall, until she was sitting on the dusty wooden floor.

'I keep thinking about that question you asked me. About why I would hurt someone I loved.' Mia looked up at Tara. 'Some people are born evil, aren't they? They hurt people because they want to. Because it gives them pleasure.'

Tara sat next to her, so they were side by side. 'Did you feel pleasure when you imagined hurting Alice?'

'No. *No.*' The disgust was evident on her face now. 'I felt sick. Having those thoughts in my mind is like torture.'

Tara needed more evidence to be certain that Mia wasn't capable of violence. She wondered if Mia's memory might be even sharper if they went out through the garden, retracing her steps down to the river.

No. It was too risky.

Tara was also becoming concerned about time. She checked her watch. If she didn't leave within the next ten minutes, she wouldn't make it back to London in time for her afternoon session. After what Mia had just disclosed though, she was reluctant to leave her out at the cottage. She definitely didn't want to leave her in such a bleak state of mind.

'Mia, I need to get back to London soon. But before I go, I wanted to ask you to remember something else about Alice. A time when things were good.'

'There were so many times like that.' Mia looked full of sadness, then.

'What did you love about her?'

'Her energy.' Mia's face became more animated as she spoke. 'Alice had this positive energy about her, and it was irresistible. And infectious. The moment she walked into a room, I would feel it too.

Mia stopped, putting her head in her hands. She took a few breaths before she continued speaking. 'Alice believed in me as much as herself. No matter how many agents or galleries turned me down, she used to say: '*You have to keep taking photographs. The world needs to see these images. It's your gift.*'

When I was with her, I felt… I felt loved. And hopeful. I never felt alone.'

Tara wondered if Mia's grief would break through then, but her eyes stayed dry.

A few minutes later, the sound of a car engine approaching shattered the quiet. Tara heard the front door open and close, and footsteps running up the stairs.

A man appeared in the doorway. Tall and heavily built, he wore his shaggy hair long to his shoulders, with a full beard to match. He was holding a very full shopping bag in one hand and a large McDonald's takeaway cup in the other.

'This is Freddie,' Mia said, 'my brother-in-law. Freddie, this is Doctor Black.'

'Good to meet you.' Freddie placed the bag on the floor and came over to hand the cup to Mia. 'Sorry, I didn't know you were here – I only brought one milkshake.'

'Don't worry about it.'

Tara was relieved to see that Mia was drinking from the cup he'd handed her, and the colour and life were coming back into her face.

'This place still stinks of damp,' Freddie said, making a face. 'It hits you every time you walk in. How much longer do you need here?'

'I'm finished,' Mia said. 'I'm ready to leave.'

NINETEEN

Tara had lost track of time. When she looked up from her desk the streetlights had come on outside her office window. She had spent the afternoon with Donna Allders, which had felt like light relief after her session with Mia at the cottage, and she'd been writing up that report for a couple of hours.

It had become quite clear to both Tara and Donna that, in fact, Donna did not want the job for which she'd been going through such an intensive interview process. It had all come pouring out. Donna's father had pressured her to go into the world of finance, probably to fulfil some of his own unmet aspirations. Donna said she had spent her life trying to please him, but the result was that she was miserable. She had been successfully working in a well-paying city job for several years but what she really wanted was to take a year off to recalibrate and to find what it was she was passionate about.

None of this information would go into Tara's formal report but it was the part of the assessment she found most gratifying. Donna was most likely going to turn the job down, even though Tara could see no reason not to recommend her for the position.

As she saved and closed the Allders document and got up to

turn on the overhead lights, Tara's mind returned to Mia, where the case was far less clear cut.

While the different symptoms that Mia was experiencing may be, as her doctors feared, signs of pre-eclampsia, they could also be signs of emotional distress. Foggy head and blurred vision were signs of a type of severe anxiety that usually began early in childhood, most often due to some kind of trauma. The headaches too could be a possible sign of repressed emotion. If Mia was able to work through her conflicted feelings about Alice's death, that could bring her anxiety levels down, and that in turn might help with the problems she was having with her pregnancy.

Whether Mia's sense of guilt was deserved because she had done something unspeakable, or whether it was a form of complicated grief over the death of her best friend, was not yet clear.

It was possible that the guilt Mia felt about Alice's death was all in her mind, a cruel trick she was playing on herself. Maybe she was a tormented soul, punishing herself for having taken over Alice's life. She could be about to destroy her family based on what could be a false memory, or even a delusion.

Or, maybe Mia was capable of extreme violence, and her child urgently needed protection.

On the one hand, it was difficult to imagine that the shy and very pregnant Mia Phillips was capable of extreme violence. On the other though, there was something unusual, unnerving even, about the way Mia behaved. The way she was never fully present, as though her mind was somewhere else, and the way she spoke so cautiously, as if she was afraid of saying the wrong thing or perhaps giving something away.

Most of the time, she was stoic, with so little emotional response, and it was difficult to read her.

The idea of speaking to one of the police officers who had been involved in Alice Kelly's case was taking root in Tara's mind. It was a long shot, and she was hardly a forensic expert, but she wondered if it might be possible to either prove or disprove that the strap of Mia's camera had been used to strangle Alice. And was there even any evidence of strangulation found on the body?

Tara opened her browser and began to look up information about Alice Kelly's death. Details were limited and the news articles didn't add much more to what she already knew: Alice's body had been found by a dog walker in the river, and there had been appeals for witnesses. Tara did repeatedly come across the name of Detective Sergeant Nina Ayola, who was mentioned as a contact person in the case.

If she did decide to speak to the police though, Tara would ideally need to discuss it with Mia first.

Tara tried to call Mia, mainly to check up on how she was feeling after the trip to the cottage. The phone rang a few times and was then disconnected. Tara was getting frustrated at Mia's inconsistency and the sense that she was constantly having to chase her client to try to re-engage her.

A nagging voice at the back of her mind whispered that something was wrong. She had felt uneasy ever since leaving Mia at that cottage.

Mia is a complex young woman.

The envelope containing Carolyn Goring's case notes was lying on the desk next to Tara's laptop. She had read these through several times and each time she did so, the lack of detail was more and more concerning.

Mia claimed that Carolyn had repeatedly pressured her to talk about the night Alice died. It was possible that this technique had in fact created a false memory, as Mia began to imagine or embellish the details. Was Carolyn worried about that? Had she left her notes as vague as possible to protect herself?

Tara sent Carolyn an email, asking if they could set up

another meeting as soon as possible. She had a feeling that this time, it would not be an easy conversation.

It suddenly felt like it had been an exceptionally long day. Tara tried Mia once more. This time the call went straight to a generic voicemail. Still with that lingering sense of unease, Tara locked up the building, leaving it in darkness and silence, and headed home.

TWENTY

The air here is pure. Bare branches shiver in the wind and the only sound is birdsong.

Mia walks, barefoot, towards the edge of the river. She feels every last ice-drop of air against her skin. Her ears, the tip of her nose, her fingers, all on fire.

The water is so dark. She watches as it ebbs and flows. It looks gentle, but then she can't see beneath the surface.

The birds are getting louder, their chattering frantic. The voice is getting louder and louder too, filling her head.

I see the devil. He is inside you.

'I'm sorry,' she says out loud.

She hesitates. Her belly protrudes under the thin fabric of her blouse.

She is petrified but she forces herself to take a step forwards. The shock of the fall sucks the breath from her chest. The freezing water numbs the terrible, terrible guilt.

She sinks deeper and deeper. In seconds, she loses all sensation, all thought. Her body shuts down.

She is no longer cold. Alice is coming back, moving across the water with strong, steady strokes.

She will be forgiven.

TWENTY-ONE

When Tara arrived back at her cottage, a large envelope had been pushed through her letterbox. The logo of Pierre Henry's law firm was embossed across the front left corner.

Tara went straight to the kitchen table and tore it open. Inside was a letter informing her that Daniel's funds had been transferred into a bank account opened in her name. Copies of the last three months' statements from Daniel's account had been enclosed and there was also a short, hand-written note from Pierre Henry. He said it had been a pleasure to meet with her and that although this was the end of the legal firm's involvement, he would be happy to be contacted if he could be of assistance at any time in the future.

Tara sat back a moment, in shock looking at the documents that were spread out across the table. This had all happened so fast. She had assumed that the bureaucracy involved would take much longer.

She took a breath and began to study the papers. First, she focused on Daniel's bank statements. There was one transaction each month where money was sent to an account identified only by a series of letters and numbers. This transfer was made on the tenth of every month, which meant there was one week to go until the next payment was due. Presumably, if this didn't happen, the recipient, whoever that was, might be short of money.

Tara needed to know the identity of the owner of that account before she could decide what to do. Either she would continue sending the money, exactly as Daniel had been doing, or she would find a way to return it to Daniel's family. The latter option would not be a simple one, because contacting Daniel's widow could cause more harm than good. The knowledge that Daniel had left Tara large sums of money would surely reopen deep wounds for Sabine.

Tara shut down that line of thought. There was no point ruminating about it before she had more information.

She briefly considered contacting the Swiss bank to request more details about the account that the money had been transferred to. She assumed though that they would not just give her the name of the owner, and there was bound to be red tape involved. There was also something else that held her back from trying the direct approach. If there was a chance this person was her brother, she did not want to risk leaving a trail which could get either of them into hot water with the authorities.

Tara had the strongest feeling that pulling on this thread of Daniel's inheritance was going to change her life, and she didn't have a soul to talk to about her decision. This sense of aloneness was suddenly unbearable.

She packed all the documents away, back into the heavy cream envelope, and she called Olivia, needing to hear a friendly voice.

Olivia answered sounding tired and harassed; Jonah was niggling in the background, calling for her attention. They ended up briefly discussing arrangements for a lunch date.

Tara missed her friend. Sometimes, she envied the all-consuming way Olivia's love and attention were wrapped up in her son.

In any case though, even if she did have Olivia's full attention, she couldn't tell her about this inheritance. She couldn't tell anyone because it wouldn't be fair. If this bank account was linked to her brother, then that meant it could also be linked to a double murder. Matthew was still the prime suspect in her parents' deaths.

After she'd said goodbye to Olivia, while she was putting a coffee on, an idea was brewing at the back of her mind. An idea she did not particularly want to acknowledge, even to herself. There was one person who could help her find out who that account belonged to, and crucially, who could be relied on for complete discretion.

I meant it when I said I could be the best friend you've ever had.

She opened the contacts list in her phone and began typing in the letters J-A-M. There he was. *Jameson, Ray.* Jade Jameson's father.

The truth was that the thought of confiding in her ex-client's father had been lurking at the back of her mind ever since she'd walked out of that first meeting with Pierre Henry. The problem was, she could not be sure whether Ray was the one person who could help her, or the last person on earth she should invite into her life.

Before she could think too hard, she sent him a message asking if they could meet. It was less than a minute before his reply came back. *Yes.*

TWENTY-TWO

Carolyn Goring agreed to see Tara again, first thing the next morning at her Harley Street office. Once again, the two women faced each other across Carolyn's desk.

'Thank you for sharing your case notes.' Tara was careful not to let her tone convey that she'd found them pretty much entirely unhelpful. 'I'd like to ask you a few more questions about Mia's treatment, if that's all right?'

Tara's notebook was open on her lap and Carolyn glanced at it briefly before answering. 'Sure.'

'Mia told me that in her last therapy session with you, she remembered killing Alice Kelly.'

Carolyn nodded.

Tara watched closely for any reaction, but there wasn't one. Carolyn was far too adept at being the blank slate. She remained relaxed in her chair, her hands resting along the armrests in a well-practiced open posture.

'That memory wasn't written up in your case notes,' Tara said. 'It does seem a significant piece of information to leave out.'

'My notes are about therapy process. I generally don't include details of too much content. There would be no point.'

Tara stopped writing and looked up. 'Even when your client confesses to killing someone?'

Carolyn frowned. 'I wouldn't have used the word *confess*.'

'What word would you have used?'

In the pause that followed, Tara was aware of the insistent ticking of the clock.

Carolyn clasped her hands loosely in her lap and crossed her legs. Subtle signs of defensiveness, perhaps. 'Mia's associations around Alice's death were no more significant than any other thoughts or images that came up during our session.'

'Okay. You used the word "associations". Could you tell me a little more about the process of reaching these associations with Mia?'

Carolyn sighed, as if she was finding Tara's questions tedious. 'Mia was lying on the couch and I asked her to speak about whatever came into her mind. In the beginning, there were random thoughts or images. That's normal. You have to be patient with the process, the connections aren't always obvious. Mia is a very visual person and she has an artist's sensibility. She described pieces of art that were on display at the gallery, for example. Then she began to see photographs she'd taken, of Alice. She described those in detail.'

That did not match Mia's version of what had happened in their final session. Mia had said that Carolyn had specifically asked her to talk about Alice, and that she had repeatedly pressured Mia to do so.

Tara looked down at the page she'd marked in her notebook. 'Mia's memory of killing Alice did not emerge during free association.'

'I beg your pardon?'

'These are Mia's exact words: "*I remember lying on my back, looking up at the chandelier, and all I could think about was the pain. It felt like my head was full of nails and it was going to explode from the pressure. But then... I was seeing all these shimmering crystal drops, shaped like tears, and I could hear Carolyn's voice, saying, "Tell me about the night Alice died." Over and over and over."'*

There was a pause. Carolyn began pushing her hair back from her face. 'Mia and I obviously remember the session somewhat differently.'

That was not impossible. Memory was unreliable and it was open to interpretation after the fact. But Tara had a lot of practice in reading people, and she had a strong sense that Carolyn was being evasive.

'Did you ask Mia directly about Alice Kelly's death?'

Carolyn didn't miss a beat. 'Of course. The violent death of a close friend is a significant trauma and it was likely to have been one of the factors causing her symptoms of depression. So yes, I would have encouraged Mia to go deeper.'

'Can you explain what you mean by "go deeper"?'

Carolyn sighed as she combed her fingers through her hair, and Tara picked up a glimmer of impatience. 'I would have asked Mia to tell me about her friendship with Alice, and the events around Alice's death. As a way to start processing her feelings about what happened.'

Tara still hadn't been able to pin Carolyn down to tell her anything specific about that last session with Mia. Carolyn was slippery. She was so good at talking in general terms that it was as though she was saying nothing at all.

Tara had to push further. She needed to know whether Carolyn may have suggested something that had influenced Mia's memory of what had happened the night Alice died.

'I apologise for telling you something that I'm sure you already know,' Tara said, 'but I need to clarify something. Research shows that repeatedly asking someone to imagine an event that did not happen can lead them to become confused between imagination and reality. Ultimately, some people will accept that the imaginary event is true. Especially people who are traumatised or severely depressed.'

Carolyn raised her eyebrows. 'You're asking me if I did something that led to the creation of a false memory?'

There was a definite edge to Carolyn's voice now, but Tara was glad to have this out in the open.

'Yes. I'm asking whether you suggested anything, or put any ideas into Mia's mind, about what she did to Alice. Even unintentionally.' Tara's words hung heavy in the air. She thought she'd overstepped the mark, but if Carolyn took offence, she was good at hiding it.

'I would regard that as unethical,' Carolyn said, calmly.

Interestingly though, she hadn't said a straight *no*.

Carolyn pushed her chair back from her desk. She uncrossed her legs and then crossed them in the other direction. Tara guessed it wouldn't be long before Carolyn grew tired of explaining herself.

'I appreciate your patience,' Tara said. 'I don't mean to question your expertise.'

'I'm not offended.' Carolyn glanced at the clock on her desk. 'So that's what this is all about? Mia is seeing you because she's concerned about that memory?'

Tara leaned forwards. 'To be clear, do you think Mia's memory of killing Alice is some kind of fantasy, or the memory of a real event?'

'I was Mia's psychotherapist. My job was to help her with unconscious processes and feelings and to treat her depression. Not to find out whether she was telling the truth.'

Tara did not believe her.

'You must have an opinion as to whether Mia has the potential to be violent?'

There was a moment, as Tara looked Carolyn directly in the eyes, of an almost imperceptible hesitation. A slow blink.

Maybe not even that; Tara wasn't sure whether she had imagined it.

Then Carolyn relaxed back in her chair, with a cynical smile on her face. 'I stick to my area of expertise, which is emotional honesty. I'll leave it to you to establish the facts.'

There was a dismissive note to Carolyn's voice which was getting under Tara's skin. 'There is a baby about to be born, who will be dependent on Mia for love and protection. I think the facts do matter. I think there is potential risk here.'

Carolyn stood up, breaking eye contact. She went over and heaved up the sash window in a fierce movement, letting in the chill air and traffic noise from Harley Street below before turning back to face Tara.

'Mia stopped her treatment so abruptly. Of course I knew she wasn't ready to end.' Carolyn ran her hands through her hair again. That was her tell. She touched her hair when she was trying to hide some rising emotion. 'It's always painful when one doesn't succeed with a patient, isn't it?'

Tara nodded.

'I have enough experience to know that you can't help everyone, but it still gets to me.' Carolyn's tone had changed and she spoke with sincerity and regret. 'I've tried to contact Mia to check up on her, but she hasn't returned my emails or calls. She knows my door is always open, but beyond that, there is nothing more I can do. As you know, you can't force someone to continue in therapy. So I'm glad she's seeing you now. Hopefully you'll get to the bottom of all of this.'

In that moment, Tara felt like an awful hypocrite. Here she was practically accusing Carolyn Goring of unethical practice, while she herself had made the dubious choice to contact Ray Jameson, father of an ex-client, for help with a highly personal matter. That was problematic in about a hundred different ways. Yes, her work on the Jameson case was over. But Jade was a very troubled young woman whom Tara had worked with intensely, and who might need Tara's help again in future. There was also the fact that Ray felt deeply grateful to Tara, which meant there was a kind of power dynamic between them which Tara should not be exploiting.

She wasn't perfect. Choices weren't always black and white, she told herself.

'My next patient is due in a few minutes,' Carolyn said. 'We'll have to end it there.'

'Well, thank you again for your time.' Tara leaned down to pick up her bag, reflecting that she hadn't got any more information out of this meeting, other than that Carolyn wasn't going to reveal her version of what Mia had told her in that last session. 'By the way, I've been meaning to ask, how was Mia referred to you?'

Carolyn pushed her hair back from her face. 'I used to work with Mia's father-in-law, David Phillips, when I was consulting to the cardiac unit at St Mary's a couple of years back. He passed on my details.'

There was something about the way Carolyn said this that set off Tara's radar. An increase in blinking; rearranging her hair yet again. It was almost as if Carolyn was embarrassed about something. Tara's gut told her Carolyn was holding something back.

TWENTY-THREE

ONE MONTH BEFORE ALICE'S DEATH

Carolyn has made all of the arrangements for their weekend break. They are staying at a boutique hotel down in Devon, in a gorgeous room overlooking the bay. This is the first time the two of them have been away together. Carolyn loves being at the hotel with him: loves walking along the beach barefoot as a couple, loves the companionship. She fantasises that one day they might come back to this place and he will be her husband.

But when the waitress brings the wine list over to their table on the first night, Carolyn's feeling of unease begins.

'I'm Kate and I'll be looking after you tonight.' She looks at him and speaks to him, ignoring Carolyn completely.

Kate is young enough to be his daughter and she knows exactly how attractive she is in that low-cut top and short skirt. Carolyn hates the way his eyes eat her up.

Stop it. You're imagining things. Again. This has to stop.

Finally, the waitress leaves them in peace. Now the sommelier comes over. He is an older man and Carolyn feels herself relaxing. She knows nothing about wine so she's happy to leave the choosing to him. They go on and on about the vintage and other things she couldn't care less about. The words wash over her. A deep red liquid swirls around the bottom of his glass and he sips it, slowly, showing off his expertise.

Suddenly, she's irritated. This all seems so pretentious, an act put on to impress the young waitress, who has returned with a basket of bread.

Finally, they've moved on to looking at the menu. Carolyn has to watch her weight and this food isn't ideal; it's full of carbohydrates, all pasta and potatoes and breadcrumbs. The bowl of bread on the table looks delicious. She touches one of the pieces, still warm and soft, but forces herself to leave it where it is.

'I think I'll go for the chicken kiev,' he says.

'Do you want to check with the waiter if that's grilled or fried?'

'What's that about?' he says.

He's a fussy eater. He doesn't like cheese on anything and he's not a fan of dishes swimming in sauce. He often orders the wrong thing.

'Remember at that Italian place, you ordered the chicken breast that came stuffed with cheese and you couldn't eat it?'

Something ugly flares in his eyes. 'You're monitoring what I eat now?'

Everything is wrong here.

She doesn't know how to respond or why he's suddenly so angry. 'I don't want you to order something you don't enjoy, that's all.'

'I'm not a child,' he says. 'I can order my own food.'

'You're misunderstanding,' she says, 'I was trying to help—'

'I don't need you to humiliate me.' His voice is raised.

The family at the next table are looking at them and she's sure they can see through everything, see through this farce to the misery underneath.

She desperately doesn't want that thought to be true. She still has hope. But her rational side has been concerned about the warning signs: moodiness, emotional distance, and worst of all, these unexplained flares of temper. But she wants this so badly. She is so tired of being alone.

She tells herself it's not personal, it's not her he's seeing. Scratch the surface and he's still relating to the mother who bullied and humiliated him. Understanding this doesn't change him though.

This is who he is. Nothing will change.

There is a white-hot silence between them.

'I apologise.' She looks down at her menu, her eyes pricking with tears. It's better not to argue. Left alone, he calms down, often within minutes.

The waitress arrives with the bottle of wine he's ordered. He's smiling again, all charm.

Carolyn adjusts the scarf that lies around her shoulders, the fabric soft and luxurious beneath her fingertips. A gift, from him.

Everything will be all right. It doesn't mean anything.

It's easier to believe the lies she tells herself than face a painful truth.

TWENTY-FOUR

As Tara rushed through the hospital corridors, she felt a weight of responsibility for what had happened to Mia. She had nearly drowned, just like Alice. That was not a coincidence.

Could she have predicted this? Prevented it somehow?

When Mia hadn't answered her phone earlier, Tara had called the gallery to try to reach her. Julia had told her that Mia had been in a serious incident, a near drowning. Tara had rushed straight to the hospital.

Mia was in an obstetrics ward, up on the second floor. Tara hovered at the door, not wanting to intrude or disturb. There were six beds in the room, and Mia was at the far end, in front of the window. She was lying on her back with the swell of her pregnancy clearly visible under the sheet. Tom Phillips was at his wife's bedside, sitting stiffly upright. An older man in a suit was standing beside Tom, with his hand resting on Tom's shoulder.

Tara was glad to see that Mia was breathing independently and not in intensive care.

After a minute or so, the man in the suit patted Tom on the

shoulder and strode across the ward and into the passageway. He passed Tara without noticing her.

Tara rushed after him. 'Excuse me—'

He stopped and turned around. He was wearing a lanyard round his neck.

'I'm Tara Black, I'm a psychologist and I've been working with Mia Phillips. Are you the consultant?'

'I'm Mia's father-in-law, David Phillips.' He held out his hand.

As they introduced themselves, Tara noted the resemblance between David and his older son, Tom. Tall and broad shouldered, David Phillips was somewhere in his sixties, with a youthful appearance. Like Tom, David took pride in his appearance, with his neat haircut, trim physique and polished shoes.

'Can you tell me anything about Mia's condition?'

'She's stable and so is the baby. They'll keep her in, at least overnight, to monitor both of them.'

Tara felt massively relieved. 'Can you tell me what happened?'

'Mia got into difficulty in the river near the cottage. Freddie got her out of the water and brought her here. That's all the information I have. Neither of them has explained what the hell Mia was doing out there, at eight months' pregnant, in this weather.' David gave a sigh of frustration as he glanced down the passage.

Tara noticed Freddie, in a leather biker's outfit, leaning against the wall further down the corridor. He had his hands in his pockets and was staring down at the floor.

'I understand you were out at my cottage with her?' David asked.

'Yes.' Tara felt another pang of responsibility.

'Why was Mia out there in the first place?'

'I'm sorry, I can't discuss that.' Tara could obviously understand his concern, but she still had to be careful about boundaries and confidentiality.

'You can't discuss it?' For a moment he looked intensely angry, but then he took a breath, as if trying to rein himself in.

'I'd like to see Mia,' Tara said. 'Is that possible?'

'She's in no state for visitors. I think it's best to wait until the obstetric consultant has been to see her.'

Tara decided it would be unwise to push the issue. It was probably too soon anyway, as Mia would likely still be in shock.

David was again looking down the corridor in Freddie's direction. Freddie was staring determinedly down at the floor, hanging his head like a guilty man. He too must feel bad, for taking Mia out to the cottage.

'Can you at least give me a view about whether Mia is capable of looking after herself, if they discharge her?' David Phillips spoke with authority and a certain arrogance. He was a man who was used to being in charge and to being obeyed.

'If Mia gives me permission, I could talk to her consultant.' The truth was, Tara could not answer that question. 'My assessment is still ongoing.'

David Phillips gave an unimpressed sort of grunt in response. 'If my daughter-in-law discloses something that means she is a danger, either to herself or her child, you do have to disclose that, correct?'

'Yes, that's right. And I am aware of safety issues for both Mia and the baby. I do think it's a good idea that she stays under observation of the staff here for the next few days.'

'That's good to know. Thank you.' David nodded a curt goodbye and began walking in the direction of the lifts.

Tara noticed that Freddie had vanished. Which was a pity, as she wanted to talk to him about what had happened at that cottage after she'd left.

. . .

Back in her office, Tara took time to review her notes on the case so far and to regroup.

Can you at least give me a view about whether Mia is capable of looking after herself, if they discharge her?

David Phillips was right to be concerned. Mia was heavily pregnant, but acted as though she was in denial of that fact. She'd been missing medical appointments and now she had put her own life and the life of her unborn child at risk. Her mental state may well be precarious and Tara could not take the chance of missing something again. She owed it to Mia and to Mia's unborn baby to make some clear recommendations.

Tara decided she needed to widen the scope of her assessment. She had to gather some collateral information from people close to Mia to form a solid opinion. Normally, she wouldn't do this without talking to the patient first and ideally getting their permission, but at this stage, she decided that the benefits outweighed the risk of waiting. She had no idea when Mia would be in a state to be interviewed. The alternative would be to contact social services if she couldn't be sure Mia's baby was going to be safe in her care, and at this point that option seemed extreme.

The first thing Tara did was call the Thames Valley Police. After what seemed like a long time on hold, she was finally put through to someone at the Oxford police station who told her that DS Ayola wasn't in at the moment. At least now though, Tara now knew where to find her.

'Would you like to leave a message?' the person on the other end of the line asked.

Tara hesitated. Then she said, 'Yes. My name is Doctor Tara Black, I'm a psychologist and I would like to talk to her about the death of Alice Kelly.'

Next, Tara tried to reach Tom Phillips. He picked up his phone straight away and agreed to come to Tara's office for a meeting late the following afternoon. He sounded pleased to have the chance to talk to her.

The third person Tara reached out to was Freddie Phillips. He had driven Mia out to the cottage, and he had been the sole witness to what had happened down at the river.

TWENTY-FIVE

Freddie Phillips lived with his mother in Hampstead, on a street called New End, which was within easy walking distance of the gallery. Julia's home was gorgeous, a free standing, two-storey Georgian house, covered in ivy. A chunky motorbike parked to the left of the front door looked somewhat out of place next to the elegant façade; Tara assumed that must belong to Freddie.

She had asked Julia for his telephone number and had arranged to come over and talk to him in a brief call, but now there was no answer when she rang the doorbell. As Tara stood waiting, she could hear the burble of children's voices from the playground of the primary school nearby. Intermittently, she could also hear what sounded like a power tool blasting out from around the side of the house.

Eventually, after she'd been waiting several minutes, Tara followed the noise down a narrow path that ran down the side of the house. Freddie was at the back of the garden, up on a ladder, trimming back the branches of a yew tree. It took her a few minutes to get his attention because he was wearing a large set of headphones to block out the sound of the electric saw.

In the meantime, Tara noticed how beautiful the small

garden was, and how well kept; sculptural trees naked without their leaves and hornbeam hedges turned brown for the winter. She thought regretfully of her own rather scruffy patch of lawn with its various mud patches and a border of unruly hedges. She also thought back to the tidy garden at the cottage out in Oxfordshire, wondering if it was Freddie who went out there to maintain it for his father.

Finally, after a couple of minutes of waving and shouting, Freddie noticed her. He took off the headphones, balancing them around his neck, and climbed down from the ladder.

'Sorry, I lost track of time.' Freddie gripped the saw with both hands, as if it were a machine gun. He seemed uncomfortable and Tara guessed it wasn't by chance he'd been out in the garden at the time he knew she was due to arrive.

They walked back to the patio area where Freddie lowered the saw, leaving it on the paving stones.

'Can I get you something to drink?' Freddie continued to avoid any eye contact with Tara, keeping his gaze on the ground.

'I'm fine, thank you.'

A large bag of seed was lying open on the teak garden table and Freddie picked it up and went over to refill the bird-feeders that were hanging from hooks along the perimeter fence.

'Once you put these feeders up,' he said, 'the birds can't do without the extra food. You have to keep filling them.' He was discharging nervous energy as he moved and still not looking at her.

It didn't seem that he was going to invite her inside the house, so Tara reached into her bag for her notebook and pen and used the table to press on. 'Freddie, I wanted to talk about what happened to Mia out at the cottage, after I left.'

'I really don't know.'

'But you were the one who found her, in the river?'

Freddie nodded. He was in a T-shirt but didn't seem to be feeling the cold.

'So how did she get down there?'

'After you left, Mia asked me to wait for her in the car. She said she wanted a few more minutes alone in the house. So I went out and waited, I was listening to music, I'd put it up pretty loud. After about fifteen minutes, when she didn't come out, I went inside to see what was going on. She wasn't in the house, and the back door was wide open. So was the gate at the bottom of the garden. I walked down to the river and there she was.' Freddie looked embarrassed as he told her this; as if he thought he was being accused of something.

'Can you describe what you saw?'

'She had her back to me, and she stepped down into the water. I yelled out at her to stop, but she didn't listen. She kept going. I ran towards her and by the time I got there, she was in up to her neck. I hauled her out.'

'Did she seem distressed? Panicked?'

Freddie shook his head. 'No. She was calm. Didn't seem to feel the cold, either. At first she was struggling a bit, when I tried to pull her out with me, but then she kind of gave up.'

'Okay, so after you pulled her out of the water, what happened then?'

'Mia was kind of dazed. Shivering like mad, both of us were. I tried to get her to change, I have some spare gym kit in my boot, but she wasn't having any of it. All I could do was get her to take off her socks and trainers and put a blanket over her. I offered to take her past a hospital, you know to check everything was okay with the baby, but she didn't want to, she wanted to get home and have a bath. She was conscious and she seemed okay, and Mia's pretty stubborn. I though the best thing was to just drive her home. And let Tom handle it from there.'

'But in the end, you did take her to a hospital?' Tara had

been wondering how Mia landed up in hospital in London, and not somewhere nearer to Oxford.

'I turned the heating up like mad and she fell asleep in the car. Around halfway back to London, she started breathing too fast, kind of panting and gasping a bit in her sleep. I was freaked out, I thought it could be cold water shock setting in, so I headed straight to the Royal Free, I know the place because it's so near where we live.'

Some elements of Freddie story seemed odd. Putting a heavily pregnant woman in wet clothes into a car for a journey that would take over an hour, for one thing. But she supposed he couldn't exactly wrestle a stubborn Mia out of her clothing. Tara would also have thought that common sense dictated that Freddie should have taken Mia directly to a hospital, but then again, waiting times at A and E could be nightmarish, and Mia had refused and stubbornly insisted on going home, and she was an adult.

'What kind of state was Mia in by the time you got to the hospital?'

'Bad.' Freddie shook his head, looking as though he felt guilty. 'I couldn't get her to wake up. Her breathing wasn't right. I practically carried her inside.'

As she scribbled her notes, Tara's fingers were turning bluish and stiffening up in the cold. 'Freddie, did Mia say anything either on the journey out there, or while you were in the cottage with her, that worried you? Or struck you as unusual? Anything you thought might indicate she was at risk of harming herself?'

Freddie thought a moment and then shook his head. 'She didn't say much of anything, which wasn't unusual. That's what Mia's like. She's always quiet. You never can tell what she's thinking.'

A red-breasted robin flew down and perched on one of the teak patio chairs right in front of Tara, looking up expectantly.

'My little gardening buddy.' Freddie came over and scattered a handful of seed onto the paving. 'Did you know these sweet-looking birds are actually highly aggressive?'

'I didn't.'

The little bird hopped down, gathered up some seed and flew off.

'They'll fight each other to the death over territory. A bit like my parents.' Freddie smiled, grimly. 'My mother got this house after the divorce, she had to fight for it tooth and nail.'

Tara's conversation with Freddie was brief, and over in a matter of minutes. He hadn't been able to give her much insight into what had happened that led Mia to go down to that river, in what seemed alarmingly like it could have been a suicide attempt.

Freddie opened the door to the conservatory and lead Tara inside the house to show her out. The room was full of large palms and cacti, with two wicker armchairs facing out into the garden. A fluffy white cat lay stretched out alongside the radiator, soaking up the warmth and the winter sun coming through the windows.

Freddie paused as he bent down to stroke him. 'This old man is Geoffrey. He's sixteen now. Mum got him from a shelter after my father moved out. She'd always wanted a cat, but my father is allergic. Or claims to be.'

The cat was purring loudly. Given this was the second comment Freddie had made about his parents' relationship, Tara gathered there was no love lost between Julia and Mia's father-in-law David, whom she'd met briefly at the hospital the day before.

Freddie straightened up and Tara followed him into a passageway that led through to the front door. Every bit of wall space was covered in paintings, mainly portraits. The overall effect was a little claustrophobic, and eerie with all those eyes watching her walk past.

A framed photograph in the midst of all the other artwork caught Tara's eye. The picture was of a group of men in army fatigues. It had been taken from a distance and they were all wearing caps; the faces were too indistinct to make out any features.

'Are you in this photo? Or Tom?'

Freddie turned around and came back to where she stood, pointing at one of the men. 'This one's me. Or it used to be. Now I'm a thirty-five-year-old, overweight, unemployed loser who drinks too much and lives with his mother.'

Under the unkempt exterior, and the few excess pounds Freddie carried, perhaps a result of the alcohol, Tara could see the vital man Freddie had once been.

'Were you on active duty?' she asked him.

'I was a paratrooper. Afghanistan.'

'Did your time there affect you?'

'The usual. Nightmares. Irritability. Flashbacks.'

'How long have you had a drinking problem?'

'Forever. It started in my early teens, but I managed to stop all that crap when I went into the army. As soon as I got back home though, it all went to hell again.' Freddie leaned back against the wall, his hands in the pockets of his cargo trousers. 'I worked in private security for a while, but I lost that job, for being under the influence, as they say. Then I lost a few more jobs the same way. So now I make myself useful by keeping the garden looking pretty and driving Julia around at night, because she's blind as a bat in the dark.'

If Freddie had started drinking that young, there was probably a good reason. That turned Tara's thoughts to her own brother. He'd also started drinking as an adolescent.

'Do you ever think about getting help?' she asked.

'Help?' Freddie laughed.

'What's funny?'

'Nothing. Sorry. No, I haven't tried to get help.' He was looking down at the cat. Geoffrey had followed him into the passage and was rubbing himself around Freddie's ankles. 'I don't go anywhere near your lot. Scares me to death. My mother's been trying to get me to see someone but it's not my scene. Being out in the garden is the best medicine.'

'I know what you mean.' Tara had a flash of her kettlebells class. She was convinced the gym kept her sane. 'Don't tell anyone but I sometimes wonder whether exercise can be as an effective a prescription as therapy or drugs. That said, let me know if you ever want me to give you some names. There is good treatment available.'

Tara watched as Freddie knelt down to scratch the cat behind its ear. Under the surface of his glib description of his suffering, she sensed a lot of emotion. Freddie was afraid of showing it, that's why he wouldn't look at her. He had described symptoms of post-traumatic stress and despite what he'd said about avoiding mental health professionals, he'd made a point of opening up to her without too much prompting. A part of him did want help. But he wasn't ready.

As Tara wound her way back to where she'd parked, through the quaint back streets of Hampstead Village, past rows of pastel-painted terrace houses, a message from Ray Jameson came through that temporarily pushed her concerns about Mia Phillips to the back of her mind.

He suggested that they meet in the bar of The Onyx Hotel.

TWENTY-SIX

Ray looked exactly the same as the last time Tara had seen him, almost a year before. Thickset, wearing a double-breasted suit, and carrying a certain feral, magnetic energy. He was leaning against the pewter bar counter in the basement of The Onyx Hotel, waiting for her.

Ray owned the hotel. It was also the place where his daughter Jade had been accused of murdering an ex-police officer. Tara had visited The Onyx several times while working with Jade on her defence. Being there again was a stark reminder of the boundaries she was about to cross by asking an ex-client's father for help.

Despite her misgivings, Tara quickly realised that the bar was the ideal meeting place. It was packed full of shiny, glamorous people flirting and laughing and drinking and she could not have felt more inconspicuous as she walked towards him.

'Doctor Black!' Ray straightened up, greeting her with a genuine smile and a strong handshake.

A former strip club manager turned hotelier, he was fabulously wealthy and intensely loyal to those people he considered friends. Tara had become one of those when she had treated his daughter.

They moved over to sit at one of the tables arranged along the wall opposite the counter. Nerves were making her cold and Tara kept her coat on as she sat down in the oversized armchair. Ray was carrying a bottle of wine and two glasses and he set these down and poured them each a drink.

'How is Jade doing at university?' Tara asked, trying to quell her nerves.

'She's amazing. Top of her class in Edinburgh.'

Ray's daughter had been Tara's client in the first murder case she had worked on for defence solicitor Valerie Bennett. At the time, Ray had put her under enormous pressure to deliver a report saying what he wanted it to say, which was that Jade's amnesia for the night of the killing was genuine. Jameson was well connected, and not only within the strictly legal channels, and he was a forceful character who was used to getting what he wanted. The friction between him and Tara had been very high at the time Daniel was killed. For a time, Tara even suspected that Ray Jameson may have orchestrated the hit-and-run, and that she may have been the real target. But as Tara had got to know Jameson better, and the police remained convinced that Daniel's accident was a random crime, she had become less sure he was involved. Ultimately, when Jameson had looked Tara in the eye and denied it strongly, she'd decided to believe him.

Now he might be about to become an unexpected ally.

Ray held out a wine glass. Tara took it from him, hoping the alcohol would take the edge off her doubts about the risk she was taking.

'You once told me I could regard you as a friend,' she said, 'and I have a favour to ask.'

Ray nodded. 'Go ahead.'

'A few days ago, I found out that I have an inheritance from

Daniel Franks' estate.' Tara took a sip of her drink. The wine was cold and crisp.

She told him about the large sum of money in Daniel's bank account and the regular monthly transfers that he had been making to a mystery account. Ray leaned forward, his hands clasped and his head down, listening intently. It was such a relief to finally share this with someone.

'At the moment, all I have is an international bank account number and I'd like your help to find out who owns this account.' Tara's voice sounded quite calm but underneath the surface, it was a different story. 'I also need to ask for your discretion because... well, there is a chance that this person is wanted by the police.'

The stripes in Ray's suit glowed white under the fluorescent pink wall lights. He had made no comment so far and he showed no sign of either surprise or judgement.

Tara sat forward, putting her glass down. Then she lifted it back up again. Having something to hold gave her a safety blanket. 'You already know that my parents were murdered twenty-six years ago. My brother Matthew disappeared the same night they died, and the police consider him a suspect. I think these bank transfers may somehow be connected to him, because Matthew and Daniel were best friends. I can think of no other reason for Daniel wanting me to have control of that account. He could have just given me the money.'

She took a breath. There, it had all been said.

Ray nodded. He gave the impression he had heard it all before and probably a lot worse besides. 'Do you think your brother is guilty?'

'I've never wanted to believe it. But Matthew had serious drug and alcohol problems and there was huge conflict between him and my father. It had got physical, before, between the two of them. So... I don't know. I've never known if he even survived that night.'

Tara was aware of how vulnerable she was making herself. But she needed Ray's help, and if she wanted it she had to be honest. There was comfort in the background blues music and the babble of voices; she felt almost as if they were inside an invisible bubble. 'The police always suspected that I knew more than I was telling them.'

'Do you?'

'No. Not consciously anyway. I've always wondered if I was drugged that night, maybe with something like Rohypnol. But by the time anyone had thought to do a blood test, it was probably too late to pick up anything, so there's no way to be sure. If my memory was going to come back though, I think it would have happened by now.'

The last thing she did recall clearly was being at her brother's party, the one he was not supposed to be having while her parents were away. She only had eyes for Daniel that night; Matthew's best friend who saw her as nothing more than Matthew's kid sister. She remembered that Daniel had been outside, smoking and talking to a group of friends, and that she had been keeping an eye on him through the kitchen window. She'd been vaguely aware that her brother and his then-girlfriend Sabine had disappeared up into his bedroom and she'd been irritated about that. It was Matthew's party and he wasn't even that interested in it. He'd done this as an act of defiance because he knew their father would have a fit if he found out. And he would find out, given the state the house was in.

That was all. The last thing she remembered was looking out of that window and watching Daniel smoking and laughing. The way he held his cigarette; the way he smiled with his whole being.

Tara did not remember her parents coming home.

There must have been screams, but she did not hear them.

Tara would never really know whether it was drugs that had made her forget, or good old repression. She had to admit there might be some things about that night she didn't want to remember.

'I was interviewed by police several times,' she said. 'They suspected that I knew where Matthew was and what he'd done, and they even questioned whether I might have had something to do with what happened that night. Probably because my brother and I were beneficiaries of my parents' insurance policies, so I guess that was supposed to be the motive. My aunt and uncle hired a good solicitor for me, and in the end no charges were ever brought.'

'I don't envy you, living with all that.' Ray refilled both of their glasses.

Tara suspected that Ray might know about all of this already, because he'd investigated her background when she'd been working with Jade. Ray was one of a handful of people who knew about Tara's past, including the fact that she had changed her name. She had never worked out exactly where he had got his information from.

In any case, she wanted to lay it all out again because it was important to her that Ray saw that she was being upfront with him.

'Will you help me trace the owner of that bank account? If there's a chance my brother is alive, I have to know.'

'I can look into it.' There was hesitation in his voice.

'If you're not comfortable with this, then would you know someone else who—'

He interrupted. 'If this person does turn out to be your brother, then he must have a good reason for going into hiding for the last twenty-odd years.'

Tara nodded, tuning in to the hum of voices and the scent of alcohol and perfume that mingled in the windowless bar. She felt a little lightheaded.

'I'm assuming that if you find out where Matthew is, you will want to see him.'

'I haven't thought that far ahead.'

Ray was right, of course.

Tara reached into her bag and took out the documents she had brought with her. Photocopies of the bank statements and a copy of the photograph page of Matthew's old passport. She handed these over. Ray took a few moments to look through them before tucking the papers into the inside pocket of his suit jacket. As usual, he was wearing his emerald pinkie ring which looked so out of place on his chunky fingers.

'Have you considered that your brother may be a dangerous man?'

'No.' The idea was so jarring and Tara was so on edge that she almost laughed.

She hadn't. Not for a single second. Not dangerous to her, anyway.

'Maybe you should think about that, before you begin this process.'

'It's too late. I've already made up my mind.'

TWENTY-SEVEN

After leaving The Onyx, Tara decided it would be more productive to go and check on Mia rather than to go home and try to sleep, or worse, find herself back on Wildway Close.

By the time she got to the hospital it was nine thirty and the car park was deserted, with visiting hours long over. On impulse, before she left her car, Tara leaned across and grabbed her old NHS lanyard from the glove compartment. As she entered the hospital she placed the blue ribbon around her neck.

There was no sign of Mia in the ward she'd been in earlier. After glancing at Tara's lanyard, a nurse told her that her client had been moved to a room in the private wing on the twelfth floor. Up there, the nurses at the front desk didn't ask any questions before directing Tara to Mia's room. They seemed quite relieved to see her, mentioning that Mia was having difficulty sleeping. The automatic trust the staff put in her was probably the lanyard effect, Tara thought with a twinge of guilt. Although maybe visiting hours were also more relaxed on a private ward.

The door of Mia's room was ajar and Tara knocked and

entered. Mia was propped up against a couple of pillows in her hospital bed. Her face was pale and her short hair had lost its spikiness, lying limp and flat.

The hospital room was dead quiet with thick glazed windows shutting out all noise.

'Do you feel like some company?' Tara asked.

Mia nodded, looking down at her hands which lay still and small on top of the white sheets. She looked so vulnerable.

Tara always imagined she could tell the age at which someone had experienced trauma by a certain way they held themselves, and in that moment she was looking at a six-year-old child who was alone and scared.

Tara pulled up one of the visitors' chairs next to the bed. 'Do you want to talk about happened?'

'It was an accident,' Mia said.

'Okay.' Tara waited. She was hesitant to put any more pressure on Mia so soon after a near drowning. She was still asking herself if she'd missed something, and if there was anything she could have done to prevent harm. Maybe it had been too much for Mia to walk through the events of that fatal night.

'After we'd been talking out at the cottage,' Mia said, 'my mind was so full of Alice. I wanted to feel closer to her. I went down to the river, because that was the last place I'd photographed her. But I didn't mean to hurt myself. I must have slipped.'

Tara recalled Freddie's description of Mia's behaviour down at the river.

She was calm. Didn't seem to feel the cold, either. At first she was struggling a bit, when I tried to pull her out with me, but then she kind of gave up.

It was difficult to get a clear picture of what had happened.

Perhaps a part of Mia had wanted to escape her pain in that freezing water.

Tara knew what it was like to feel loss and guilt wrapped

like tentacles around the heart and brain. She knew what it was like to live with not knowing. Daniel's death had been the most recent loss in her life, and the wound was still raw.

Mia sank back into her pillows, turning her head away so that she was staring at the window. Her reflection looked back at her with wretched eyes.

Tara sat quietly at her bedside. She did not ask any more questions, because she suspected Mia did not know the true answers herself. Those were buried in her unconscious, making her act in ways she could not understand or explain.

After a while, Mia spoke, breaking the silence. 'It's a girl,' she said. 'They did a scan to check that everything was all right, and they told me it's a girl.'

Tears dripped down onto the sheets.

Tara wanted so badly to reach out to offer a comforting touch, but she knew it was unwise to cross that line. All she could do was sit there and hope that was some comfort.

After a while Mia's eyes drifted closed. Her cheeks glistened with tears.

'I'll come back and see you tomorrow,' Tara said.

Mia didn't respond. Perhaps she was asleep.

Tara stepped out of Mia's room, leaving the door ajar the same way she'd found it earlier. An older man she didn't recognise was walking down the corridor towards her.

He stopped and looked at her lanyard. 'Are you one of Mia's doctors? I'm John Clarke, Mia's father.'

He was an ordinary-looking man, with a slight paunch, greying hair and glasses. There was nothing of Mia's edginess or style about him.

'I'm Tara Black, I'm a psychologist.' Tara held out her hand to shake his.

'How is Mia doing?' His grip was weak, and he quickly

withdrew his hand and tucked it back into the pocket of his overcoat.

'She's physically stable and I understand the baby is doing fine too.'

It's a girl.

'Good. Good. Tom's been keeping me updated. I wanted to get here earlier but it's been one of those days.'

Tara was still standing in front of Mia's door and now she closed it softly behind her. 'Actually, I'm glad I've bumped into you because I was going to contact you to make a time to talk. Mia has just dozed off. Would you have a few minutes to talk to me first before you go in to see her?'

John glanced around, hesitating before he answered. 'Uh... I suppose that's all right. What is this about?'

Clearly he wasn't keen.

'I was hoping you could give me some information about Mia's childhood.'

Mia had said she remembered very little from the first ten years of her life, and very few details at all about her mother.

John gave small sigh. 'I can't stay too long, I live out in St Albans and I don't want to miss the last train back. What is it you need to know?'

'Anything you can tell me would be helpful. Anything significant.'

'Such as?'

Tara was getting a sense of John's detachment, as though he was reluctant to become involved in his daughter's problems. His tone and demeanour gave the impression that he would really rather be somewhere else. She found herself irritated with him for his apparent lack of concern.

Tara tried her best to keep the impatience out of her voice. 'For example, what was Mia like as a baby or a toddler, and how did she get along at school?'

'She wasn't an easy child.'

'In what way?'

'She didn't ever seem to sleep. She'd be constantly crying and nothing seemed to help, it didn't matter what we did. It was exhausting for Sarah, and I freely admit I didn't help enough, I left all of that to her mother.' He smiled, which was disconcerting because he was talking about something sad. It wasn't a genuine smile, but more of a reflex. 'The second time around, it was different. I've remarried you see, and I have two boys now.'

'Right. When you say Mia wasn't an easy child, can you say more about that?'

John sighed, a deeper one this time. 'Mia wasn't happy, I suppose. When she was a little older, there were constant temper tantrums. I used to find weekends at home quite exhausting. At nursery, she couldn't get on with other children; she used to bite and lash out, and we ended up having to move her a couple of times. As I say, I was at work and Sarah took the brunt of it so I can't really give you many more details.'

For Tara the question was why Mia had been so unhappy and angry. It sounded like this pattern had begun even before she lost her mother, and perhaps that relationship hadn't been a close one either. It was clear from the way Mia's father talked that he couldn't empathise much with Mia's emotional state as a child and had kept his distance.

'The death of Mia's mother at such a young age must have been very difficult. How did she react to that?'

John looked at Tara strangely, narrowing his eyes. He seemed confused. 'I don't follow?'

'Mia's mother died of cancer when she was seven, is that right?'

'Is that what Mia told you?'

Tara nodded.

'Sarah's never had cancer. And she is very much alive.'

TWENTY-EIGHT

So Mia had lied about her mother dying of cancer.

John had explained that when Mia was seven years old, her mother hadn't been ill, but she had left the family, abandoning both Mia and her husband. At the time, the three of them had been living in the Netherlands and according to Mia's father, Sarah had packed up her belongings, taken a bus to Schiphol airport and never returned. She apparently didn't want any more contact with John or their daughter. The reason for this, John believed, was that she was struggling with depression and living abroad was too difficult for her. John, who was out of his depth having not had much of a hands-on role as a father before, had hired a series of nannies to look after Mia as he continued to move countries for his job. Mia's difficult behaviour graduated to school truancy, and sometimes she barely left her bedroom. When she was older he had sent Mia to boarding school and there her behaviour seemed to settle down. John had not had any further complaints from the school other than remarks that Mia was quite solitary and had trouble making friends. The two of them had remained distant from each other.

John had gone on to explain that Mia's mother lived in an

apartment in Buckinghamshire, which she had inherited from
her parents. She worked as an assistant in a local pharmacy. He
and his ex-wife had no contact, but it didn't sound like the relationship was hostile.

It was becoming clear that Mia had never had much of a
secure bond with either of her parents. Her father, by his own
admission, had been uninvolved in her life and, for whatever
reason, Mia's mother had abandoned her. Tara wasn't sure why
Mia had lied about that, but perhaps it was something too difficult to face. And her mother's abandonment could certainly be
linked to Mia's conflict over her own pregnancy.

Tara spent most of the following day with a new client, a
twenty-year-old young man from a wealthy family who had
been caught shoplifting several times. His solicitor questioned if
he had a learning disability or any other condition which meant
he couldn't tell right from wrong. Tara had administered this set
of IQ tests and personality questionnaires many times and she
welcomed the fact that this was a case with straightforward
answers.

'All finished.' Her client, Timothy, looked up at her and
grinned. With his big blue eyes, he was used to charming his
way out of trouble.

Tara smiled back. Unfortunately, she could already tell
from these few hours of being with him that there was no
evidence of serious cognitive impairment or mental disorder.
He was going to have to face the consequences of his actions.
But that conversation would be between him and his solicitor.
All Tara had to do was write the report.

After she'd let Timothy out of the mews house, Tara had a
couple of hours free until her scheduled appointment with Tom
Phillips. She called the hospital and was reassured to hear that
Mia had been settled overnight. There was no set discharge

date yet and that too was a relief to know that Mia would remain in a safe environment for the time being.

It felt like perfect timing when a few minutes later, Tara received a phone call from DS Ayola. Tara began by saying how appreciative she was to the detective for making the time to speak to her.

'My colleague said you're a psychologist?' DS Ayola sounded quite intrigued.

'That's right. I'm trying to find information about the investigation into Alice Kelly's death.' Tara explained that she was doing some trauma work with Alice's close friend, Mia Phillips.

'Sure. What sort of details are you after exactly?'

'It's been three years,' Tara continued, 'and because my client was in shock at the time, she's having trouble remembering some of what actually happened.'

That wasn't a million miles from the truth.

'For one thing,' Tara said, 'can you clarify Alice's cause of death?'

'I'm afraid I can't. The coroner returned an open verdict.'

'Could you explain more about why that was?'

'Okay, sure. So there was water in Alice's lungs, which indicates that she was alive at the time she went into the water, although she could already have been unconscious at that point. But how Alice got into the river is a more difficult question to answer. It's possible that she could have been assaulted before she entered the water, or that she may have slipped or fallen into the river, or even that she entered the water deliberately.'

'Deliberately? You mean she could have been suicidal?'

'It's a possibility, but it seems unlikely. No one who knew Alice had any evidence that she was at risk of suicide. But Alice did have cannabis in her system and it's possible she had a bad reaction to what she'd smoked, or it was a particularly strong batch – it happens. So, for example, maybe because Alice was under the influence, she decided it was a good idea to go out in the dark for a walk, and maybe a swim too, and then once she was in the water she could have got into difficulty or succumbed to cold water shock.'

'Okay. That's really helpful, thank you.'

Mia had not mentioned the fact that there had been cannabis used at the cottage. Tara wondered who had supplied the drugs and if Mia had been high too. That would explain both her memory loss and her confusion over what she did remember.

'I understand that there were some injuries on Alice's body though?' Mia had mentioned bruising in their first interview.

'That's right. But again, when a body has been in the water for some time, it can be difficult to identify the cause of the injuries. For example, Alice could have hit her head as she fell into the water. She was also found some way from where she most likely entered the water, given that she left the cottage on foot, so her body could have been battered along the way. Plus, if she didn't die immediately, her injuries would behave as pre-mortem injuries even though they happened after she entered the water – sorry, is this too technical? I'm not quite sure what you're looking for?'

'No, no, not at all. This is brilliant, thank you. Can I check if there was any sign of sexual assault?'

'Not that we could tell. And Alice was fully clothed,' the detective said. 'That was at least some consolation we could give to her family.'

Tara was making notes as fast and as comprehensively as she could. 'I was also wondering if you might have inter-viewed my client? Mia Clarke was her name at the time and she was staying with Alice in the cottage at the time of her death.'

'I didn't personally, no. That would have been one of my colleagues.'

'Would that interview have been recorded?'

'Uh, not necessarily. There will be written notes some-where. I'm afraid I don't think I can get you access to those.'

'I understand. I have one last question. Would you have tested for DNA, to see if Alice had been assaulted, you know, in the wounds, under her fingernails, anything like that?'

'The short answer is no. Because her body had been in the water for several hours, and we know that DNA can dissipate quite quickly – things like loose hair or skin cells – we couldn't allocate resources to that. Testing is expensive, and it's hit and miss too. If you don't take samples from the exact right area, there's no result anyway. It's not the magic bullet people think it is. There just wasn't enough to justify it.'

'That's really helpful. Thank you again.'

'I'm glad I could help,' DS Ayola said. 'It's one of those cases that stays with you. It's hard when you can't even give the loved ones closure, let alone justice.'

TWENTY-NINE

Tom Phillips took off his coat and draped it neatly over the back of the armchair in Tara's office. When he sat down, there was a stiffness about his posture and his back was ramrod straight. It was the same tense position Tara had noticed in the hospital next to Mia's bed.

'How is Mia today?' she asked him.

'The registrar seems happy with how she's doing, but the consultant was called away to an emergency so he never turned up. They'll keep her overnight and Mr Rance will hopefully see her in the morning.' Tom adjusted the cuffs of his white shirt. 'I'm glad you contacted me. I really don't know how to help her anymore. This has all been going on for months.'

'Tell me what you've noticed,' Tara said.

He kept fiddling with his shirtsleeves as he spoke, 'Basically, Mia's been struggling ever since we found out she was pregnant. Most of the time, she behaves as though the baby doesn't exist.'

Tara felt a sudden chill, even though the heating in the building was up high.

'She's due in a few weeks, and we don't own a single baby item except for the stuff my mother bought us. And that's all still wrapped in plastic.' Tom rubbed his jaw, trying to ease the tension he carried there. Then he leaned forward, his hands clenched. 'Mia never talks about our child. If I raise the subject, she ignores me, so I've stopped trying. I've even stopped being excited. Mia is usually incredibly reliable and responsible, but somehow she forgets her antenatal checkups. Obviously – well, I've actually got no idea how she feels because she doesn't talk to me – but I'm assuming she's very unhappy.'

Tom seemed grateful to get all of this off his chest and his words poured out with a sense of urgency. 'I've been trying to convince her to talk to someone for months. When she started seeing Carolyn, I was so relieved. And then I found out she'd stopped going.'

It struck Tara that Tom had referred to Mia's psychotherapist by her first name, in a familiar sort of way.

He was sitting upright, staring at her intently with his hands still clasped tight in front of him. 'I'm afraid of what's going to happen when the baby is born.'

'What specifically are you afraid of?'

Tom cleared his throat. After a slight hesitation, he said, 'Sometimes I don't know who Mia is. She probably told you that we got together after Alice died. Maybe it was all too fast and too intense. Too complicated.'

There were a few minutes of silence where Tom looked deeply sad and his eyes welled up.

Tara was still left with the sense there was something more he wanted her to know. 'Tom, you said you're afraid of what will happen after the baby's born. What are you afraid of?'

He was fidgeting, pulling at his sleeves again, and then rubbing his tight jaw. 'A week ago, I came home early from work and I found Mia in our bedroom. I guess I surprised her. She was standing in front of the mirror, in her underwear, looking at herself. And she was wearing Alice's pendant. It's in the shape of a heart, and it was a gift from me.'

Tara remembered that pendant. Alice had been wearing it in the photograph Mia had shown her.

Tom was clenching his teeth so hard that muscles bulged along his jaw. 'Alice never took that pendant off. She showered with it on. She even slept with it around her neck. But it was missing when they found her body and I always wondered if someone… if someone who hurt her may have taken it. Even though I suppose the most likely thing was that the chain had broken in the water and been washed away. And then it turns out that Mia has had it all along. She's been hiding it.'

'Did you ask Mia how she got hold of it?'

Tom looked down at the blue rug. He shook his head. 'I couldn't. Everything had been building up between us and I was too worked up. I thought it was better to just leave the room and get some distance until I calmed down. I slept on the sofa and when I left for work the next morning, Mia was still asleep. I knew she had a session with Carolyn, so I thought maybe she'd talk about it there and then come to me and explain, when she was ready. But she never did. Not a word. Then a couple of days later, she went out to the cottage and had this accident. Or whatever it was.'

Tom closed his eyes, covering his face for a moment. When he lowered his hands, he sighed with frustration. 'Is she having some kind of breakdown? Please, tell me what is going on.'

I'm worried about what's going to happen once the baby is born.

Tom seemed to be implying that Mia had a hidden side; that she might be dangerous.

'Maybe when Mia is up to it, we could set up a joint session and talk this through, if you both agree that would be helpful.'

'So you won't give me a view now? Advice on how to handle this?'

'I'm sorry, I can't do that.' Tara didn't blame him for being frustrated, but her hands were tied for now. Mia was her client.

'I can give you the name of a psychologist you can talk to. He's excellent—'

'That's it? Really?' Tom gave a cynical laugh. 'Okay. Well, you asked me to come and see you. Is there anything else you want to know?'

'That's enough for now. I appreciate you coming in.'

'Well, I won't take up any more of your time.' Tom stood up and shoved his arms into the sleeves of his coat.

Tara was left with mixed impressions about Tom Phillips. On the one hand, he came across as sincere and genuinely concerned for the welfare of his wife and his unborn child. But on the other, he had become irritable quickly when Tara could not give him what he wanted.

It was interesting too that Tom seemed to have a habit of walking in on Mia by surprise. The last time he'd done so had been when Tara was with Mia at their home. Sometimes caring and controlling behaviours were hard to distinguish from one another.

In fairness though, Tom was under immense stress with Mia in the hospital and she couldn't assume this was a fair reflection of his personality.

Tara opened her laptop and did some online digging. She found the profile of the secondary school where Tom was the newly appointed deputy head. Further googling revealed various reports of the school being in 'special measures', with problems ranging from drugs and violence to truancy. Parental unemployment was high and student results were much lower than the national average. Tom had been appointed about a year earlier with the hopes that he would be an important part of the team responsible for turning the school around. On the surface at least, Mia's husband seemed to be well respected and he held a responsible role caring for vulnerable children.

Tara wrote up a summary of the meeting with Tom Phillips. She ended by listing a few questions she could not yet answer. Tom had painted a picture of his wife as someone unravelling, as a person who couldn't be trusted. Did that mean he had mentally checked out of the marriage? Was he already anticipating a custody battle?

And did he have his own suspicions about his wife's involvement in Alice Kelly's death?

Tara sat at her desk with a cup of strong coffee and stared at the screen.

It's a girl.

Some people are born evil, aren't they? They hurt people because they want to.

Mia had looked so defenceless in her hospital bed. It was very difficult to imagine her committing an act of extreme violence. But then killers did not behave like killers all the time. Violence could lurk, provoked by rage.

Mia is a complex young woman. I hope you can help her.

The more Tara found out about Mia, the more contradictions there were. In their first meeting, Tara had asked Mia what had happened to trigger her memory of murder, and Mia had by no means given her the full picture. Mia had not mentioned the incident with the pendant at all, even though it sounded like that moment with Tom could well have been the catalyst for the memory that surfaced in Carolyn's office.

Mia not only had a tendency to leave out sensitive information, but she sometimes gave out entirely false information, such as the claim that her mother had died. She was not entirely reliable.

Tara got up, closed the shutters, and then went to rinse out her mug in the kitchen. As she moved around the clinic, a different view of what was going on was developing in her mind.

Maybe Mia needed someone who would empathise,

someone who saw her as fragile and in need of help. Maybe she wanted someone on her side, just in case Carolyn, or even Tom, went to the police with what they knew.

What if Mia *wanted* Tara to suspect a false memory had been created in that session with Carolyn? The phenomenon of false memories being created in therapy was well known and there was a great deal of suspicion around recovered memories. If Tara, an expert on memory, wrote a report saying the memory was unreliable, then Mia would be out of the woods.

If she trawled through Mia's internet searches, would she find the question *How to implant memories in therapy?*

Was it possible that Tara was being used? Had Tara in fact been hired so that Mia could convince Tara, and other people in her life, that she was innocent?

She had to consider that there could be a lot more damage in the depths of Mia's psyche than was visible on the surface. That could mean her client was truly, deeply disturbed and highly manipulative. Even capable of murder.

Something else was beginning to prey on Tara's mind too, and that was the uncanny similarity between Mia's situation and Tara's own. Could Mia have found out that Tara was also struggling to remember a night when a violent murder took place? Other people knew. Ray Jameson had uncovered it all and Tara herself had confided in her colleague Anthony Edwards, her colleague who had referred Mia.

Had Mia chosen Tara because of her weakness?

That was so unlikely. A far simpler explanation was that Tara had devoted much of her career to working with memory problems and so obviously these kinds of cases were bound to come her way.

She shook herself out of this spiral of thought. Time was running out before the baby was born and she urgently needed to unravel the truth about what was going on in this case – whether that was mental turmoil or a calculated deception.

When Tara called the hospital hoping to set up a visit though, she was informed that Mia had requested that she not be disturbed and she did not want any further visitors that day.

Despite saying how motivated she was to get to the truth, Mia was constantly finding ways to avoid and delay.

THIRTY

The call from the hospital came through around midnight.

'I'm so sorry to disturb you.' The woman's voice was raspy, as though she had a long history of chain smoking. 'It's Kim here, from the Royal Free. I'm looking after Mia Phillips tonight.'

'What's happened?' Tara sat up, dragging herself out of a deep sleep full of vivid dreams. She and her brother had been back in the house on Wildway Close, and young again. They had been happy, laughing. She was reluctant to leave that place to come back to the real world.

'Mia's very agitated. She woke up around two hours ago and she can't get back to sleep. She doesn't want to take anything to settle her anxiety, but she's been asking to see you.'

The streets of London were dead quiet in the early hours of the morning and Tara was at the hospital within half an hour. She found Mia sitting up in a chair which she had backed into the corner of her room, between the window and the bed. She was directly facing the door as Tara walked in and her eyes were wide with fear.

As soon as she saw Tara, she began talking. 'I had that headache again this afternoon. The nurses put up a drip for me. They said it was only paracetamol, but it knocked me out. I fell asleep and I started to remember, or I fell asleep and I had a nightmare, I don't know which it is—'

Tara had the sense Mia wasn't quite awake, that she was still in a dreamlike state. 'Mia, you've had a high dose of IV painkillers and I think you're confused. You were dreaming—'

Mia shook her head vehemently. She stood up, becoming more and more agitated. 'I was in the water and someone was pushing me under, he was holding my head down. I felt this hand on me... I heard his voice.'

'Mia, you need to slow down. Try to slow your breathing right down.'

'I can't. My chest is closing, I can't get enough air.' She was hyperventilating, right on the edge of a panic attack.

'Okay. Listen to me. Don't worry about telling me what's happened. Just focus on your breathing. Slow it down.'

Mia nodded, finally taking in Tara's words. She placed her hands in the small of her back and managed a few deeper breaths. 'It was so real. This hand on the back of my head, pushing me under. And a voice. Yelling at me.'

'Whose voice, Mia?' As far as Tara knew, Freddie was the only person who had been out at the cottage with her.

'I don't know. He was there with me. In the water, but I couldn't see him.' Mia began biting down hard on her thumbnail.

Tara remembered Freddie's frank description of his own difficulties, including alcohol and irritability.

'I understand that Freddie dived in to save you, right?'

Mia nodded.

'Do you think it felt as though he was trying to push you under, but he was actually trying to pull you out?'

'Maybe. I don't... I know Freddie would never hurt me. He said I was fighting him, in the river, but I don't remember that.'

Mia was clearly afraid. Whether it was of something inside herself, or of her brother-in-law or even her husband, wasn't at all clear.

'There's no air.' Mia was on the edge again, her breathing rapid as she turned to the window, trying to find a way to open it. Her fear-filled face looked back at her. 'It's driving me crazy being up here with all the windows sealed. I need to get out of this room.'

'You need to get back into bed. You're safe in here—'

Mia grabbed her dressing gown from the foot of her bed, trying to get her hands into the sleeves. 'I can't take this feeling. Get me out, please.'

Tara did not want Mia leaving the ward on her own, and she was entitled to do that. Maybe it could help to get her out of the confines of the hospital room. A walk might settle Mia's breathing and lessen the panic.

'Okay. Okay. Let's take a walk. Together.'

Mia was so frantic that she had got herself tangled in the sleeves of the dressing gown.

'Here we go. Let me help you.'

Mia's breathing settled as Tara helped her with the gown. She became calm enough to tie the belt around her swollen middle and then she slipped her feet into a pair of trainers that were beside the bed.

Tara opened the door and they entered the hushed passageway. The nurses' station was at the end of a long corridor and beyond that, a set of lifts. They began walking, side by side. Dim light bounced off the white walls and blue floors. Yellow signboards warned of wet, just-mopped floors and the smell of antiseptic was strong.

After leaving her room, Mia had gone quiet. She walked with her hands tucked into the pockets of her gown, which had fallen open. When they reached the nurses' station, Kim looked up at the two of them briefly, smiled and looked down again. She looked reassuringly competent in her smart blue uniform, with her hair and make-up pristine in the early hours of the morning. Tara imagined that she probably looked less than impeccable herself having rushed out of the house at midnight without checking the mirror.

They walked as far as the lifts and then turned back. With the low light and a distant beeping, the place was almost hypnotic, like being underwater.

As Tara inhaled that sharp chemical smell, her own memories pushed their way to the surface. She lay in a hospital bed, other patients groaning and whispering. Nurses looked down at her with pitying eyes; the damage inside exposed, for everyone to see.

Why does Daniel not come?

After a few roundtrips up and down the corridor, walking to the lifts and then back to the emergency exit door at the other end, Mia's breathing had settled and she showed no sign of the panic she'd experienced in her hospital room.

'Mia, is there anyone in your life you're afraid of?'

She ignored Tara's question. The next circuit of the corridor was completed in silence.

'I'm wondering what that dream was trying to tell you,' Tara said. 'It was so powerful. It must be about feelings of fear, or anger.'

Mia still did not say a word in response and it was clear she did not want to acknowledge what Tara had said. She wasn't ready to say more.

There were other issues playing on Tara's mind too. The first was the fact that Mia's mother was still alive. Tara was waiting for the right moment to delve into that, and this wasn't it. The second issue was Tara's meetings with Mia's father, Freddie and DS Ayola. And then there was the meeting with Tom where he'd expressed serious concerns. She wanted to tell Mia about all of this herself, rather than wait and have Mia feel her confidence had been betrayed.

Tara spoke carefully. 'Mia, while you've been in hospital, I've been talking to a few people in your family, as well as a police officer who was involved in Alice's case.'

'Tom told me he was in your office.' Mia stopped and looked into Tara's eyes for a few moments, but Tara couldn't read her expression. Her eyes were flat again. 'What did he say?'

'He's worried about you and the baby.'

'Is that all?'

'No. He also told me that he saw you wearing Alice's necklace. A necklace that went missing when Alice died.'

Mia began walking again, heading back to her hospital room. She pushed open the door and pulled off her shoes roughly, then went to sit on the edge of the bed, looking down at the floor.

'Why didn't you tell me?' Tara asked her.

'It wasn't important.'

'I don't think that's true. That incident with Tom happened the night before you had this memory in Carolyn's office, right?'

Mia nodded.

'So it is important.'

Mia did not respond. She was such a strange combination of vulnerable and defiant. She kept shifting between the two and Tara couldn't get a hold of the real Mia, the core of her.

'Tom said that Alice never took that pendant off.'

'Tom didn't know Alice as well as I did. He thinks he knew her, but he didn't. I knew Alice for years before he ever met her.' Mia stopped speaking. Her small, bare feet dangled a few inches above the floor.

'So what happened? How did you end up with Alice's necklace?'

'I didn't steal it,' Mia said stubbornly, as if it was important to her that Tara did not see her as a thief. 'Like I told you, I went to bed early with a headache. Then later, Alice came into my room and we talked, about what she'd done in Julia's office. Then she said she was going for a walk, but before she left, she asked me to help her with the clasp of her chain, because she couldn't get it off. When she went out, she left the necklace with the pendant on my bedside table. And afterwards... I kept it.'

'Did you find it strange that Alice wanted to take her necklace off before she went out? Did you ask her about it?'

Mia shook her head as her legs swung gently back and forth. 'Like I told you, it was complicated between us that night. Because of what I'd seen in Julia's office, and because Alice was leaving the gallery. I think the real reason she wanted to talk to me was because she was scared of what I was going to do.'

'What do you mean?'

Mia shrugged off her dressing gown and climbed back into the hospital bed, pulling the sheets up to her chin and leaning back against the pillows. 'I think Alice was scared I was going to tell Julia what she'd done. And then Tom would have found out too.'

Tara pulled the visitors' chair up beside her. 'Mia, I spoke to DS Ayola. She said that Alice had been using cannabis that night. Were you both high?'

Mia shook her head.

'That could explain why Alice was behaving a little strangely, taking her chain off and wanting to go out for a walk in the countryside in the middle of the night.'

'Maybe. I didn't realise she was out of it. She was talking normally.' Mia was starting to look very tired. 'She knew I wasn't happy about what she was doing. I'd already—'

Kim knocked on the door, interrupting them as she came in to do her observations. Mia's breathing and blood pressure had settled, which she was pleased about. Kim offered to put up another paracetamol drip if Mia was still in pain from the headache, and Mia agreed.

Once the nurse had left the room, Tara stayed awhile, watching the colourless liquid fall, drop by drop, from the IV bag into the plastic tubing connected to the canula at the back of Mia's hand.

It was almost two in the morning.

Mia was staring up at the ceiling. 'Sometimes I wear the necklace so I can feel her with me. But other times, I wear it to punish myself. I put it around my neck and I stand in front of the full-length mirror we have in our room so I can see the reflection of our bed behind me. I imagine Tom and Alice, together, in our bed. I watch them.'

Tara shuddered at the thought of Mia torturing herself.

This went far back to the beginning. To the night at the gallery where Tom had chosen Alice, and Mia had pretended not to care. But she had cared, deeply. She just hadn't admitted it, to herself or to anyone else.

Mia's eyes drifted closed.

Working with her was a balancing act. On the one hand, Mia was fragile and there was the danger that if pushed too far, she could do harm to herself or her baby. But if Tara treated her with kid gloves, Mia would never get to the truth and that would help no one. So Tara walked a fine line, pushing Mia as close to her threshold as she could, while being there to support her.

'Are you awake?'

Mia nodded though she didn't open her eyes.

'Mia, you lied to the police and to Alice's family. You let everyone believe that the necklace was missing. That may have had an impact on the investigation.'

'Everybody lied.'

'What does that mean?'

'Nothing.' Mia's eyes stayed obstinately closed.

'It's not nothing. Who else lied? Is it the same man whose voice you heard in the river?'

Mia gave a deep sigh. She massaged her throat and then she yawned. 'I have to sleep now.'

THIRTY-ONE

On her way out of the ward, Tara stopped at the nurses' station to talk to Kim. Before she left, Tara had Kim's assurance that the nursing staff would check on Mia frequently. Kim also said that there were no plans in place to discharge Mia yet. Tara was planning to come back the next morning as soon as ward rounds were over.

As she exited the glass doors of the lobby, the chill air was invigorating. Mia was right, there wasn't enough oxygen in that sealed hospital room. Tara headed back to her car, pulling her lanyard over her head and tucking it back into her bag. She was still mulling over the fact that Alice had been so determined to take her necklace off before she went out for that mysterious late-night walk. Could she have been meeting someone? Another man? Mia behaved as though those questions had never crossed her mind, which Tara found odd.

On the other hand, could anything Mia said be assumed to be the whole truth? She had been feeding Tara fragments of information about that last weekend with Alice and it was clear she'd been holding things back. For someone who wanted to get to the truth about her own mind, that was a strange way to behave.

As Tara walked across the parking lot, she was looking down into her bag and fishing around for her keys, which had disappeared somewhere into the depths. It was only when she was a couple of metres away from her car that she looked up and saw the man who had been waiting for her.

He was tall and dressed all in black, and she couldn't make out his face in the dark. The way he was so still and so tense set off alarm bells.

There were only a few cars scattered across the lot and not another soul in sight. The hospital entrance was too far away to try to run back. Tara had found the keys and she gripped them tightly in her fist, feeling the sharp edges dig into her flesh as she scanned the area for the best escape route. It was then she noticed the motorbike that was parked at a haphazard angle a little way away from her car.

She realised she knew the man who had been waiting for her. 'Freddie?'

'That's me. Freddie.' His words were slurred and his tone belligerent. 'You're working late tonight, Doctor Black.'

'What are you doing here?' Tara's voice was a little shaky.

'What are *you* doing here?' Freddie lurched forwards and Tara felt a fresh wave of fear.

She had to find a way to get past him to reach the driver's door, to get inside the safety of her car, but for the moment she was rooted to the tarmac. Frozen.

Freddie took a couple more unsteady few steps forward. 'I came to talk to Mia, but the nurses wouldn't let me see her.'

Surely someone else had to come out into the parking lot? But there was no one.

'Why are you fucking seeing her at midnight?' Freddie was right up close now, right in her face, and his breath was pure alcohol.

'Mia asked me to help her. That's what I'm trying to do.'

'What's wrong with her?'

Tara pressed the button on her car keys and there was a burst of orange light as the doors unlocked. Distracted, Freddie looked up. Tara took her chance, running past him towards her car, but she felt him grabbing at the back of her jacket. In her mind's eye, she saw Jade Jameson holding a knife and with a rush of terror, she swung her bag wildly, trying to get away. It connected heavily with the side of his body. For a moment, Freddie lost his grip and Tara ran forwards again, reaching the driver's door, yanking it open, getting inside.

But she couldn't get the door closed. Freddie was right there, blocking it with his body.

Tara heard herself screaming like a banshee. 'Get away from me! Get away from my car! Get off me!'

She surprised herself with her strength as she swung her legs round and kicked out at him with all the force she had. As Freddie staggered backwards, Tara grabbed for the handle and slammed the door shut, desperately fumbling for the lock.

Freddie wasn't done. He was banging on the window with his fists, furious and red-faced.

Tara wondered how much force it would take to break that window.

'Open up. I have to talk to you. Open up!' He would not stop pounding.

Tara watched him, trembling. There was rage in his face and in the sound of his fists against the glass, but her fear was settling now that she was safe inside the locked car. She took out her phone, ready to call emergency services.

Suddenly though, the energy drained out of Freddie's arms. He stopped banging on the window but he stayed right there, looking in at her with tormented eyes.

Tara felt a certain responsibility. She couldn't leave him there in that state. If he drove that motorbike he could end up either dead or killing someone else or both. She also did not want him going up to Mia's ward and causing a scene, or worse.

She opened her window a crack. 'Freddie, you can't get back on that motorbike in this state. I can call someone to pick you up or I can get you a taxi.'

'You need to tell them to let me see Mia. Please. This is all my fault. I need to talk to her.'

'Why do you think it's your fault?' Tara's throat was raw from yelling.

Freddie took a few steps backwards and then sat down heavily on the pavement, with his head in his hands.

Tara called Mia's ward and spoke to Kim. She asked her to please get hold of Tom Phillips urgently and tell him to come and get his brother. Then she sat in her car and waited, watching him.

Around twenty minutes later, a large Mercedes pulled up next to Tara's car. David Phillips stepped out of it and he approached Tara's window first, before going anywhere near his son.

'Are you all right?'

'I'm fine.' Tara rolled down her window a little more but she was still cautious about getting out of the car. Freddie had not moved from where he had collapsed but now he lay on his back, half on and half off the pavement, with his arms splayed out on the grass and his legs sticking out into one of the parking spaces.

'I'm so sorry about this.' David looked seriously concerned, frowning down at her. 'Has he been aggressive?'

'I'm fine, really.'

'You're sure?'

Tara nodded and David looked relieved. She had to wonder how many of these situations he'd had to deal with before, and how bad Freddie's aggression might have become. She had a flash of him beating his fists on the window. If she hadn't been able to get to the car and lock herself in, she could have been in real trouble.

'I wanted to make sure he got home safely,' Tara said. 'And I didn't want him going up to see Mia in this state.'

'Of course. Thank you. I really appreciate this.' David stayed close to Tara's car and seemed reluctant to approach or speak to his son.

Freddie had not moved or looked up at his father since David had arrived.

'Tom called me and asked me to come and pick up his brother since I live much closer than he does. Of course, Julia's right around the corner, but she doesn't deal with these situations.' David sighed deeply. 'I'm so ashamed. I really can't apologise enough.'

'That's not necessary. I know Freddie has been badly affected by his time in the military.'

'How long can he use that as an excuse?' David gestured towards his son, who was still lying prone on his back. 'This is who Freddie is. A pavement drunk. Literally. He's a lost cause.'

It was obvious that David had been through a lot of these nights with Freddie, but Tara was still shocked at the way he spoke so ruthlessly in front of his son. Freddie, who was close enough to hear every word of what David had said, still did not move a muscle.

Tara remembered that photograph of a very different Freddie in his days as a paratrooper.

Despite his frightening behaviour, Tara did feel some sympathy for him. Probably because on some level he reminded her of her own troubled brother. The worse things had got at home, the more Matthew had taken refuge in alcohol. He too had spiralled into aggression and self-destruction.

'Freddie needs professional help. He urgently needs a rehab programme.'

'We know. We've tried everything. His mother and I have both tried, believe me.' David walked over and stared down at Freddie, but it was as though he couldn't bear to reach down and help him up. 'Julia still holds out hope but I gave up a long time ago. But yes, I'll talk to Julia and let her know what's happened. And I'll try to make sure that Freddie is better supervised.'

David positioned himself behind Freddie, bent down and hooked his arms under his son's armpits, and heaved him to his feet. It was a practiced move. 'Right, here we go.'

Freddie leaned against his father's shoulder a moment, bleary-eyed, then he threw himself forward and began heaving. Tara looked away as the contents of his stomach spewed onto the tarmac.

She heard David saying, in a voice both resigned and tender, 'Come on, my boy. I'll take you home.'

Tara felt terribly sad for both of them.

THIRTY-TWO

Tara surfaced on Saturday morning, after around four hours of sleep, to a phone call from a frantic-sounding Julia Leonard.

'David dropped Freddie off in the early hours, and I nearly had heart failure when the doorbell went. Freddie couldn't find his keys, apparently. My first thought was—'

Julia stopped there, but Tara had a good idea of what she was thinking. She must be terrified of what Freddie could do to himself on that motorbike.

'How is Freddie today?' Tara asked.

'Sleeping it off. I can't talk to David about this, but he said you were there, with Freddie at the hospital. Can you tell me what happened?'

Tara explained that Freddie had been waiting for her in the parking lot. 'It was obvious he'd been drinking,' she said, 'and he was intimidating. Physically threatening.'

'Why did Freddie want to see you?' Julia said. 'What did he want?'

'I'm not sure. He was asking about Mia. He seemed worried about her.'

It struck Tara that Julia had chosen to ignore what she'd said about Freddie's aggressive behaviour towards her.

'What exactly did Freddie say to you?'

Again, Tara was surprised by Julia's question. She had assumed Julia would want to apologise and express her dismay at what her son had done, or ask for advice to get Freddie some help.

'Freddie seemed worried that it was somehow his fault that Mia was in hospital,' Tara said. 'He said something about feeling guilty, but he wasn't making a lot of sense. As I said, he was clearly intoxicated and confused.'

Frustratingly, Tara could not remember the details of what Freddie had said to her; it was all a blur because of her initial shock and fear response.

'Do you know why Freddie would think that Mia's accident was his fault?' Tara definitely remembered that Freddie had mentioned a sense of guilt.

'Could you come over to the house?' Julia said. 'Please? As soon as possible. I'd like to talk more about this, but not over the phone.'

It did not seem to occur to Julia that it was the weekend.

Tara agreed without giving it much thought. She had no pressing plans anyway and the truth was that working evenings and weekends didn't bother her. If anything, she welcomed it; report writing kept her company over empty weekends spent in her cottage. Work was her life.

As she dressed and made a coffee before leaving, Tara was mentally running through her late-night session with Mia and then the encounter with Freddie in the hospital parking lot.

Someone was pushing me under, holding my head down.

She had no idea of the significance of Mia's dream, or whether it could be linked in any way to Freddie's loss of control. There was still so much to unpack in this case.

Before she left home, Tara called the hospital to check how

Mia was doing. To her relief, Mia's condition was stable. She asked the nurse on duty to pass on a message that she'd be there for afternoon visiting hours. She left her mug in the sink and then headed out to her car.

When Tara arrived at the house on New End, Julia, Tom and David were all in the conservatory, sitting in the wicker chairs in sombre silence.

'I'll start, shall I?' David said. 'It should be obvious to all of us that Freddie cannot be allowed to carry on like this.'

He glanced at his ex-wife as he spoke. Tara noticed how Julia couldn't bring herself to look at David, even when he spoke to her directly.

'Freddie cannot be waiting for women in the parking lot at night. He cannot be driving that motorbike drunk. Julia, you are encouraging this by letting him live here, rent free, and letting him get away with—'

'Freddie would never hurt anyone.' Julia spoke over her ex-husband, cutting him off and looking at Tara.

'If you want to go to the police, Doctor Black,' David said, 'I wouldn't blame you.'

'I haven't had a chance to think about it,' Tara said. 'But my feeling is that if we can get Freddie to agree to treatment, it won't be necessary.'

Julia had slumped back into her chair. She was clearly devastated.

'He's really surpassed himself this time, hasn't he?' David spoke with a deep bitterness.

Julia's expression changed, and Tara saw not only distress, but something else: a combination of venom and fear. This time, she did look directly at her ex-husband. She hissed at him. 'You have never taken responsibility for what you did to that boy.'

David jerked forwards in his chair, clutching the armrests as if to hold himself back, and raising his voice. 'Oh, grow up, Julia! If anything, it's your constant indulgence that's ruined him. But go ahead – you keep deluding yourself that it's my fault for not loving him enough.'

Tom stood up, positioning his body between his warring parents.

'Enough.' He spoke calmly, but his voice was full of controlled anger. 'Listen to me. I know you two hate each other, but we have to sort this out as a family because I need your help. Mia is falling apart. My child is about to be born – *your* grandchild. Mia and the baby need all of our support. Isn't that right?' Tom turned to Tara with this question.

Before Tara could answer, Julia spoke. 'Freddie was such a gentle little boy, so loving. Neither of you have ever understood how sensitive he is.'

A tear ran down her cheek and she wiped it away.

David ignored her as he responded to Tom, his tone much calmer and kinder. 'Of course, you're right. Anything you need from us you'll get.'

'It makes it worse for Freddie that Tom is your golden boy,' Julia said, looking at David. 'And Tom worships you. Which is everything you ever wanted from a son.'

With the intensity of negative feeling still so strong between Julia and David, Tara felt sorry for Tom. He was stuck in the middle of the two of them.

'Mum,' Tom said, 'he is my father. He is part of this, whether you like it or not. I need him.'

'Julia, enough.' David held one hand outstretched in a gesture that Tara could see only inflamed Julia's anger, but she managed to contain herself. 'I'll talk to Freddie's GP. You talk to your son and tell him he needs to get into a substance abuse programme or he's going to end up in a police cell. Tom has to concentrate on keeping Mia well and stable. Doctor Black is a professional, and if she is going to continue to help Mia – which

I hope she will – she cannot be drawn into these family issues with Freddie. You shouldn't have dragged her into this.'

Julia pulled a tissue out of her pocket, dabbing at her nose delicately. 'Thank God for Mia and the baby, or I'd probably go mad, thinking about what's to become of Freddie.'

Tara could see that Julia wasn't really listening to what anyone else in the room was saying. She was having trouble accepting how severe Freddie's problems were; perhaps she could only let reality through in small digestible pieces.

Freddie is a lost cause. This is who he is. A pavement drunk. Literally.

As ruthless as David's approach was to his son's difficulties, Julia's attitude was perhaps a little too forgiving.

And no one else in the room had any idea about Mia's confession of violence.

The threads of what was left of this family were pulling apart.

'I take it this meeting is about me?'

At the sound of Freddie's voice, all four of them looked towards the doorway. He looked even worse for wear than he had the night before, extremely dishevelled and unshaven, in a grubby tracksuit. Tara could pick up the smell of sweat and alcohol from across the room.

The contrast between the two brothers was stark as they stood across from each other. Tom was so impeccably put together, not a hair out of place, in his well-fitting coat.

'Doctor Black was kind enough to come and check if you were all right,' Julia said. The tone in her voice was pacifying.

'I'm sorry about last night,' Freddie said. 'I don't remember much of it, to be honest. I hope I didn't do anything stupid.'

Tara saw how Julia put her free hand to her throat as she glanced at her son in the doorway.

David let out a half snort of derision. 'Maybe instead of

hoping, you shouldn't get so bloody drunk you can't control yourself.'

'Apology accepted,' Tara said, quickly. 'And if you're interested in a referral for treatment, I'd be happy to talk through some options with you. I'll give you my mobile number. You can call me when you're ready.'

'Maybe I should do that, thanks.'

But Tara could tell from his tone he had no intention of getting help.

Freddie was looking past her at his mother.

'Don't look so scared, Mum.' He spoke softly, smiling.

The discord between the smile and the sadness behind his words was jarring.

Julia swallowed. 'Freddie, please, that's enough.'

'You think I've done something. I see it in your eyes.'

'Don't be ridiculous. Don't say anything stupid.' Julia stood up and took a few tentative steps towards him. She reached for his hand, looking up to him. 'You are my kindest, gentlest boy—'

'Stop it, Mum.' Freddie wrenched his hand away and Julia stumbled, managing to clutch hold of the table to stop herself falling. Tom rushed over to her.

'I'm fine, it's nothing.' Julia stepped back, massaging her hand. 'Don't make a fuss.'

The conservatory door had been left wide open and Freddie had disappeared. Seconds later, they heard the revving of a motorbike engine.

THIRTY-THREE

'Doctor Black, do you have a moment?' David Phillips had exited the house shortly after Tara and was rushing down New End to catch up with her. Tara had been heading towards her car, which was parked a block or two away. She paused, waiting for him.

'I wanted to thank you again, for last night and for this morning. And I know you've been spending a lot of time with Mia, including after-hours work.'

'Yes.' The hours had climbed higher than Tara had anticipated, but working with Mia had become a matter of safety and she had no choice.

'I imagine it didn't cross Julia's mind to check what you charge for coming out over a weekend and I know Mia and Tom might struggle to afford your rates, so please, if there's any issue, I'll be responsible for your fees. It's the least I can do.'

'I appreciate the offer. Thank you.'

David looked back towards the house, but lingered where he was. 'I also wanted to make it clear that you shouldn't feel in any way pressured to give in to what Julia wants.'

'I'm not sure what you mean?'

'I know my ex-wife. She invited you here today because she's worried you might make a report about Freddie's behaviour. She has always over-protected him, and it has only caused more problems. I wanted you to know that you have my full support, whatever route you decide is best.'

'Okay. Thank you.' Tara had a sense she was being invited to take sides, and she had no intention of being dragged into the politics between David and Julia.

She wanted to extricate herself as soon as possible but David was lingering beside her as if he had more to say.

'I know you can't say too much,' he began, 'but as a father and a medical professional, I am really concerned about Mia. I know she denies it but that business down at the cottage looked very much like some sort of self-harm. I take it this has something to do with Alice?'

If she was to keep Mia's trust, Tara could not disclose the reason why Mia had gone out to the cottage.

'I understand your concern,' she said, 'and I am aware of issues around risk.'

'Well,' David said, taking the hint from her vague answer, 'at least it was some relief when Mia left Carolyn and started seeing you.'

'Why is that?'

'Frankly, I could see that Mia was getting worse as opposed to better during her treatment with Carolyn. I obviously had misgivings from the outset, but I didn't want to interfere.'

'Why would you have misgivings?'

'Ah. I see from the confused look on your face that you aren't aware that Carolyn and I have a personal connection. We were in a relationship for a while, a few years back. When I ended things, let's just say she didn't take our break-up very well. Maybe I'm being conceited here but I did wonder if she took Mia on as a patient to try to reconnect with me. I worry she's still... fixated on getting back together.'

Tara stood in the biting cold, absorbing this new information. Carolyn had said that Mia was referred to her because she and David had been colleagues. Obviously, that was not the whole truth.

THIRTY-FOUR

Later that afternoon, Tara walked into Mia's hospital room to find her packing her few pieces of clothing into an overnight bag lying open on her bed. Mia was dressed in jeans and a fitted long-sleeve top, and she had her trainers on. Tom was standing at the window, watching her. As usual, he had his long navy coat on, with his hands deep inside the pockets, and as usual, his jaw was tensed.

'Have you been discharged?' Tara put her bag down inside the door, noting the strained silence between the couple.

'I've told the nurses I want to leave.' Mia was folding the dressing gown she'd worn the night before. 'They're trying to reach the consultant or the registrar or whoever to sort it out. All my tests came back fine.'

Mia did look better. There was no sign of the rapid breathing and wide eyes she'd had in her panicked state the night before. The change in her demeanour was quite dramatic. The question crossed Tara's mind as to whether Mia could have been faking, but she didn't think so.

It was also interesting that Mia's tests had come back clear. Although there had been concern that the symptoms of blurred vision and headaches could be pre-eclampsia, it seemed that they could well be signs of anxiety and emotional distress.

Mia had opened the bedside drawer and collected a set of keys and a phone charger and dropped them into her bag. 'I can't take another night in this place. I want to go home.'

'I don't think that's a good idea,' Tom said.

Tara agreed with him. Her heart sank at the thought of Mia leaving the safety of the hospital when everything about her situation still felt so precarious.

She didn't know yet if Mia was safe to take care of either herself or her child. Mia's father was barely involved in her life, and while the Phillips family members might be watching Mia more closely after that incident at the cottage, they could not provide twenty-four-hour care. And then there was Freddie, who should not be allowed anywhere near his sister-in-law at this point.

Let me see Mia. Please. This is all my fault. I need to talk to her.

After the state Mia had been in the night before, Tara had assumed she'd be in the hospital at least a couple more days. But if there was no pressing medical reason to keep her in hospital, and Mia could not be persuaded to change her mind, she may well walk out of there.

'Mia, I think Tom's right.' Tara had to be careful what she said in front of Tom, who still wasn't aware of the full nature of what Mia had disclosed. 'Last night, you were in a panic with a severe headache, and that concerns me. Why not stay here until the medical team are ready to discharge you?'

Mia paused, looking down at her bag which was full to bursting. 'I need to be at home. Where I can sleep.'

She turned around to Tom, as if seeking his support, but he shook his head. 'I agree with Doctor Black.'

Mia looked defeated. She leaned down and with some effort

managed to zip the bag closed, but then she looked down at it as if she didn't know what to do next.

'I've been waiting for you to get here,' Tom said to Tara. 'I need to show you both something.'

He reached into a backpack that was placed on the visitor's chair and lifted something out of it with both hands. Mia drew back, as if she'd seen a snake.

It was a camera case.

'I picked this up from the gallery earlier,' Tom said, looking at Mia. 'Julia wanted me to bring it to the hospital to give to you. She's convinced it might help if you started taking photographs again. She would have brought it herself, but she's tied up with Freddie; he's been on another bender.'

Mia's eyes were fixed on Tom as he carefully removed the camera from its case. The long, black, silky camera strap dangled down from his hands.

Suddenly, it was as if all the air had been sucked out of the room.

'I don't want to upset you any more than you are already,' Tom said, 'but then I can't live my life being afraid of upsetting you. I thought it was better we had this conversation here, while you're still in the hospital.'

Tom held the camera out to his wife but she refused to take it, shaking her head.

Mia sat down heavily on the edge of the bed. She didn't move or speak. Tom's jaw was tensed up rigidly again. Something was going on between the couple but Tara didn't understand it yet.

Tom turned the camera on. 'When I found this at the gallery, the memory card was still inside. I charged it and I took a look at the photographs that are on there.'

Mia sighed and hung her head. 'Those are the last photographs I ever took. The day Alice died.'

Tom walked over and handed Tara the camera. He turned

away, staring out of the window as Tara looked down at the screen feeling a gut-twist of unease.

Alice had been posed as if she were already dead. She lay on her back, on the riverbank, wearing only red underwear and heels. Her head was turned to the side, her eyes staring blankly at the camera. Her arms were at right angles from her body, one facing up, one down, and her legs were splayed.

Tara looked up. 'Did you ask Alice to pose this way?'

Mia nodded.

Tara clicked the arrow and another photograph appeared. In this one, Alice floated on her back in the shallow river, her arms by her sides and her eyes closed. Her long hair fanned out across the surface of the water.

Tara's eyes were glued to the small screen. There was an element of the grotesque about the pictures, with their combination of female beauty and murderous fantasy. They felt disturbingly real.

'Why would you make her pose like that?' Tom had turned his back to them, his hands in fists, pressing down on the windowsill, knuckles turning white.

'I can't explain.' Mia was looking up at him beseechingly, but Tom would not turn around. 'Those were the images that came into my mind that day. That's how it works for me. Alice didn't mind. She loved to pose for me. She loved images that were unusual. Disturbing.'

Tom had turned around but he was keeping his distance, staying on the other side of the room. 'It's as if you knew what was going to happen to her.'

Mia shook her head. 'That's not true.'

She couldn't bring herself to tell Tom about her memory. She was terrified of losing him.

'Why won't you tell me what's going on?' Tom asked her. 'You've barely spoken to me in months. You walked out on

Carolyn. Then there was this insanity at the cottage. You have to talk to me. This is my child too.'

Mia was gripping the bedsheets with both hands. Her bitten-down nails left smears of blood. 'I'm not the only one holding things back.'

'What is that supposed to mean?' he said.

'I was angry at Alice that weekend, and that feeling came out, through the photographs.' Mia's voice was stronger and she sat up straighter. 'That night at the cottage, I went to bed early. I wasn't feeling good, the pain in my head was getting worse and worse and I wanted to sleep it off. But then—'

Mia stopped speaking as she squeezed her eyes shut and began rubbing at her temples. Tara hoped that yet another one of her headaches would not interfere with the process. She did not want Mia to stop speaking; it felt as though she was finally opening up. 'Mia, what happened next?'

'I heard something.'

'What did you hear?' Tara asked her.

'Voices.' Mia opened her eyes and looked at Tom. 'I heard voices coming from downstairs. There was someone else in the cottage with Alice.'

THIRTY-FIVE

TWO HOURS BEFORE ALICE'S DEATH

When Mia opens the door of her bedroom, all the lights in the cottage are on and everything is strangely bright. The voices that woke her are coming from downstairs.

She is confused. Disoriented. The pain in her head pulses as she makes her way down the narrow staircase, one hand pressed against the rough-painted wall for balance. The whole cottage stinks of dope.

From the bottom of the stairs, she can see through to the living room. Alice and Tom are sitting on the floor in front of the sofa. Alice takes a deep draw on her joint, then, slowly, she leans forward and blows a perfect smoke ring into Tom's mouth.

Mia doesn't move or make a sound. She watches them, unseen.

Alice and Tom lean into each other, laughing. It hits her then: they are in love.

A wave of envy rises inside of her. And another. Wave after wave, crashing up into her throat, moving through her shoulders and into her hands. When she looks down, they have tensed up into fists.

Be careful.

She has to drag herself out of this black mood. She is so full of poison. She should leave, but she can't take her eyes off them even though it is torture.

Alice climbs on top of Tom and he moans. Their lips touch, gently.

'We can't,' Alice says, drawing back.

'Yes we can.'

'Mia might still be awake.'

'So what? Mia's a grown up.' Tom's hand snakes through Alice's hair, grabbing a fistful, pulling her to him with force.

'No, seriously, we can't.' Alice pushes him away, stands up and picks up the joint that is lying on the coffee table. 'She'll freak out if she finds you here.'

'What are you talking about?'

Alice goes over to the window, inhaling deeply. Tom goes over to stand next to her and she hands him the joint. He inhales too.

'She's in one of her moods,' Alice says. 'She has these headaches all the time and she gets really weird when she's like this.'

'Weird how?'

'I don't know – I think it's some kind of mental problem or something. Her mum's the same, there's something weird about her. Anyway, Mia can't help it.'

'Really?' Tom nuzzles into Alice's hair. 'I had no idea.'

Mia feels as though someone has delivered a blow to her gut. She gasps for breath, her hands wrap around her belly, protecting herself.

Alice reaches behind her, snaking her hand around the back of Tom's neck and winding her fingers through his hair. 'Mia isn't easy to live with. I have to be really careful around her because I never quite know what will set her off. She scares me, sometimes.'

Alice is poisoning Tom's mind. She is punishing Mia for

threatening to tell Tom and Julia what she had done at the gallery. Alice is setting her up.

Tom pulls away, concerned now. 'Should my mother know about this?'

'No, please, you can't say anything to Julia. Please. Please don't.'

Alice is so cruel. Why had Mia not seen it before? Alice lies and steals and destroys. She will do anything to get what she wants. And Alice wants everything.

THIRTY-SIX

'I was so humiliated,' Mia said. 'All I wanted was to get away from that cottage. But it was the middle of the night and we were stuck out there, so I went back up to bed and I lay there wide awake and I kept hearing what Alice had said about me, it was on a loop in my head. I kept seeing the two of you together, laughing at me, and there was this stench of cannabis. I felt like I was going crazy.'

Tara was trying to get her head around the implications of what Mia had just told them. She looked across at Tom, who was standing at the window, stiff and pale and saying nothing.

'A while later,' Mia continued, 'I don't know how long it was exactly, but Alice came upstairs and climbed into bed next to me. She wanted to talk, to make things right between us. I suppose she felt bad about what she'd said to you. She told me you'd turned up out of the blue. That you had trouble staying away from her.'

Tom's eyes kept going back to rest on the camera that now lay on Mia's bed, inches from her hand. Tara too had those disturbing photographs hovering in her mind's eye.

'I couldn't speak,' Mia said. 'It literally felt like I was choking. Alice was my closest friend and she used the things I was most ashamed of to hurt me.'

'Tom, is this true?' Tara asked. 'Were you at the cottage that night, with Alice?'

He nodded as he finally looked at his wife. 'Why didn't you tell me you knew?'

'Because you never brought it up.' Mia's hands gripped the sheets, clenching and unclenching. 'I've never told anyone. Everyone seemed to believe you were at some bachelor party, but I knew you couldn't have been there the whole night.' Mia was so naïve and so trusting as she looked at him. 'I thought you lied because you were scared. I knew you would never hurt her.'

'So you both lied to the police?' Tara said.

Mia looked at Tara with those innocent, deer-in-headlight eyes. 'I just left that part out. I thought that if the police knew Tom was at the cottage, then he might have been under suspicion, and I didn't want them to waste time—'

'I didn't need you to lie for me,' Tom said. 'When I left the cottage, I was high. I didn't realise at first, but after I started driving I knew I had to pull over. I was in no state to get to the party. I stopped as soon as I could, at some services. I had a coffee and sobered up a bit and got a taxi over to Oxford to join the others. I told all of this to the police, Mia. It's all on CCTV. They were satisfied that I'd left the cottage long before Alice went out.'

Tom went over and sat down on the visitor's chair, leaning forwards with his hands clasped as he spoke. 'I understand that you were angry after you overheard what we were saying downstairs, but those photographs of Alice were taken in daylight, much earlier that day. So something was already going on.'

Mia nodded. Calmly, she told Tom about finding Alice copying data from Julia's hard drive. It was obvious from his expression that he was shocked. He'd had no idea.

'Why would she do that?' he asked.

'I'm not sure,' Mia said. 'I had an idea she was going to use Julia's contacts to try to get more sales in her new job at The Sharp Gallery. She was going to be working on commission. You know how Alice was about money.'

Tom nodded.

'Alice asked me to help her take the necklace off,' Mia said. 'I promise you, that's what happened. She turned around and I undid the clasp for her and then she said she was going out to get some air.'

Both Mia and Tom seemed more relaxed. The tension had dropped from Tom's jaw as he went to sit next to Mia on the bed, though he was careful to still leave a gap between them.

'I let her go,' Mia said. 'It doesn't make sense, does it? Why would I let her go out into the night, and then just fall asleep?'

She was hinting at her recovered memory now, but she did not come out and reveal it to her husband. She shifted slightly further away from Tom. 'There is something wrong with me. I've always known that. That's why I never wanted to have children. Every minute of being pregnant has been torture. Alice was right about me.'

Briefly, Tom reached out and laid his hand over hers. 'Mia, that is not true. Alice and I were both high that night, and Alice was obviously feeling guilty for what she'd done to Julia. She was looking for excuses.'

Mia's eyes filled with tears. 'I don't want to hurt the baby, I promise you. I have to fix this. That's why I asked Doctor Black for help.'

'Then please, stay here. At least one more night.'

Mia nodded.

Tom stood up. 'I'm sorry. I need some space.'

Mia didn't look up and she didn't protest as Tom walked out. Her small hands lay still on top of the sheets, those bitten-down nails a reminder of her turmoil. Once again, Tara thought, Mia looked terribly young and terribly alone.

. . .

Mia seemed to have given up on the idea of discharging herself and would at least be safe in the hospital overnight. But Tara was left with several concerns.

She had witnessed Mia swing from flatness to panic and back again in such a short space of time. Mia's father had described her difficulty regulating emotions, with anger outbursts and temper tantrums starting in early childhood. Alice, if she could be believed, may have seen evidence of this too.

Mia herself feared she was capable of violence. Of evil, even.

But it was also dawning on Tara that Mia's confession could be a covert way of expressing her doubts about Tom's innocence; doubts she could not even admit to herself. Part of Mia needed to know the whole truth to keep herself and her baby safe, but the other part didn't want to face it because she was in love with her husband.

According to statistics, if Alice Kelly was murdered, she was more likely to have been killed by a male. A male who was an intimate partner, or at least was known to her.

Could Tom have been suspicious that Alice was cheating on him? Is that why he turned up at the cottage that night, taking her by surprise? Could he have followed Alice when she left the cottage, believing she was headed to a secret rendezvous? Tom was already high. Did he become enraged, too?

If Mia did end up going to the police with her confession, they might end up looking more closely at Alice's case. And that may lead them to look again at Tom, and to dig deeper into his alibi. So, in a roundabout way, Mia could bring the spotlight back to her husband.

With all of this swirling in her head, Tara made a second

phone call to DS Ayola as soon as she got back home. She had saved the detective's mobile phone number after their last conversation, and now, feeling slightly guilty about doing this on a Saturday evening, she used it.

After apologising profusely for disturbing her on the weekend, Tara got straight to the point. 'I have some information about Alice's boyfriend at the time of her death that I wanted to share with you. His name is Tom Phillips.'

'I remember Tom actually. I interviewed him myself.'

'Was Tom automatically under suspicion, being the boyfriend?'

'There were never any reports of aggression or violence in the relationship with Ms Kelly. He was interviewed of course – not under caution, it didn't get that far – but he was put under a fair amount of pressure and I found him very genuine. Did you say you had new information?'

'According to Mia Phillips, she saw him at the cottage that night with Alice. He didn't tell anyone in his or Alice's family about that.'

'I see. Well, he did share that information with us. Tom had an alibi that we were able to verify.'

Tara was reassured by her response. So Tom had been telling the truth.

There was a pause where it sounded as though someone else came into the room and DS Ayola apologised and said she'd be there in two minutes and the candles were in the drawer next to the fridge and please to also get the matches.

Tara thought she heard a sigh as DS Ayola resumed their phone conversation. 'Was there anything else?'

'Well, what I'm wondering is, does this fully exonerate Tom? Because I assume that Tom's alibi is solid only if Mia's timeline is correct, and if she was the last one to see Alice, at around midnight?'

'Uh, that sounds right. Obviously I don't have my casefile in

front of me and it's been some time. What I do remember is that
Tom said he'd made a visit to the cottage that only he and Ms
Kelly were aware of, but that he'd left fairly early that evening
to get to this bachelor party. He admitted he'd been driving
under the influence of marijuana, which he and Ms Kelly were
smoking together during this visit. He said shortly after leaving
the cottage he'd felt too intoxicated to drive and he'd stopped in
the services to get something to eat. We managed to get CCTV
footage from there. Then Mia confirmed that Alice left the
cottage sometime around midnight, if my memory is correct,
and Tom was at the services until around ten.'

Tara saw Mia, alone in her hospital bed, with her eyes
changing from sad to empty.

Who are you, Mia?

'One minute, darling!' DS Ayola called out. 'Sorry, I'm back
with you. Look Doctor Black, if Alice Kelly was murdered, then
we have a very good idea of who was responsible. We just can't
prove it.'

THIRTY-SEVEN

DS Ayola's revelation about the potential identity of Alice's killer was entirely unexpected. It was also, to some extent, reassuring. The detective had explained that suspicion had immediately fallen on the dogwalker who claimed to have discovered Alice's body. The police believed this was a calculated strategy to ensure that any of his DNA found on her body could be explained away. This individual had previously been charged with sexual assault of a teenage girl in the woods near where Alice's body was found. The other interesting thing was that he didn't actually own the dog he was walking. It belonged to his neighbour, and it was odd that he'd suddenly offered to take it out with him that morning.

The police however could obtain no confession and no forensic evidence, and the man's wife and son insisted on sticking by their alibi for him. DS Ayola also mentioned that fibres had been identified in Alice's mouth and throat which were light in colour and cotton, but they had not managed to find any match for those anywhere in the suspect's home or car.

Tara had made a mental note that these fibres did not sound like those that might come from a black camera strap.

DS Ayola said that while the investigation into Alice's death was still ongoing, the dogwalker had been imprisoned for the other sexual assault charge he'd been facing and had subsequently died after suffering a heart attack in prison.

While Tara was still digesting all of this, and before she could ask any further questions, DS Ayola had needed to end the call to return to her duties at her daughter's sleepover party. Tara had not raised Mia's recovered memory with her; she needed to be sure of her own opinion about that first.

The rest of Tara's night was undisturbed. There were no further emergency calls from the hospital and when she called the ward much later, Kim told her that Mia was sleeping peacefully.

Tara slept in late on Sunday and woke up determined to take the day off. She did not intend to do any work on the Phillips case for at least twenty-four hours unless a new urgent development cropped up at the hospital. She needed a break to decompress, but she also felt she needed some distance from the complex case so that she could come back to it with fresh eyes.

Like old times, she and Olivia met up at their favourite sushi place near Baker Street station for lunch. This time, Jonah was with them, sitting in his highchair and entertaining them with his antics. Olivia had brought him a tub of pasta which he was mostly smearing across the plastic tray, while every now and again dropping a piece over the side before peering over to see if it still existed.

Olivia looked tired but happy. She was even talking about coming back to work two days a week, if she could find a good nursery place for Jonah, which Tara was delighted about. Olivia paused mid-sentence as she was discussing childcare options, and examined Tara's face.

Tara put her hand across her mouth. 'Do I have seaweed between my teeth?'

Olivia shook her head. 'Something's going on with you though.'

'This case I'm working on is taking up all my headspace. Without you to chat to in the kitchen at work, my brain is working much slower.'

'No, it's not that. You look like... like you're not saying something that you want to say.'

Olivia was distracted by Jonah banging a spoon on the table of his highchair. Hopefully she didn't notice the look of disquiet that had flitted across Tara's face before she could hide it. She had not said a word about Daniel's inheritance, or the favour she had asked of Ray Jameson.

Tara watched as Olivia and Jonah played hide and seek with the menu. The baby's laugh was a tonic. A pure, infectious sound. She felt a sudden sadness come over her, seeing the two of them together. It was so different when things went right between parents and children. Perhaps her own life would have been very different if her mother had been able to feel joy. Her mind wandered to Mia's mother too, who had walked out on her child, and how much that profound rejection must have hurt.

'Listen,' Olivia was saying, 'I know we mentioned it vaguely before, and please feel free to say no, but is there any chance you might have Jonah overnight one weekend? Rohan and I are desperate to get a full night's sleep.'

'Oh, I'd love that.' Tara reached out and stroked Jonah's silky baby hair.

After lunch they walked up Marylebone Lane. Jonah was exhausted and had fallen asleep in his buggy; Tara pushed him while Olivia tried to flag down a black cab to drive them home.

The weight of what Tara was hiding from her closest friend had grown heavier and heavier until she felt physically tired. But it wouldn't be fair to open up to Olivia, because then she too would have to carry the burden. The murder case was still open and Tara's brother was still a person of interest.

If someone knew about Matthew's whereabouts, would they be legally or morally obliged to report that information? Tara didn't know the answer and for now she was avoiding the question.

Meanwhile, she herself had just reported Tom Phillips to DS Ayola. What would she do if she found out that Matthew had committed an act of violence?

Tara reminded herself that she still didn't know if any of this inheritance business even had anything at all to do with her brother.

At the sound of her message notification, Tara glanced down at her phone. Ray's message was short and simple.

Let's meet in person, ASAP.

A cab was drawing up alongside them and Tara helped Olivia to lift the buggy into the back, before kissing both Olivia and Jonah goodbye. Left standing on her own, waving as she watched the black cab pull out into the traffic, Tara felt a pang of loneliness followed by an urgent sense of anticipation as she sent Ray her reply.

THIRTY-EIGHT

Tara had never imagined that she would find herself back at the Jameson family home in St John's Wood. The four-storey townhouse was at the top of a cul-de-sac, one of three identical modern homes all in a row. Ray Jameson owned all of them; he had bought the land and commissioned the development over the last decade.

The last time she'd been there, only the Jameson house had been occupied and the other buildings had seemed eerily vacant. Now the situation was reversed: the two adjacent properties were full of life, with cars parked on the driveways and verges, and ornaments and art visible through large windows, while the Jameson place was a ghost house. The shutters on all four floors were shut tight. The two pots outside which had once held beautiful bay trees stood empty, as did the parking spaces out front.

As Tara approached the front door, her heart lurched between dread and excitement. If Ray wanted to meet up in person then he must have something significant to tell her. She was trying to ignore both her gut instinct and her common sense, both of which were informing her that this meeting was inappropriate in about a thousand different ways.

As she approached the house, she heard a dog barking. A few seconds after she'd pressed the bell, Ray opened the front door.

'Doctor Black.' His greeting was less effusive than usual. There was no handshake and only the vaguest smile.

He also looked uncharacteristically casual, in a thick jumper over black jeans. This was the first time Tara had ever seen him without of one of his trademark pinstripe suits, and it took her a few moments to adjust to the new – cuddlier – look as she followed him inside.

The house was noticeably chilly, as if Ray couldn't be bothered to heat it while living there alone. As Tara stepped through the door of the kitchen, Ziggy, the Staffordshire terrier belonging to Ray's daughter Jade, came bounding up to her as though she was an old friend. He seemed thrilled to see her, licking her hands as she reached out to pat him, wagging his tail and wriggling around.

'He remembers you,' Ray said.

Tara stroked his silvery head as he settled down next to her. 'He's so much more relaxed.'

'Ziggy was as stressed out as the rest of us when you first met him.' Ray put down a large bowl of kibble in the corner and the dog rushed over to scoff it down.

As she watched Ray with the dog, in this house that echoed with emptiness, the loneliness of his situation struck Tara for the first time.

She and Ray had never spoken about Sandra. They had discussed his daughter Jade's progress during her treatment, usually in the form of brief written updates, but Tara had never raised the subject of Ray's wife. She feared it may be a sore point because Tara's work with Jade had ultimately led to Sandra's confession. As far as Tara knew, Sandra's defence had gone with manslaughter by diminished responsibility, and she was serving a sentence of seven and a half years. In practical terms that meant that she could be released in half that time.

Now that Tara was inside their home, she felt she had to clear the air. 'How is Sandra doing?'

'Surprisingly well.' Ray's eyes brightened a little. 'In a strange way, I think this has all been a relief for her. She has nothing more to hide, and she's paying her dues. She's started a fitness programme in prison.'

Tara smiled. She had a clear image of Sandra, still stunning in Lycra, but now in a room with bars rather than up on the lavender-scented rooftop of The Onyx Hotel.

Ray offered her a coffee and she accepted. Ziggy dozed on a mat near the back door, snoring, while Ray handled his state-of-the-art coffee machine. The kitchen was filled with noise and the delicious smell of freshly ground coffee beans.

Tara was impatient to know why she was there, but Ray seemed to be delaying getting to the point, which was most unlike him.

Please let this not be bad news.

Please let Matthew be alive. Please.

She only had one close family member left.

Ray came over and placed the two cups down on the marble countertop. He sat down on the bar stool opposite hers. 'I've located the owner of the bank account.'

An octopus thrashed around in her belly, tentacles reaching for her heart and lungs so she could barely get the words out. 'Who is it?'

Matthew might have changed his name; that would not surprise her. Which was why she had given Ray the photograph page of his passport.

'Her name is Maria Scalera.'

'*Her* name. A woman?' Tara's heart sank.

Ray nodded. 'Maria is sixty-one years old and she lives in a town in southern Italy called Tricase.' Ray held out his phone, showing her a blurry image of an older woman walking along a street. It looked like she was carrying shopping bags. She had a squat build and short dark hair. 'Do you recognise her?'

Tara shook her head.

'She's local to the area, she's lived there most of her life. She works as a cleaner for a wealthy ex-pat family who have a holiday home in a nearby town. She has a husband, three grown-up sons and four grandchildren. That's about it.' Ray put his phone away.

Tara sighed, frustrated and disappointed. Why would she choose to continue to transfer large amounts of money to a stranger? How was this woman linked, either to Daniel or to Matthew?

'Daniel never mentioned a woman in Italy, nothing like that?' Ray asked.

'Nothing. Not a single word.' Tara sipped her coffee.

If Daniel had not died, she may never have known about any of this. She had no idea that he was keeping secrets from her, or that he was so good at it. Which was pretty naïve, now she thought about it, because he had been deceiving his wife about his affair with Tara for years.

'Do you know anything about Maria's ex-pat employer that might be relevant?' Tara asked. 'Could there be any connection to Daniel there?'

'I know enough. He's an attorney from Milan and I don't think he's the person you're interested in.'

'Right.' Tara didn't ask how Ray had come by all of this information. She assumed he had private detectives involved, very possibly the same ones he'd used to look into Tara's own background when she was assessing his daughter. This time round, she was simply grateful for his connections.

'Did you say this woman is a full-time cleaner?' Tara asked.

'She works six days a week and apparently pops in to feed the cats on a Sunday too.'

'She probably wouldn't carry on working as a cleaner if she was receiving all of Daniel's monthly transfer, right? It adds up to a significant amount of money.'

Ray nodded. 'Maria withdraws the money each month in cash. I'm guessing she takes a cut but not the whole amount.'

The spark of hope was back. The money could still be ending up with her brother. This woman, Maria, might lead her to Matthew.

Ray went over to the cupboard and took down two glasses, which he filled with water from a dispenser on the fridge. Ziggy was still lying at the back door, but now he lifted his head, watching Ray closely as he moved across the kitchen.

Ray set one of the glasses down in front of Tara.

'Could you email me that photograph of Maria, and the address of the bank where she goes to collect the money?'

'Sure.'

Tara took a long drink of ice-cold water as a possibility took shape in her mind. Once she had completed her work with Mia Phillips, she might take a holiday. To a small town in southern Italy.

'You're hoping that this woman might lead you to your brother?'

Tara nodded.

'If this person receiving the money does turn out to be Matthew,' Ray said, 'then your Daniel was a very good friend to him, all these years. I have to wonder why Daniel would be quite so loyal and so generous?'

Tara didn't want to think about what he was implying. Not yet.

'I have no idea. Daniel never said a word to me about any of this.'

'To be absolutely clear though,' Ray said, 'Matthew himself has never once tried to contact you in all this time?'

'No. Never. I don't even know if he's still alive.' Tara looked at him. 'That's the truth. It isn't a story I made up for the police.'

'So if he is alive, then for whatever reason, Matthew does not want contact with you.'

Tara appreciated his bluntness even though it hurt. 'Yes. If Matthew survived, then he doesn't seem to want to have anything to do with me. But I need to understand why that is.'

Ray was leaning forwards and speaking in a low voice, even though Tara assumed they were alone in the house and in no danger of being overheard. 'Look, I know you don't want to hear this, but we have to consider that your brother may have done exactly what the police say he did.'

She liked the fact that Ray had used the word *we*. It made her feel less alone.

'I need to know what happened the night my parents died.'

'I understand. I'd feel the same way. But before you rush over there, you have to consider that Matthew may not want to be found, and that you can't predict how he will react if you track him down.'

'I'm not afraid of him.' The numbness that had protected her was thawing and Tara felt raw. 'Or, rather, I'm not afraid that he'll do anything to hurt me. What really scares me is that he'll refuse to have anything to do with me.'

There were a few moments of silence. Tara knew that her pain was showing in her face, in the set of her mouth. Their eyes connected and Ray saw everything.

If anyone understood, it would be him. Here he was, alone in this mansion, when all that really mattered to him was his family. Come to think of it, Ray did not look himself either, and it wasn't only the absence of the suit. She had caught a glimpse of desolation in his eyes.

'Is everything all right with you?' Tara asked him.

'Jade barely speaks to me.'

'I'm sorry.' Ray and Jade had always been close. He had made his mistakes, terrible ones, but at the core he was a loving and protective father.

'At first she was in shock, after everything that happened,' Ray said, pausing to clear his throat, 'but now she's angry. Furious that we let her go through all those police interviews without telling her the truth. I can't even understand it myself now. All I can say is that at the time I was half crazy, trying to rescue my wife and my daughter. I nearly screwed everything up. I would have done, completely, if you hadn't been there.'

Tara let the depth of his gratitude sink in. 'I know how much Jade loves you. The anger is healthy, in a way. It will pass and she'll come back to you.'

Ray lifted his glass of water as if to make a toast, covering his pain with a half-smile. 'To family, Doctor Black.'

Tara lifted hers too. 'To family. And truth.'

After a few moments, she said, 'Are you ever going to call me anything other than Doctor Black?'

'Sure. As soon as you tell me your real name.'

THIRTY-NINE

After her meeting with Ray, Tara was too full of adrenaline to sleep. They had agreed that she would send a money transfer through exactly as Daniel usually did. Ray would then arrange to have the woman collecting it followed.

As she set up the transfer online, Tara's hands were shaking. She knew she was about to implode the almost normal life she had worked so long and so hard to create.

At around one in the morning, she gave up on trying to sleep and got up and went downstairs. From the kitchen window, she looked out at her cherry tree. Underneath it, she had buried the last bottle of red wine she and Daniel had drunk together. The spot was marked with a small rosemary bush.

With a blanket around her shoulders, Tara walked out into the garden, knelt down and cut a few sprigs from the plant with sharp kitchen scissors. She held them to her face and inhaled.

Ray was right. If Matthew was alive, then it was obvious he did not want Tara to find him. Matthew could have found some way to contact her at some point during the last twenty-seven years.

But the need to get to the bottom of it all had become so

strong that it drowned out any doubt and any need for self-preservation. The answers to questions she'd lived with for decades might be within reach.

Tara stood up and took the sprigs of rosemary inside and laid them on her kitchen table.

She had made her decision and there was no going back. She was going to take one more week to tie up the Mia Phillips case and a few other loose ends in her practice, and then she was going to take some time off and travel to the small town where the bank branch was located.

She went to find her laptop and made the booking there and then.

Tara woke up on her sofa with sunlight shining in through the half open curtains and that flight booking confirmation sitting right at the top of her inbox. There was time pressure now from both sides: her own trip as well as Mia's impending due date.

While she dressed and then made a coffee, thinking wistfully of Ray's state of the art coffee machine and wondering what beans he used, she rationalised that if the police had been satisfied with Mia's and Tom's explanations of their movements on the night Alice Kelly had died, then she should trust that the investigation had been solid and let go of her concerns about risk. For now, anyway.

She had to refocus on what she'd initially been hired to do, which was to understand the psychology behind Mia's confession. There was an obvious place where she needed to dig deeper. She wanted to understand more about Mia's childhood and the impact of that early separation. It must be significant, or Mia would not have lied about it. Tara needed to talk to Sarah Clarke, Mia's mother.

She used the contact details Mia's father had given her a few days earlier, and called Sarah first thing that morning.

Although Sarah had sounded surprised and not particularly pleased to hear from her daughter's psychologist, nonetheless she said it would be fine for Tara to come out and see her. It would have to be at her workplace, she insisted.

She was based in Little Chalfont, a village northwest of London. It took Tara about forty minutes to get out there by train and then it was an easy walk to the pharmacy, located in a small row of shops near the station. The place was small and unassuming, with a hushed atmosphere. There was a dispensary area behind a glass partition at the back, and in front of that a woman standing behind the counter. Tara walked towards her through the narrow space where shelves on either side of her were filled with all manner of medicines and toiletries and various other essentials.

'Can I help you?'

Sarah had the same petite build and elfin-type face as her daughter, but that was where the similarity ended. She had none of Mia's spikiness. Her eyes were dull, and she looked far older than she probably was. She was dressed in shapeless clothing, and an air of defeat hovered in the air around her.

'Are you Sarah Clarke?'

She nodded.

'My name is Tara Black, we spoke on the phone earlier?'

Sarah looked at her blankly, as though she didn't remember the conversation they'd had only a couple of hours before.

'I'm the psychologist working with Mia,' Tara reminded her.

'Oh.' Sarah glanced behind her at the pharmacist, a kindly looking man in tortoise-shell glasses who was busy in the dispensary area. He gave Sarah a reassuring smile and raised a hand in greeting to Tara.

'How long will this take?' Sarah asked.

'I'll be as brief as I can. Do you have a break coming up? I can wait until it's more convenient.'

'I've already taken my morning break. I can't leave the counter unattended.'

'Right.'

Tara was reluctant to speak to her in the middle of the store. Though they were alone for now, other customers could walk in at any time, and the pharmacist could overhear every word.

'You're welcome to use the consultation room,' the pharmacist said, coming to the rescue. 'I can keep an eye on the counter for you.'

Reluctantly, Sarah emerged from her spot and took Tara through a door into a tiny, clinical space where there were two plastic chairs, a table and a blood pressure monitor.

Tara took out her notebook and got straight to the point, sensing Sarah might give her limited time.

'John tells me Mia is in hospital?' Sarah said.

'Yes.'

'I'm sure she'll be fine.'

'I hope so.'

If anything, Sarah seemed even more detached from her daughter than Mia's father had been. Tara wasn't sure if she even knew Mia was pregnant and that she was soon to be a grandmother.

'I was wondering if you could you tell me a little about Mia's early childhood?' Tara said.

'It was a horrible time. We left England when Mia was only six months old, because of John's job, and then there was all the moving around to different countries and I hated it when I couldn't speak the language. I wasn't well and John was always at work.'

'When you say you weren't well, what do you mean?'

'The doctors didn't really know what was wrong with me. I've seen so many of them, and had all sorts of tablets. When I was younger I didn't always take my medication properly. I do take it now, more regularly. I came back to England when Mia was seven. It's better for me here. My cousin is not too far and she helps me.'

'Right. Okay.' Tara wasn't sure if Sarah was referring to physical or mental illness and her explanation was rather disjointed. She had also noticed that although she'd asked about Mia's childhood, so far, everything Sarah had said was about herself.

'Sarah, you said the doctors weren't sure what was wrong, and they gave you medication. Can you describe what symptoms you were having?'

'It was mostly the thoughts. I would have these terrible thoughts and I was scared all the time, so that's when the doctors started giving the pills. But to be honest, I'm still not sure if they were just thoughts, or if it was real.'

'Could you tell me more about those thoughts?'

'I worried there was something wrong with Mia. She cried all the time. She had these eyes... She wasn't like the other children.' Sarah cleared her throat. 'I had three miscarriages, after Mia was born, and I started to worry that Mia was doing something, to make me lose all the babies.'

Tara nodded, feeling her own mouth go dry. Sarah's belief that her two-year-old daughter was responsible for her miscarriages was very disturbing. 'What did you think Mia was doing?'

Sarah was not able to make eye contact at all. She looked past Tara, her eyes fixed on the door. 'We had a bird, you see, and I told Mia never to leave the cage door open; she knew she wasn't allowed to do that. But she must have, you see, because the bird got out of the window and I found the poor little thing later, out in the garden, ripped to shreds. Only the wings left. No head. Heart and guts all exposed. Feathers everywhere. John said a cat must have got hold of it.'

For the first time, Sarah was showing emotion. She was frowning and looking distressed. 'Mia knew how much I loved that bird. She was so jealous. I kept telling John, but he didn't take any notice. He didn't believe me. And then I kept losing all those babies. So that's why I had to leave. They always told me it wasn't true, but I know I was much more ill when I was around Mia. I'm much better now I'm back here, in England. It was better for Mia too, after I left. It was the right thing to do. She's happier now, isn't she? She's having a baby soon?'

There was a tinge of regret as Sarah made eye contact, briefly.

Tara nodded, feeling empathy for her. She imagined that in foreign countries, moving around often and perhaps not being able to communicate easily because of a language barrier, some of Sarah's mental health difficulties and her struggles to parent Mia might have been missed or misdiagnosed. She had clearly needed professional help and support.

'When was the last time you saw Mia?' Tara asked her.

'Oh, I suppose around twenty years ago now. Maybe a bit more.' Sarah checked her watch. 'I don't want to stay in here too long. I worry about my job.'

'Of course. I think that's really all I wanted to ask you.' It had taken almost an hour to get out there, and the meeting was over in ten minutes. But Tara was glad she'd decided to come and meet Sarah in person. She certainly had a sense of what Mia would have had to deal with in her early years. She imagined there had been little comfort, and the interactions with Sarah could have been quite frightening for a small child.

Tara tucked her notebook back into her bag and lifted it onto her shoulder. 'Do you enjoy your job?'

'The customers can be difficult sometimes, but usually it's all right.' Sarah held the door of the small room open for Tara.

'Thank you again for seeing me at such short notice.'

'I hope you'll be careful.' Sarah leaned towards Tara so she was right up close, her breath stale as she whispered, 'Mia has the devil inside.'

FORTY

Tara did not believe in the devil, but she did know that some people were born with a greater propensity for evil than others. There were children that lacked empathy and enjoyed causing pain. This lifelong pattern often began with warning signs such as cruelty to animals. Mia's history of biting other children at school and perhaps intentionally causing the gruesome death of her mother's pet bird could potentially fit this pattern. But Tara was far from convinced that was the case.

It was clear that Sarah had disturbed thought patterns and struggled to empathise with her daughter, and that was a form of emotional trauma. Mia's behaviour could have been a symptom of her pain at feeling unloved, rather than driven by an innate capacity for aggression.

Tara thought about Jonah, Olivia's baby, the feel of his plump body and the smell of lavender in his hair, his contented babbling and his sense that all was secure in his world as long as he was in his mother's arms. Tara herself had never really felt she had a mother, in the sense of being comforted and loved. But she understood the absence of one and she felt Mia's pain.

Tara thought of Mia, forcing herself into that freezing

water. Maybe on some level, Mia was afraid. Afraid of developing her mother's illness, afraid of being a damaging mother, afraid of herself.

But the question remained: had Mia acted out her pain with Alice at the cottage?

When Carolyn Goring arrived at Tara's office building later that afternoon, she looked weary. The shadows under her eyes were darker and the lines around her eyes and mouth deeper than Tara remembered.

Tara had sent her a brief but firm email from the train on the way back from seeing Mia's mother, saying that they needed to talk and that it was urgent. Tara had requested that this time Carolyn come to her Marylebone office.

It was interesting that Carolyn had made herself available so soon and also that she had been so accommodating about coming out to Tara's office, without asking questions. That probably meant that she was keen to know what Tara had to say. Perhaps she was even worried about something Tara might have uncovered.

Carolyn was taking a while to disentangle herself from her coat and scarf in the entrance hall. She looked around appreciatively as she hung these up on the hooks beside the door. 'How many psychologists are in the practice here?'

'At the moment it's just me.'

'Really? Well, it's a lovely space. The rental must be quite something too, I imagine.'

Tara smiled. Carolyn would probably be surprised to hear that Tara owned the mews house, and she might well be curious about how Tara could afford such a piece of prime London real estate. But this meeting was about the skeletons in Carolyn's closet, not Tara's own.

She led Carolyn upstairs to the first floor without making

any further small talk. In Tara's office, they sat facing each other in the matching armchairs.

'I went to see Mia's mother today,' Tara said. 'Sarah explained to me that she'd had significant mental health difficulties when Mia was little, and it sounds like she may have had a form of psychosis. She was having delusions that Mia was evil, which was part of the reason she left the family. I believe that Mia's experience of living with a very disturbed mother and then her mother's abandonment left her vulnerable to depression. Mia herself is possibly experiencing a psychotic depression, and her memory about killing Alice may be a type of delusion.'

'That makes sense,' Carolyn said.

'So my question is this. You're a very experienced therapist. How could you miss the possibility of a psychotic depression, and her need for urgent treatment?'

Caroline sighed. 'We've been through all of this. I'm not going to explain it all to you again and I'm not here to justify my treatment approach.' But Carolyn wasn't leaving, either. 'I remind you that Mia walked out of treatment early—'

'And why focus so much on the death of Alice Kelly? Is that because you were biased because of your feelings for David Phillips?' The words came out bluntly. Tara wanted to jolt Carolyn into being more upfront.

Carolyn was looking at her in shock, taking a while to regroup.

'You were in a relationship with David Phillips at the time of Alice's death. But you deliberately didn't tell me that when I asked how Mia was referred to you. You said that you and David were colleagues.'

'That was true.' Carolyn was flustered but trying to regain her composure, taking a few deeper breaths. 'David and I were colleagues first, and then yes, we dated for a while. We ended things a few weeks after Alice passed away.'

'Why would you not mention that when I asked you?'

'Because it's personal.'

'David Phillips had concerns about you seeing Mia as a patient. He believes you still have feelings for him, and that those feelings clouded your judgement. David is concerned you took the break up badly and that you may be... fixated on getting back together with him.'

At that, Carolyn laughed. 'Are you serious?'

Tara nodded.

Carolyn sighed, alternately rearranging her hair and changing her position in the armchair. She was not finding this conversation easy. Tara could relate; she knew what it was like to feel like an imposter: helping people with their own emotional difficulties all day while your own personal life was a train wreck.

'Do you want to tell me the way you see things? Otherwise I only have David's version to go on.'

Carolyn sighed. 'As I said, David and I worked together on a cardiac unit for a couple of years. At some point, David was going through a rough time after his divorce, and I was having a rough time after mine. We'd go out for a meal now and again, and gradually, things developed. A few months after we'd started dating, I felt something was wrong. David was emotionally distant, and he started disengaging – he'd be late for our arrangements or cancel last minute, or he'd claim he had to work when I knew otherwise. I think he wasn't ready to commit to another relationship so soon after such a toxic divorce. I on the other hand very much wanted to get married again.'

A car alarm began going off outside Tara's window, interrupting them. Carolyn was looking pensive. When the noise finally stopped, she continued talking.

'For a while,' she said, 'I convinced myself I was imagining things, even though alarm bells were ringing loud and clear. But eventually, it sank in that David would never love me in the way

I wanted to be loved and I'd already been down that awful road with my first husband. I suppose I was a comfort blanket for David at a time when he needed one.'

'That sounds painful.'

'It was. Very. After I told him I thought we should end it, I never heard from him again. I suspect he was relieved. But I really didn't think I would be spending these years of my life on my own.'

The two women sat in silence for a few moments. From the way Carolyn described the breakdown of their relationship, she did not come across a woman who was 'fixated', as David had described her. Although Tara couldn't help but wonder if Carolyn was playing her by opening up – or seeming to open up.

'Did you have concerns about taking Mia on as a patient, given that you'd had this painful experience with David?'

'No. I didn't. I was with David the weekend Alice died, and I'll never forget it. Tom called his father, first to tell him that Alice was missing, and then to say a body had been found. Tom was in pieces, he was absolutely devastated. The whole thing was so tragic, with Alice being so young. I'd always been very fond of Tom, and by the time he contacted me about his wife, it had been three years since I had anything to do with David. Tom sounded desperate. Mia is a vulnerable pregnant woman and I thought they both deserved a break. I wanted to help.'

What Carolyn had done by taking Mia on as a patient didn't officially break any rules. The code of ethics for therapists was clear that 'dual relationships' with patients were not permitted, but Carolyn taking on Mia as a client didn't exactly fit that definition. Yes, Carolyn had once dated Mia's father-in-law, but the connection was a distant one and apparently Carolyn hadn't had contact with the family in years.

Still, the situation wasn't entirely without complications, and Tara pushed a little harder, to see if there was anything else that might be hidden under Carolyn's perfectly reasonable and rational façade.

'But wouldn't it have been the safer option to simply refer Mia to someone else?'

'Hindsight is always perfectly accurate, isn't it?' Carolyn was fidgeting again, adjusting and readjusting her hair. 'In hindsight, yes, maybe it would have been a better option to send Mia to someone else. And of course I've been asking myself what I could have done differently, especially with Mia landing up in hospital. But there are also a lot of mediocre, or even terrible, therapists out there, and all the good ones are full and a lot more expensive than Tom and Mia could afford.'

'Can you be one hundred per cent sure that your feelings about David did not affect your treatment of Mia in any way?'

'I believe I acted with integrity.' The blank mask was slipping and Carolyn was visibly upset. 'My reputation matters to me. Very much. It's all I have. I'm sure you understand that.'

'I do.'

Tara was feeling more sympathetic towards Carolyn, who appeared to be genuinely pained by her inability to help Mia. Her reasoning for taking Mia on as a patient was persuasive. Almost. But then Carolyn was good at building trust, and being persuasive was her business. Tara could not shake her scepticism. Her gut was telling her something. Something about the way Mia had described that last session was not right.

'The first time we met,' Carolyn said, 'you told me that you weren't seeing patients because of personal circumstances.'

Tara nodded.

'What happened to you?' There was an intensity in Carolyn's gaze.

'I lost someone. A partner.'

'So you're on your own too.'

'Yes.' For a moment, Tara's whole body yearned for the comforting weight of Daniel's arms around her.

'I imagine you and I are alike,' Carolyn said. 'We both work hard to be self-sufficient. We keep tight control of our own feelings. We focus our energy on what other people feel and need.'

Carolyn's eyes were warm. Comforting.

But then, that was her job. To convey empathy, whether real or not. Was Carolyn genuinely caring, or was she a skilled manipulator, turning the tables so she could find Tara's weak points? Had she done the same with Mia?

It struck Tara again that she may have committed a worse boundary violation than anything Carolyn had done. She had asked Ray Jameson for his help with a highly sensitive personal matter, even though she had been his daughter's therapist. There was a power dynamic there, and a debt of gratitude. Tara could be taking advantage of him. She was in no position to judge Carolyn Goring.

Tara picked up the glass of water she'd put on her side table and drank half of it down.

Carolyn picked up her glass too and sipped at her water. 'Being on my own suits me fine. I don't know about you, but I've had enough trouble with men.'

Without waiting for Tara to respond, Carolyn put her glass down and then stood up, rearranging her hair one last time before walking out of the office.

'Such a lovely building,' she commented again, having regained her composure by the time they reached the bottom of the stairs. Carolyn peered through to the reception area as she rearranged her scarf, shrugged on her coat and picked up her umbrella.

Tara held the front door open for her and Carolyn stepped outside, looking right and left before crossing the street. As Tara watched her walk away, she was left with the nagging feeling that there was still something more about that last session with Mia that Carolyn was hiding.

FORTY-ONE

THREE MONTHS BEFORE ALICE'S DEATH

David had invited Carolyn to go with him to a photography exhibition, something Tom's girlfriend Alice was involved in, apparently. Carolyn was conflicted about it. One the one hand, she was happy that David was including her in his family life, especially after the doubts that had been gnawing at her over the last few months in the face of his withdrawal and irritability. On the other hand, she was uneasy because this event was taking place at his ex-wife's gallery. This would be the first time she'd meet the infamous Julia.

The divorce had not been easy and David was still licking his wounds years later. After something like twenty-seven years of marriage, Julia had blindsided David with a divorce petition as soon as their son Freddie left home to join the army. David had never talked about what the problems in their marriage actually were, but he did say that Julia had gone after half of all his assets, including his pension. There had been no prenuptial contract and Julia had, in David's words, fleeced him. He accused Julia of squirrelling away money at her gallery for years, making much more than she declared to the tax man, and hiding her own assets which included several valuable pieces of art.

Worst of all, his ex-wife had contrived to keep the house on New End, which David loved with his heart and soul.

The therapist in Carolyn couldn't help but see it from both sides. Julia had, after all, looked after David's two sons while he went out and forged a career. But Carolyn also knew how the NHS took its pound of flesh, and she knew that after the incredibly long hours David had worked over several decades, now at almost retirement age, he did not have enough years of work left to recoup his losses.

Carolyn's parents had always been comfortably well off and generous, so she had never experienced financial hardship herself. She didn't judge David for the deep bitterness he held towards Julia, but it did nag at her. Carolyn only hoped the strong negative feeling was purely about finances, as opposed to the kind of bitterness that might stem from David still being in love with his ex-wife.

Well, she would soon find out. At the exhibition she would have her chance to observe the two of them together for the first time.

Carolyn walked into the Leonard Gallery with butterflies in her stomach. She was in one of her flowing linen outfits to hide those extra pounds she could not shake, and she felt like a total frump compared to David's ex-wife. Julia was as stylish as she had feared. Rake thin, too. The whole gallery was infused with an air of sophistication, and the art students brought with them a youthful energy. This was a different world.

Surprisingly, Julia greeted her with genuine warmth. David stayed by Carolyn's side the entire time and was courteous and affectionate in public. She did have the fleeting thought that she might be being used to provoke Julia, but she brushed that aside.

Insecurity was her Achilles heel. For the most part, the exes avoided looking at each other and contrived never to be on the same side of the room. Carolyn could not see any evidence of residual passion between them.

There was cheap prosecco on offer, but the stuff always gave her a terrible headache and so Carolyn stuck to water. Out of nerves, she drank a lot of that and so she needed the bathroom a couple of times. The poky toilet was down a narrow passageway at the back of the gallery, past a small office, which was far more utilitarian in appearance than the whitewashed gallery out front,

Carolyn spent a minute or two more than she needed to in there, relishing the break from the crowded room. She avoided the mirror, aware of her dowdy outfit, her hair with too much frizz and the lines on her sagging face.

What is wrong with you? David brought you to introduce to his family. He's proud to be with you.

Envy had already destroyed her first marriage. But she'd been right; her husband *had* been unfaithful. Carolyn had never felt confident in holding a man's attention; her own therapist had traced her insecurities back to her father, of course. Being in possession of these insights about herself though unfortunately did not change the way she felt inside, or the resentment that sometimes spilled out.

Right. She couldn't hide any longer. There was probably a queue outside. Carolyn took a breath, gathered herself and opened the door. As she did so, she heard a giggle. She paused, peering through the gap in the door. David was in the passageway with a young woman. Gorgeous, auburn hair to her waist, in a barely-there mini-skirt. The two of them were standing a little too close together for Carolyn's liking. *They're only talking*, she told herself. *Probably getting bored waiting for the bathroom because I'm taking so long.*

She opened the door fully, put a smile on her face, and walked back outside.

FORTY-TWO

'All the tests keep coming back fine,' Mia said. 'They won't keep me here anymore.'

Tara was in the car, on speakerphone. She was heading to the gym after an afternoon completing Timothy's assessment report, which had been due that day. 'Okay. When are they discharging you?'

'Tomorrow, after ward rounds. But I can't go home.'

'What do you mean?'

'Tom can't even look at me, let alone sleep in the same bed. I've asked Julia if I can stay with her for a while. I told her the doctors said it was safer because the house on New End is so near to the hospital.'

Tara suspected that Tom might be relieved about this decision. The problem was, she wasn't convinced that Julia's house was a good option, given that Freddie lived there.

The situation was getting more and more complicated. Mia's due date was approaching fast and Tara had five days left before she was scheduled to leave the country.

'I'll come and see you at Julia's tomorrow afternoon. I'd like to spend the rest of the day working with you. I have an idea how we can get through this.'

'Okay.' But there wasn't much hope left in Mia's voice.

Tara felt a sudden weight of responsibility for her vulnerable client. Mia was so isolated from her own family, and the Phillips family was not exactly a safe haven.

Vulnerable and potentially dangerous, she reminded herself. A part of her kept wanting to ignore that option.

Tara turned the music up louder as she drove.

Louis, the gym owner and principal trainer, regularly put together playlists for his clients on Spotify, compilations of high energy tracks which he sent out with inspirational titles such as '*Music to get you moving*'. This one was a pop mix stretching back to the nineties, ranging from Miley Cyrus to George Michael. Even with the volume up loud though, Tara could not drown out her concern about Mia being released from the safety of the hospital the next day.

The traffic queues were driving her nuts. She had to move. She wanted to be lifting weights, sweating, and physically worn out so that she could not think about work or her trip to Italy for at least the next hour. She craved an intense, sweaty mental cleanse.

She arrived at the gym just in time for the kettle bells session and in that class, she had forty-five minutes of escape. Afterwards, she delayed leaving the studio. She had a feeling that if she went home, she would be drawn to Wildway Close in the darkness.

She decided to stay for the cool down class, the last session of the day. Usually this one was too slow for her, but as it turned out, the deep stretching exercises ended up being exactly what she needed.

The low light and instrumental music made for a mellow atmosphere. The class started gently but progressed to increasingly intense and at times agonising stretches that seemed to be held forever. The studio was small, so there were only eight people in the class, and Tara vaguely recognised them all as regulars. Since Daniel had been gone, she was in the gym at least four times a week so she'd started to notice the other people who turned up as frequently as she did. She kept herself to herself though. She talked to people all day in her job and in here she relished both the lack of conversation and relative anonymity.

Louis was hands on, walking around to make adjustments. He was in a vest and shorts, showing off the impressive results of his own training regime. He knelt behind Tara, pulling her shoulders back into a strong stretch. 'Is this pressure okay?'

'Mm. Yes.'

He knew to be gentler on the right side where she'd fractured her clavicle the year before in the hit-and-run.

Later, as Tara sat with her legs outstretched in front of her, folding herself forward, he pushed down on her lower back, releasing the tension. By the end, she felt a welcome stillness inside. After the class, she lingered again, rolling up her mat and then pulling on her sweatshirt and coat in the lobby area. She realised she was the last person to leave the studio.

Louis was behind the reception desk. He looked up and smiled.

'What time do you close up here?' she asked, inanely.

'Depends. Sometimes I hang out and clean when I'm in the mood for a really wild night.'

She laughed. 'I know the feeling.'

When she'd first joined the gym and Louis had been showing her around, he'd told her he had been an accountant in a city firm but found himself unsuited to corporate life because his passion was exercise and wellness. He'd taken a chance, opening the boutique gym offering personal training and small group sessions. Since then, they hadn't talked much but she'd overheard someone in the changing rooms saying he was divorced with young sons.

'How is your shoulder feeling after those stretches?'

'Great actually.' She pulled the elastic band out of her hair.

'Do you still get much pain?'

'Sometimes.' Tara wasn't entirely sure if the ache she still felt was only in her mind. 'It's more stiffness now, I think. The stretching really helps. I should do more.'

Tara felt a prickle of embarrassment. She'd just been thinking that the closest she'd been to intimacy for over a year was when Louis had put his hand on her lower back.

'Would you like another round?'

Was he flirting with her? Or was she flirting with him? She had not felt attractive or attraction for so long.

'Yes,' she said, 'I really would.'

FORTY-THREE

The cobbled alleyway in Hampstead had come to life around lunch time and the cafés and vintage stores and hairdressers bustled with clients and passers-by. The unsettling red painting still had pride of place in the window of the Leonard Gallery. This time when Tara looked at it though, she saw shades of a vibrant pink. And then she had a glimpse of an image of what had happened the night before, in a deserted gym studio with the lights turned down low.

Inside, Julia was taking delivery of several cases of champagne and a delivery driver was stacking these beside the door. Once Julia had signed for the items and the man had left, she and Tara were alone together in the gallery.

'Morning, Doctor Black.' Julia had retreated behind the desk. 'How can I help?'

'I wanted to talk to you in person. I know Mia is being discharged today and I understand she's planning to stay with you?'

Julia gave a sigh. 'Apparently so. Neither she nor my son will tell me what's going on and frankly I don't really understand why she's not going home.'

Tara took a few steps further inside the gallery. 'Julia, I don't think it's safe for her to be in the house while Freddie's there.'

Julia emerged from behind her desk and stood in front of it with her arms folded. 'Freddie's fine.'

She was immediately wary. Prickly at the mention of her younger son.

'Julia, I don't think you believe that. You know that Freddie is unstable. That night at the hospital – he was threatening and he said he felt guilty about Mia. I don't think this situation is safe for her. I haven't raised this with the police, but I—'

Julia's eyes widened as she looked past Tara's shoulder. When Tara turned around, Freddie was standing behind her.

He looked down at the floor and greeted her monosyllabically. Tara knew he'd overheard what had been said. She took a deep breath. He was easily triggered and she had not anticipated running into him.

'She's right,' Freddie said, looking up at Julia. 'Everything Doctor Black said is right.'

'Freddie, stop it.'

'Mum, I don't need you to lie for me.'

Julia was frozen with dread as she looked at him.

'I heard you and Tom last night.' Freddie turned to Tara now. 'My brother was over at the house last night and he was telling Mum a bunch of stuff about Mia. He said that Mia stole Alice's necklace after she died and that she's been hiding it. Wearing it in secret. And then he showed her the photographs Mia took. Pictures of Alice, posing as though she was dead. Out at the cottage, near the river.'

This time, Freddie was lucid and completely sober. 'Tom said that he doesn't trust Mia to be alone with the baby after it's born. I don't know what he's going to do.'

Tara nodded. She didn't ask any questions, not wanting to interrupt the flow of what he was saying. She was keeping an eye on Julia, who looked like she wanted to spring forwards and physically make Freddie stop talking.

'I don't know what's going on with Mia, or why she went into that river,' Freddie said, 'but I do know she blames herself for what happened to Alice. I don't know why, maybe because they were together that last weekend.'

Julia walked forwards, placing herself between Tara and Freddie. 'Look, we can find somewhere for Freddie to stay until Tom and Mia sort themselves out. Will that put your mind at ease?'

Freddie interrupted his mother, speaking to Tara. 'You have to make Mia see that she isn't responsible for what happened. Mia is a good person. She has always been kind to me. That's why I want to tell you something, before I change my mind. I'm just going to say it.'

'No. Freddie—' Julia faced him, her hands on his shoulders. 'Listen to me. You don't have to do this.'

Freddie barely noticed Julia as he looked past her, keeping his eyes on Tara. 'You should record this.'

'Okay.' Tara took out her phone and pressed record.

She was no longer nervous around Freddie. He was distressed, but clear-headed.

Julia looked as though she wanted to throw herself at Tara and grab the phone, but Freddie had taken hold of her hands.

'My brother needs to know,' Freddie said, 'that if anyone hurt Alice that night, it was me.'

FORTY-FOUR

THIRTY MINUTES BEFORE ALICE'S DEATH

Freddie leaves the motorbike tucked away on a dark lane, about half a mile away from the cottage. There are no cameras around here and no streetlights, either. Dressed all in black, motorcycle leathers and heavy boots, he makes his way on foot along the path that runs alongside the river. He feels powerful again, adrenaline pumping through his veins. People say paratroopers are like junkies, addicted to danger. They're right.

When he reaches the back of the cottage, he vaults over the wooden gate into the garden. From there, he has a clear view of the house. The lights in the kitchen are turned on, but the upstairs bedrooms are in darkness. He has a key to the back door, but decides to delay a while, until those lights go out. He wants the element of surprise.

He waits. The only sound is the eerie hooting of an owl. The lights stay on. He is on edge. He's been drinking, but not enough to dull the anger.

Impatient now, he makes his way up to the back door. Through the window, he can see the girls have left a mess. Dirty dishes and glasses all over the place, and a couple of open bottles of wine. He can smell dope, too.

Maybe Alice and Mia forgot to turn out the lights; maybe they've fallen asleep, drunk and high. That doesn't seem like Mia though.

He wonders if Tom is with them. Tom has a hard time staying away from Alice. And Alice is partial to a smoke and doesn't like to get high alone. Tom is not part of this plan.

Just then, Alice walks into the kitchen and Freddie draws back, sharply. He flattens himself against the back wall of the house and watches in surprise as the door opens and she steps outside, closing it behind her. It takes him a second to adjust. But only a second.

Alice heads down the path and unlocks the back gate, leaving it open behind her.

Where is she going? This doesn't make sense.

As Alice steps out onto the lane, Freddie comes up behind her. He clamps his left hand firmly across her mouth and presses his right forearm against her throat.

'Shhh,' he whispers, close to her ear.

Alice goes limp. She doesn't struggle, doesn't try to speak.

'You took something that doesn't belong to you. I've come to get it back.'

Freddie doesn't take his arm off her throat. The pressure is enough to scare her, but he lets in enough air to breathe.

He doesn't want to hurt her. Or maybe he does. Part of him craves this.

Alice hasn't moved a muscle.

'If I take my hand away, can I trust you to be quiet?'

She nods.

'I hope you're telling the truth. Or you'll be sorry.' He lifts his hand away from her mouth.

She turns to look at him, her pupils dilated with shock or dope, or both. 'Freddie?'

She massages her throat with one hand, then she starts coughing. Maybe he'd pressed down harder than he'd meant to.

'Where is the memory stick?' he asks her.

'What memory stick?' The cogs begin to turn behind Alice's eyes. 'What are you talking about?'

'Don't underestimate me. I'm not stupid. I know what you've done.'

'Did Mia tell you?'

Freddie grabs her by her hair and shoves her down on her knees. Alice makes a small, desperate sound.

'Don't make me hurt you,' he says.

She's trembling now.

'Answer me. Where is it?'

She reaches into her pocket with a shaking hand and pulls out a small memory stick.

Freddie lifts it out of her open palm. 'Have you made a copy of this?'

'No. I swear. This is it.'

He thinks she's telling the truth, but he can't be sure. He might be too late.

'Has anyone else seen what's on here?'

She shakes her head. 'No, honestly.'

'Where were you taking this at eleven thirty at night?'

'Nowhere, I just needed a walk—'

'Bullshit!' He slaps her face. He didn't mean to. He's losing it. Losing control. He hates himself so much and the rage is spilling out all over the place and he can't control it. 'Don't fucking lie to me! Who were you going to give this to?'

'No one.' She can barely get the words out. She's crying, covering her face with her hands.

He sees red. He wants to make her pay and he's shaking her, hard. Next thing, she falls.

His breath comes in jolts and gasps and he's ashamed and he's not sure what he's done.

Alice doesn't resist, doesn't put up a fight. Just lies there.

'Alice? Alice, come on, get up.'
She's still not moving.

FORTY-FIVE

Tara was holding her phone in her right hand and it was still recording. 'Did you tell anyone what happened?'

Freddie shook his head. 'Alice was alive when I left her, I swear to you. She must have got confused, maybe slipped, or... I don't know. She stood up. I swear to you.'

When Tara caught Julia's eyes, she saw her guilt. Somehow, Julia had known about this all along.

Freddie's breathing was growing heavier now as he became more distressed, his chest tightening. 'I didn't kill her. But with my record, no one would have believed me.'

'It would only have caused more pain to Alice's mother and her sisters if they knew she suffered twice,' Julia said.

Tara ignored her, speaking only to Freddie. 'I'm going to give you the name of the detective you can speak to about Alice's case. And the name of a psychiatrist specialising in addictions. You have to contact both of these people, today. Right now.'

Freddie remained mute as Tara wrote both contact details down on a page she tore out of her notebook. But when she held it out to him, he refused to take it.

He rammed his knuckles into his temples. 'My father is right about me. I'm garbage.'

'Freddie, stop,' Tara said. 'Alice's family deserve the full truth. And this might help in many ways you can't understand. You need to focus on them.'

Tara was thinking about Mia too as she said this.

For a moment, she had Freddie's attention, and she knew there was a part of him that wanted to atone, to do the right thing. But then he turned to his mother. 'I'm sorry,' he said.

He walked to the door of the gallery, opened it and stepped out into the alley.

'Freddie, wait!' Julia ran after him.

Through the glass window, Tara saw her trying to hold Freddie back, grabbing on to his arms, as he shrugged her off and left her standing helpless in the alleyway, staring after him.

Julia was tearful when she came back into the gallery. She closed the door and then turned the latch, locking it. 'Are you happy now?'

Tara was uneasy, alone in there with her. 'Being in denial of Freddie's problems won't help him. Or anyone else in your family.'

'Thanks for the advice. Right out of a textbook.'

Tara had walked into a situation she wasn't prepared for. Freddie's confession of assaulting Alice had come out of the blue. But looking into Julia's eyes, Tara had a strong feeling that she either already knew, or at least suspected, that her son had been involved in the events leading up to Alice Kelly's death.

'I want you to delete that recording.' Julia pointed to the phone Tara was gripping in her right hand.

'I can't do that. The police need to be aware there is new information.' Her mouth was very dry.

Julia had taken a step forwards and Tara instinctively

moved backwards, clutching her phone tighter. She could see, given Julia's heightened anxious state, that it might be possible to pressure her to talk. Tara was convinced that she knew something more, and could give her another piece of the puzzle.

'This recording is going to be included in my report, which I am going to pass on the police.' Tara could not help but glance at that locked door. It struck her that in the few times she'd been in there, there had been no other customers. 'If you think there's something else I should include, then this is your chance to tell me.'

Julia rubbed nervously at her throat.

'Did you know that Freddie had gone out to the cottage to retrieve your data?'

'I won't let my son take the fall for whatever is going on with Mia,' Julia said. 'Freddie was not responsible for Alice's death. I have proof.'

FORTY-SIX

NINETY MINUTES BEFORE ALICE'S DEATH

Julia knows she has made a terrible mistake. She paces up and down her living room, unable to stay still, praying that Freddie will come back home before he does something dangerous. She is sick with fear and guilt. She has done it to him again, done what she always does: she has dragged her son right into the middle of her problems.

After that message from Mia had come through to her phone, Julia had been half-hysterical; part furious, part terrified. She had been kind to Alice, she had given her a foothold into the art world, and now Alice had betrayed her.

The information on that hard drive could sink her.

Julia hadn't been thinking straight when she'd gone upstairs to wake Freddie. She had been ranting, telling him that Alice Kelly would destroy everything. She had told Freddie she could land up in jail if those files got into the wrong hands.

Seeing her distress, Freddie had become more and more wound up, until he'd grabbed the keys of his motorbike and stormed out of the house.

Julia is so furious with herself. She had panicked. She hadn't been thinking straight. She'd tried to call Freddie, over and over, but there was no answer. Then she'd seen his phone and the sight of it turned her blood cold. It was lying on the kitchen counter and it had been switched off. Freddie had left it behind deliberately. He did not want to leave any trace that he'd gone down to the cottage to find Alice.

Freddie. Her beautiful little boy, smiling and gap-toothed. So gentle and so loving. When was the last time she'd seen him truly happy?

She could not sit and do nothing while Freddie destroyed himself. What if he had an accident on the motorway on his bike? What if he'd been drinking? What if he lost control? What if he did something they would all regret?

She has to find him. To rescue him, for once.

In the car, Julia's hands are shaking. She's looking for motorbike accidents on the motorway, dreading that she might see the body of her son. And it would all be her fault.

She hates that motorbike. It feels like a death wish.

Freddie, please. Stay calm. I'm nearly there.

Half a mile to go. When she reaches the cottage, she tells herself, Freddie's motorbike will be parked outside, safe and sound. She will knock on the door, go inside and find Freddie and convince him to come home with her, and everything will be all right. She will ask Alice politely to give the stolen property back or she will threaten to report the theft to the police.

She will do what she should have done in the first place: she will handle this herself.

Only none of that happens. As the car inches slowly along one of the back roads leading to the cottage, Julia struggling to see in the pitch darkness, a figure appears in the glare of her headlights. A woman. Tall and slim, with waist-length auburn hair, making her way along using a flashlight.

Alice.

The lane is so narrow that there is no choice but to brake suddenly and stop the car. Julia reaches for the torch she keeps in the side compartment. She steps out and shines it into Alice's face.

Alice is squinting in the glare. 'Julia? What's going on?'

There is a sound from behind them, like a car door opening.

'Who's there?' Alice says, peering into the darkness. 'Is someone there?'

'Where's Freddie?' As the words come out of her mouth, Julia realises she has made another mistake.

'Oh my God. *You* sent him after me, didn't you? You really are a piece of work, Julia.'

'What happened?'

'*What happened?*' Alice comes right up close, shrieking at her. 'He fucking threatened to kill me, that's what happened.'

That'll teach you to steal.

'You're exaggerating as usual.' Julia shines the torch on the ground so she doesn't have to look into Alice's eyes. 'He's protective, and you stole from me.'

'Well, according to your ex-husband, you stole everything he'd ever worked for, so I guess what goes around comes around, right?'

'David said that?'

'Forget it,' Alice says.

'No. Tell me. When did he say that?'

Alice tries to get past her, but Julia won't move.

'Why is David talking to you about his personal life?'

'What are you so afraid of, Julia? What's in that data?'

Alice is screaming and now Julia yells back at her. 'You don't care how many lives you destroy, do you?'

'Your *son* threatened to kill me. Do you not give a shit about that? Freddie is a fucking lunatic, he should be locked up. I should go to the police.'

Alice has the power to destroy everything Julia has worked for, and Freddie too.

Julia remembers all those times she did not protect her son. She remembers Freddie's eyes, full of pain.

Alice won't stop shouting.

She bears down on her, spit flying onto Julia's face. 'You really are a crazy bitch! David was right about you. Should I show the police the memory stick too, when I report Freddie?'

Julia lashes out, trying to get away. The torch, still in her hand, connects with something, she's not sure what.

A cracking sound.

When Julia lifts the torch again, she sees blood trickling down Alice's temple. Did she do that? How did that happen?

She panics. The torch slips from her hand and everything flies into darkness and silence.

FORTY-SEVEN

When Julia had finished speaking, she went to the window, looking outside anxiously as if she was hoping for Freddie to come back.

'What happened to Alice?' Tara said.

'I've no idea. I was so wound up, it was all a blur and so dark. I knelt down, feeling around on the road for the torch. I'd dropped it and I heard it hit the tarmac. It took me a while to find it, and when I turned it back on, Alice was gone.'

'She can't have vanished?'

Julia shook her head. 'I know, I know. Maybe it took me longer than I remembered to find the torch on the ground, it's so hard to piece it all together after so long. But I'm telling you, Alice *was* there. She was screaming at me.'

Julia left the window and went behind her desk. She collapsed down on a stool, taking off her high heels and opening the button of her jacket. 'The point is that I saw Alice *after* Freddie had left. She was furious with him and she was very much alive.'

Tara wasn't sure what to make of Julia's confession. She could be making the whole thing up, lying to protect Freddie.

The Phillips family had turned out to be festering with secrets.

In a strange way, Tara found this reassuring; it reminded her that she was not alone. The myth of the happy family was so often just that. A lie. Sometimes on her more cynical days she wondered whether any family truly offered a place of comfort. But that was an occupational hazard, she supposed, because she spent most of her time with people who were victims of damage inflicted in the home, and that included herself.

'Julia, first of all, how did you know about the memory stick?' Tara was trying to work out the timeline; that might help her to figure out whether there could be any truth in what Julia was saying.

'Mia called me from the cottage. She told me she'd caught Alice copying data from my hard drive.'

'And why were you so worried about that data?'

Julia stood up and began walking along the walls of the gallery, looking at all of those red canvases. 'My boys don't know this because I try not to burden them, but finances have always been a struggle. The rental rate at the gallery space keeps doubling. I've lent Freddie a fortune for his stays in a private rehab clinic, and his flat rental, and the course in marketing he never finished. The list goes on and on. I've had to re-mortgage the house on New End and at my age that's frightening.' Julia sighed. 'I don't know why I'm telling you all this.'

'Maybe you want to. For yourself as much as Freddie. Maybe if everything is out in the open, you can fix this. I think Freddie needs that, to heal.'

Julia had stopped in front of the small painting that Tara had been drawn to a few days before. 'You have no idea what I had to do to set myself up to leave David. No one does. I had to claw my way to freedom. I put years of blood, sweat and tears into this gallery and I've had to do things I'm not proud of.'

'What kind of things are we talking about?'

'Things like having two sets of invoices, to make it look like I'd sold paintings at much lower prices, so I didn't have to pay exorbitant tax bills. Fake expense claims. Different email addresses. Freddie helped me with all of it. I was under so much pressure and what Alice did was the last straw. I had this feeling that everything was about to unravel. I had no idea what she might have had access to on my computer. I barely understand how these things work.'

If their confessions were true, could either Julia or Freddie have snapped and gone further than they'd admitted?

Freddie claimed that Alice fell to the ground and was unresponsive for a few moments. She might have been injured in that fall, in a way that somehow contributed to her death. Could she have had a concussion, been confused, and then stumbled into the river?

Or, she may never have got up again after his blow.

Julia had mentioned seeing a trickle of blood, but she wasn't clear about whether or not she'd actually struck Alice with her torch. Julia wasn't really clear about anything that happened that night, other than her guilt at sending Freddie out after Alice.

Hearing Alice say she was going to report Freddie, and knowing that Alice and her ex-husband had been mocking her, would have been a powerful trigger for Julia's rage.

'I feel like I've failed Freddie his whole life.' Julia turned back to Tara. 'But I swear, I saw Alice and she was all right.'

'You said that you saw blood on her face,' Tara said. 'And Freddie said she fell earlier, and was unresponsive. So Alice was not all right. She was injured and distressed.'

'If you go to the police' – Julia was quite calm now – 'I want you to include what I have told you in my report. All of it.'

Tara nodded.

Julia went behind her desk where she reached into a drawer and took out a box cutter. She flipped the blade out, went over to the boxes of champagne that had been delivered earlier and slit one of them open.

'Freddie will come back, he just needs to cool off.' Julia paused, absent-mindedly holding the yellow boxcutter still in her hand. 'He'll come back, for Tom's birthday drinks. He wouldn't miss that for the world. I know he'll be here.'

Feeling nervous at the sight of that blade, Tara walked slowly to the door of the gallery and unlocked it. To her relief, Julia didn't even seem to notice that Tara was leaving. She had dropped to her knees and was cutting open box after box with savage movements.

FORTY-EIGHT

That afternoon, Tara fetched Mia from Julia's house and they drove together to the Hampstead ponds. It was peaceful there, with trees all around encircling them in nature. A kind of magic place of solace in the middle of London. Wildway Close, where Tara had grown up, was not too far away; she knew the area well.

The freshwater swimming pools were almost deserted, with only a handful of swimmers in the distance braving the cold.

Tara and Mia stood at the end of the long wooden platform at the water's edge. Mia's eyes were fixed on the dark surface of the water.

Freddie had not been back to Julia's house and had not been in contact with anyone in his family since he'd left the gallery. Tara knew that at some point she would need to inform the police about what he'd told her, in case Freddie himself chose not to do so. But she wanted to talk to Mia first.

Freddie was not her client and that decision could wait one more day. It was Mia she had to help.

Tara had just finished playing the recordings she had made of Freddie and Julia's confessions earlier that day. She was aware of her heartbeat speeding up as she waited for Mia's reaction.

'I had no idea,' Mia said. 'I really had no idea. I didn't expect all of this to come out.'

'Do you remember that dream you had, about someone holding you under the water?'

Mia nodded.

'I think a part of you knew that someone close to you might be dangerous, even if you didn't want to see it.'

'Maybe.'

Mia was still numb, still absorbing what she had heard. The saddest part for Tara was that when it all sank in, and when Mia understood what Julia had been hiding, it could damage their relationship. Julia was the closest thing to a mother Mia had ever had. Mia needed her, especially now she was about to be a mother herself. Tara hoped there was room for repair.

'If Alice had the memory stick with her when she went out for that walk,' Tara said, 'then Freddie was right, it does seem as though she was intending to give it to someone. Do you have any idea who that might have been?'

Mia shook her head. 'None.'

'The important thing is that Alice was alone when Freddie followed her that night. You weren't there.'

'But I can never unsee what I remembered in Carolyn's office.' Mia began biting her thumbnail.

'Mia, stop. You're hurting yourself.'

Mia didn't seem to hear her. Gently, Tara reached out and pulled her hand away. She kept hold of it a second before letting go. Bringing Mia to the ponds had been a calculated risk. Tara believed that the water would be a trigger for Mia's memories of Alice.

'You're right,' Tara said, 'you can't unsee those images. But there is another way to understand what you saw.'

'What do you mean?' Mia glanced at her.

'I know about your mother,' Tara said. 'I know she's still alive. Why did you lie to me about her?'

'My own mother hates me so much she can't be anywhere near me. I lie because it helps. It makes the pain go away, for a while.'

Tara felt tears pricking in her own yes, but Mia's were dry. And flat again.

'I went to talk to her,' Tara said. 'I know that she was very ill and that she put some damaging ideas into your mind when you were a tiny child.'

Mia moved closer to the edge of the platform. She slid her right foot forward, so that it hung over the water. Her centre of gravity looked dangerously unbalanced with her swollen belly. She was dressed in warm layers, with a beanie hat, coat and boots. If she went into the water wearing all that heavy winter clothing, the weight would drag her under.

Would a lifeguard be able to reach her in time? Tara looked around. She couldn't see any of them, but they must be there, she told herself.

'Please take a step back from the water,' Tara said. 'You're making me nervous.'

Mia looked at her, surprised, as if she'd been somewhere else. She moved a couple of steps back.

Tara felt herself breathing a little easier. 'Mia, I believe you are having trouble distinguishing between reality and imagination. You've had a very complicated emotional reaction to your pregnancy, and you've been depressed. All of that makes you vulnerable to self-punishing thoughts. Thoughts that are so extreme they are almost like a delusion.'

'So Alice was right. I'm losing my mind, like my mother?'

'That is not what I'm saying. I'm trying to explain that you are suffering from a depression that is much more serious than you realise. You've carried severe emotional trauma since childhood and this was probably retriggered when you lost Alice, and again when you found out you were pregnant. None of that is your fault.'

'Tom is right. When I look at those photographs it seems as though I wanted Alice to die. As though I planned it.'

Tara wasn't reaching her. It might be too late to untangle fantasy from reality in Mia's mind. The imagery work that Mia had done with Carolyn Goring, while in the depths of a severe depressive episode, could well have impacted her memory system. Memory and imagination may now be inextricably confused. But she had to try.

'Mia, I know there is a voice in your head that tells you you're evil.'

'What if it's true?'

'It's not true. It's the voice of your mother's illness.'

Mia did not answer.

She had to help Mia push through this. But if anything happened to her, it would be on Tara's shoulders.

'I do not believe that you are evil. Let's think about this logically, okay?'

Mia nodded. A small nod, but at least it was something. She was listening carefully now.

'When Tom walked in on you wearing Alice's locket, you were already in the middle of a depressive episode. And the next morning you had your last session with Carolyn, right? The session with the memory of Alice's death.'

Mia nodded.

'You were highly emotional after the incident with Tom. You had a migraine and you hadn't slept. In that state, when Carolyn put pressure on you to talk about Alice's death, I believe you confused what you imagined you'd done with reality, because you were so hurt by Alice and you felt so much anger and then so much guilt over your life with Tom. That image is not what you remembered, but what you *imagined* you'd done.'

'I wish I could believe you.' Mia wasn't convinced yet. But she was still listening.

'Our brains do not record events accurately, especially when emotions are involved. There's a ton of research to show that memory is not reliable and that memories change constantly over time. A memory is not like a photograph that's fixed and doesn't change. It's not a recording of what happened.'

Mia had turned back to the water. In the distance, smooth heads in swimming caps bobbed along the surface. She placed her left hand lightly on the top of her belly, perhaps without even being aware of it. That small gesture gave Tara courage that she was on the right track.

And she needed courage, because what she had in mind would pressure Mia to go further towards the truth, and that may be as painful as a murder confession, or even more so.

'Do you want to go deeper into that visualisation of killing Alice, so we can test how reliable it really is?'

Mia nodded. Her hands dropped to her sides. It seemed as though she was in an almost hypnotic state by the water.

'Take me through what you remembered again. One more time.'

Tara wasn't happy doing this with Mia standing so close to the edge of the pond. The wind was coming off the water and the slate clouds overhead made everything feel ominous.

This wasn't the first time she had looked so deep into that darkness with a disturbed patient. Her work with Jade Jameson had been right on the borderline, or perhaps over it, of safe practice.

Mia had closed her eyes, waiting for Tara to guide her.

Tara hesitated. She had to question whether the craving for answers was so unfulfilled in her own life that she pushed too far to find them in the lives of others.

If they didn't at least try to get an answer though, then Mia's child would not have a mother. Either physically or mentally, Mia would be absent.

'Picture the moment you felt most enraged with Alice,' Tara said.

Mia's answer came easily.

'I see Alice and Tom in the living room of the cottage. I can hear what she says about me. I can hear her lies.'

Mia closed her eyes again, concentrating.

'Follow the energy in your body. What does it feel like?'

'Like a fire, in my belly.' Mia began unzipping her coat, pulling off the sleeves and then dropping it to the ground. 'It's burning, through my shoulders and my hands. I feel like I'm going to explode.'

Mia half stumbled and Tara grabbed her arm, steadying her.

That water was so close.

'What does the rage want to do to Alice?' Tara asked.

Mia's hands were rigid, in claws. She raised her arms, picturing herself until she was throttling Alice, her own face turning red with feeling and effort.

Tara took a breath. She too had to be open to these feelings and images, or Mia would not trust her. It was only visualisation. Imagination, not reality.

Suddenly, the tension dropped and Mia's arms fell to her sides. She took several steps back and looked down, as though seeing Alice's body lying on the wooden slats.

'She's gone.' Mia knelt down beside her friend's body and reached out as if to stroke Alice's hair. 'I'm so sorry.'

In the distance, there was the sound of thunder. Raindrops caused ripples across the surface of the pond.

Mia's tears poured down onto the wood below. 'I'm so, so sorry. I didn't protect you.'

Tara waited until Mia's sobs had passed, then she asked a question. 'In your image, can you look into Alice's eyes?'

Mia shook her head. 'They're closed.'

'Imagine that Alice's eyes are open. Look into them. What colour are they?'

Mia seemed calmer now. The pent-up anxiety had flowed out of her body and her breathing was regular. 'Brown,' she said.

'Brown eyes. Dark eyes. Like yours?'

'Yes.' Mia looked up, confused.

'I saw her photograph. Alice's eyes are light.'

'Green,' Mia said. 'She had the most beautiful green eyes.'

'So whose eyes are there on the ground in front of you?'

A sharp intake of breath. Mia looked down again, holding her stomach, as if she was in pain.

'It's not Alice, is it?'

Mia shook her head.

'I think you see your mother.'

Mia was bracing herself, on her knees now; she shuffled backwards, as if away from a snake. Her eyes were wide open. 'It was Alice at first. But when you asked me to look into her eyes, they changed colour.'

She folded forwards, as if in pain. Tara picked up the coat Mia had discarded and placed it around her shoulders. After a while, her breathing became less jagged and more even again.

'There isn't a single photograph left of me as a little girl. She destroyed them. She destroyed everything.' Mia was looking at Tara now, the tears running down her cheeks mixing with rain and her hair soaking wet. 'My memory of being a child is gone. Completely gone. All I have left are these flashes – nightmares, where I can't breathe. And the headaches. That's all that's left.'

Mia huddled under her coat as Tara sat next to her.

'She told me that the devil was inside me,' Mia said. 'In the end, I believed her. I remember loving her so much. I didn't understand what I'd done. I was always trying to be better, but it never worked. I could never make her love me.'

'I'm so sorry.'

When Mia looked up, her eyes were swollen and her face was blotchy. 'Can you promise me that I didn't hurt Alice?'

'I can't promise, but I can give you my strong opinion. I don't believe you had anything to do with Alice's death.'

As they sat there on the damp wooden platform, Tara was struck by the similarity between Mia's situation and her own. How strange she hadn't seen it clearly before. Tara knew what it was like to feel guilt after the death of someone close. On a bad day, she would do almost anything to escape the pain of not knowing and the frustration of not being able to remember.

Both she and Mia might live their lives not knowing. They could spend a lifetime atoning for crimes they did not commit.

'We may never know the absolute truth about what happened to Alice,' Tara said, 'but I can tell you that you're not evil. If you were, you wouldn't feel this sense of guilt or this need to suffer.'

She stood up and reached down to help Mia to her feet.

'When I write up my report, I want to include everything from all my interviews. Then I would like to give one copy of that report to you, and another to the detective involved in Alice's case. I'm asking for your permission to tell her everything we know. That way, you don't carry the weight of it on your shoulders alone.'

Mia looked unsure, but only for a moment. Then she nodded. 'Okay.'

Once again, Mia rested her hand on her belly. This time she looked down, realising what she had done. She left her hand there a few moments more.

FORTY-NINE

When Tara delivered Mia back to the house on New End, Julia looked like a different person when she opened her front door. Her face was scrubbed clean of make-up and her hair was unkempt. She looked desperate.

Freddie was still not home, and Tara could see that Julia needed Mia's company as much as Mia needed hers. Julia was afraid that Freddie had gone on a binge of drugs and alcohol, and she had been contacting various hospital emergency rooms in fear that he might have come to harm on his bike.

From what Tara could see, it seemed that Mia had taken her mother-in-law's story at face value and had already forgiven Julia for the part she claimed to have played the night of Alice's death.

Whether or not it was deserved, Tara suspected that Mia shouldered some of the responsibility for Julia's actions, since she herself had alerted Julia to the fact that Alice had copied the contents of the hard drive at the gallery.

The human brain was pragmatic, after all, and programmed for survival; Julia was all Mia had left. Perhaps more anger would come later, maybe when Mia had fully forgiven herself.

Much later that afternoon, Tara was at her desk, putting the finishing touches on her report. Her notebook lay open next to her laptop, the pages filled with her purple-inked scrawl.

She worked through her detailed notes, documenting everything carefully, including the fact that Mia Phillips had had a memory of following Alice out of the cottage that night, and strangling Alice with the strap of her camera.

The opinion section was the most challenging to write without solid evidence.

> *My clinical opinion is that Mia's memory of causing Alice's death is likely to be a false memory that was created in a therapy session, in the context of a severe depression with psychotic features.*
>
> *This memory is most likely related to longstanding emotional difficulties. Mia is emotionally vulnerable after severe childhood trauma, due to her mother's mental illness and abandonment. She carries unprocessed and complex grief over Alice Kelly's death and these feelings were retriggered by her pregnancy.*
>
> *I would also like to stress that memory is not an accurate record of reality. Instead, memory is full of errors and omissions. Memories are not fixed, either. They change and mutate over time. Memory can be so unreliable and so open to manipulation that it is entirely possible to remember events that never happened. Memory is not truth.*
>
> *Mia's recollection of how Alice Kelly died is highly unlikely to be a true reflection of what happened.*

Tara felt some regret as she wrote those lines. She had not succeeded in delivering what Mia had asked of her: the whole truth.

Tara ended with an urgent recommendation that Mia go back into therapy. She made three possible suggestions, all of them excellent clinicians who could be trusted to have Mia's best interests at heart.

She closed her laptop. She was finished, but she would wait to send the report through to DS Ayola because she wanted Mia to have a chance to read it first. It would be a relief to share everything she had learned about Alice's last hours with the police officer, so she could help shoulder the burden of the secrets and lies that had been uncovered.

Tara stood up and as was her usual habit, she went to look out of the window to decompress, stretching her arms above her head and then behind her back. Coltrane Mews was quiet at the end of the working day.

This case had become about more than helping Mia find the truth about her recovered memory. The more she found out, the more questions were raised.

Mia's fearful dream about a man attacking her that night at the hospital.

The fact that Tom had never spoken openly to anyone in his family about having been at the cottage the night Alice died, and the fact that his alibi for that night was only solid if Mia's memory of the timeline was reliable.

Freddie's admission that he had threatened and assaulted Alice.

Carolyn's suspiciously brief case notes and her intense interest in the night Alice died.

David Phillips' claim that Carolyn was fixated on him.

All of these disparate pieces must fit together, and it frustrated Tara that she could not see the whole. There were so many unexplained loose ends.

She felt a sliver of concern that Freddie might come looking for her again. If he did, he may not be sober or rational. Would he regret what he had told her about assaulting Alice?

She would feel better once he was found. Although that could raise other problems. Tara did not think it was safe for him to be in the same house as Mia, and she had made that crystal clear to both Mia and Julia.

As she stretched her neck, Tara's mind wandered to what had happened on those exercise mats in the darkened gym, to the weight of Louis' body on top of her. She closed her eyes a moment. It was a good feeling.

She had no idea if it would happen again. It had been an impulsive moment between two lonely people who barely knew each other. She really hoped it would not be too awkward between them now, because those gym classes were her life saver. She could not imagine how she'd survive without them.

She checked her watch. There were a few minutes to go before her meeting with Ray.

At five thirty precisely, Tara saw a familiar figure approaching the gates of the garden square opposite her clinic: a solidly built man with prematurely silver hair and craggy features.

FIFTY

Tara and Ray sat next to each other on a bench in the square. Ziggy was beside them, keeping a close eye on the squirrels.

Tara was feeling the cold, even huddled inside her long puffy coat, but she was glad to be out in the open air for this conversation. A part of her didn't want the complications in her own personal life to enter her workplace, where she was the professional, and in control.

She had put through the money transfer as usual, exactly as Daniel had been doing all these years, and now she hoped that Ray might have more information for her about where exactly it was landing up.

Ray was once again the Ray Jameson she remembered, not the man in the cosy sweater she'd met in his kitchen. His tailored coat fitted precisely over his pin-striped suit and his shoes were impeccably polished. His Rolex glinted in the winter sun.

'So,' he said, 'our Maria collected the money as usual, at ten thirty sharp on the day it dropped into her account. Afterwards, she drove to another, smaller town, about ten minutes south.

When she got there, she handed it over to a man at a café on the main piazza.'

A man. Tara's heart nearly stopped beating. 'Do you have a photograph?'

Ray took out his phone and showed her the screen. The picture looked like it had been taken from a distance, and then enlarged, so it was grainy. The man had a full beard and was wearing a cap pulled down low over his forehead. He was thin, maybe somewhere around middle age. His face was in shadow.

'I can't be sure if that's Matthew,' she said.

Tara felt a knife-twist of grief. There were shards of that lodged all over her body, and sometimes, if she moved the wrong way, one of them would pierce her heart, or her lungs. She could no longer be sure if she would recognise her own brother.

Ray tucked the phone back into his pocket. 'I'll send it to you. Maybe if you look at it a little longer, you'll know.'

'Do you have his name and address?'

Ray handed her a piece of paper with all the details. The man's name was unfamiliar, but that didn't mean much.

'He goes to that café most mornings. Same time.'

The chill from the damp wooden bench was seeping through Tara's trousers. Her coat was still damp from the session with Mia out at the ponds.

'I've booked my flight,' she said. 'It's in two days' time.'

She would leave from Stansted Airport at a ridiculously early hour. Her suitcase was already packed.

Ray had his sturdy hands clasped tightly in his lap. His fingers were an angry red with cold. 'Doctor Black, please don't go alone.'

'I need to do this.'

Mia's case had brought home to her, yet again, the impact of not knowing. Tara could not give up a chance to fill in the gaps she had lived with for most of her life – not only about what her brother had done, but what part she herself might have played. Matthew must know something.

'I could go in your place.' Ray leant over, patting Ziggy's head, avoiding looking at her. 'I can get you the answers you need.'

Tara's stomach flipped over. His offer was deeply kind. She already knew that Ray would do anything to protect his family; now he was extending this protective circle around her.

'I'm grateful for the offer. But no. I need to go myself.'

Impulsively, she reached for his hand, squeezing tight so she could feel his ring pushing into her skin.

Ziggy looked on with interest, pricking up his ears.

Tara pulled away. When she stood up to leave, she did not look back. For some reason, when she was with Ray, when he was kind to her, she felt more acutely how alone she was in the world.

She passed the ancient gravestones in the far corner, many of the inscriptions too faded to read, and headed straight for the gate before crossing the small street to her clinic. She slid her key into the door, pushed it open and entered the welcome warmth of the building, shutting the door behind her. As she slipped off her shoes, her toes were numb from cold and her eyes were still damp.

FIFTY-ONE

That night, sitting in the dark on Wildway Close, Tara let her imagination take her through the house, as though she was lying on a therapy couch. Free association. She allowed in anything that came to mind, not searching for memory but letting the images appear.

She found herself wandering through the house. Through the front door, up the stairs and into her parents' bedroom. Her mother was awake, sitting at her dressing table. She was taking off her make up with face oil and cotton wool balls. Tara watched for a while before she spoke.

'Why won't you help us?' she said.

Her mother did not turn around. She was looking at herself in the mirror, her face gaunt and her eyes vacant.

'Did you hear me?'

She didn't answer.

'Can't you hear them downstairs? Dad and Matthew are going at each other again.'

You are a pathetic piece of shit. I want nothing to do with you. Get out of my house.

Her mother dabbed a cotton wool pad over one eye. She

threw the blackened cotton ball into the bin and picked up another.

'Why won't you do something?' Tara asked her.

'You know your father. He won't listen.' She stood up, walked over to her side of the bed and drew back the covers.

'You have to try to stop him. Please.' Tara was so angry. So helpless. 'Mum, I'm talking to you.'

She was lying on her back with her eyes closed. 'It's late. I'm very tired.'

Tara was next to the bed, looking down. She saw herself placing her hands around her mother's white, bony throat. Then she felt herself recoil. She stepped back. She never could bear to touch her mother. Not even in anger.

When she looked down again, her mother was cold and still. Tara was holding a pillow in her hands. This time, in her image, there was no blood. Nothing. Nothing on the pillowcase, no blood spatter up the wall. Only a clean, white pillow.

Tara dropped it. It fell to the floor next to her mother's side of the bed.

Tara blinked, snapping out of her reverie. That was so strange.

She had walked into that bedroom on the morning she'd discovered her parents' bodies. She'd seen the blood-soaked bed and the stains on the wall. Or she thought she had. But she'd been in shock, and there had been so much blood in the living room, perhaps the two images had become confused in her mind?

She had never wanted to read the autopsy report.

Was her mind trying to erase the evidence of violence she'd seen that morning? Or had it been playing tricks on her all along? Tormenting her.

As Tara walked home, slowly, enjoying the cold, her mind clear, it wasn't guilt that she felt. Or the usual anger. She simply felt compassion, for everyone in her family.

FIFTY-TWO

With the sense of something unfinished, Tara had not hesitated to accept Mia's invitation to the cocktail party Julia was throwing for Tom's birthday. Mia had wanted her there for support and from Tara's perspective, it was a chance to see the whole family together. Plus, her flight out was first thing the next morning, and she welcomed a distraction from her nerves and excitement, which were difficult to disentangle.

Julia had apparently gone to a significant amount of both effort and expense to organise the cocktail party, and although she was in a fragile state with Freddie still missing, she had insisted that it go ahead as planned.

The event was due to start at six o'clock at the Leonard Gallery. The dress code was formal, which meant Tara only had one option: her black velvet dress. It still fitted her well, but it felt wrong, as though she was playing dress up. She looked at herself in the mirror and considered letting her hair down to look a little less... repressed, but then decided that since it was an event with a client, she'd leave it tied back.

Tara arrived exactly on time and walked in alone.

The atmosphere in the gallery was hushed. Around ten

people were milling around the small space, in tight groups, talking in low voices. A table had been set out along the back with several bottles of wine and champagne, so it seemed as though quite a few more people were expected.

Mia and Tom were standing in front of a wall of red paintings, deep in conversation with Julia and a couple Tara didn't recognise. Mia looked well, with good colour in her face. She wore a stunning, red tartan-print dress and chunky boots. Tara noted how Tom's hand rested protectively on his wife's back. Julia was back to her polished self again too, in a white suit with silver stiletto heels.

In time, Tom would find out what his mother and brother had done that night out at the cottage, but from his relaxed body language, Tara guessed that he hadn't yet been told. As she watched the three of them a while longer, Tara could see that their smiles were a little muted; Freddie's absence must be playing on their minds. Julia in particular kept glancing at the door, probably hoping to see her younger son walk through it.

For Mia, Tara suspected, the party was a form of closure, a symbolic acceptance that she deserved to be part of Tom's family.

Something about how quickly things had been smoothed over in this family troubled Tara. She hoped she was over-thinking things. Given all the facts she had so far, her diagnosis of Mia's depression with psychotic features was the most likely explanation. It did seem that her intervention with Mia at the ponds, processing some of her complex mixed feelings towards her mother, had been effective in lifting her mood.

It was hard to shake that lingering doubt, though. Tara could not be absolutely sure that Mia's memory in Carolyn's office did not contain at least some kernel of truth.

More and more people were trickling in through the gallery door. David Phillips was on the other side of the room now, looking down at his phone with a steely expression. He did not look at all comfortable to be in Julia's gallery.

A waitress came past with a tray of fizzing champagne flutes, which Tara regretfully declined. Officially, she was still working. She was starting to feel conspicuous, standing alone, and it was strange to be at a social event in a fitted velvet dress with her client and several other people she'd interviewed while working on the case. She missed her anonymous suit.

Tara crossed the room to join David Phillips, who looked equally out of place. He also happened to be in front of the small red painting that Tara had grown fond of.

He looked pleased to see her, shaking her hand warmly. 'I'm glad you're here, Doctor Black. I wanted to thank you for everything you've done for Mia. She seems far more settled. For now, anyway. I suppose we'll all have to keep an eye on things, to see how she's coping with the baby. I know Tom will be a hands-on dad, so she'll have a lot of support.'

Given his breezy manner, Tara guessed that he had no idea what Julia and Freddie had confessed to that afternoon. It would seem he either didn't know or wasn't concerned that no one could get hold of Freddie.

'David, something you said has been on my mind. Do you mind if I ask if there was a specific reason why you were worried about Mia being in treatment with Carolyn?'

'I've been hesitant to talk about this.' David was looking down into his champagne glass. 'But then I raised it with you, didn't I?'

Tara nodded. There was classical music playing in the background, and a muted chatter which gave them a sense of privacy even as the room grew more crowded.

'Carolyn has a problem with jealousy,' David said. 'A serious problem. I'd go so far as to say she is pathologically jealous. That's why I ended things.'

'Pathologically jealous?'

He nodded, downing most of the drink in his hand. 'Carolyn couldn't bear for me to have even the most basic interaction with any female that crossed my path – shop assistants, waitresses, nurses, my ex-wife, even my secretary. If a woman so much as walked past me on the street and I happened to look in her direction, Carolyn would accuse me of having an affair. In the beginning, frankly, it was quite flattering, especially at my age. I found it charming. I assumed that as time went on, Carolyn would feel more secure and that would all settle down, but it was quite the opposite. And everything became more intense when Alice came on the scene.'

David paused as he scanned the room, his eyes resting on Tom and Mia. Julia had moved away from the couple and was mingling with other guests.

'Tom was always serious about Alice,' David said, 'right from the beginning. He introduced her to me very early on. Somehow that triggered something for Carolyn. She was so envious of Alice, of her youth, of her beauty, and especially of any attention I paid her. That's when it became unbearable. When I think back, I believe Carolyn was almost... stalking me. She would turn up at my apartment and let herself in at odd hours. I'd find her going through my credit card statements...'

David paused as the waitress came past with a fresh tray of champagne glasses. He smiled at the young woman as he swapped his empty glass for a full one. Tara declined.

'Anyway,' David continued after the waitress had moved away, 'I finally came to my senses after a rather nasty incident. Carolyn and I had been arguing over something trivial, I don't even remember what it was now. I suppose Carolyn accused me of something or other, and we were in the kitchen, and she grabbed a hot frying pan off the cooker and took a swing at me.'

David cleared his throat, then laughed, as if he was embarrassed. 'Sounds ridiculous, doesn't it?'

'No, not at all. It sounds serious.'

David nodded, still looking across the room. His hand holding the champagne glass shook a little. 'I ended up with a burn on my hand where I tried to protect myself and a very bruised cheekbone. I remember sitting in A and E, waiting to be seen, and sending Carolyn a text saying it was over. I can't express the relief I felt. And I thought that was the end of it. Until this business with Mia becoming her patient.'

It was hard to imagine Carolyn, the self-assured and experienced therapist who ran a successful Harley Street therapy practice, as the woman David had described. Which wasn't to say it wasn't possible. Private and public personas could be very different.

Tara was still concerned that Carolyn's behaviour in that last session had somehow caused harm to Mia, and intensified Mia's turmoil, but there was no way to prove it.

'Did you report the incident?' Tara asked.

'No, the thought didn't cross my mind. Frankly, I felt humiliated. I'd kept the whole messy part between Carolyn and myself private and no one in the family has a clue about any of it. Tom always liked Carolyn – as most people do. I'm sure this side of her only comes out in private.'

Mia and Tom had spotted the two of them and were approaching across the room, making slow progress as they stopped to speak to various guests.

David lowered his voice, keeping his eyes on his son and daughter-in-law. 'I suspect that Carolyn is still a very bitter woman, even after all these years. It wouldn't surprise me if she put ideas in Mia's head, to get back at me.'

'What sort of ideas?'

'It's just a feeling I have.'

Something about the way he had said that raised the hackles on Tara's neck. Could there be some truth in Carolyn's suspicions about David's behaviour with other women?

Things were not necessarily black and white. Carolyn's problems and David's indiscretions could co-exist.

'I assume you have access to Carolyn's case notes about their sessions?' David said.

Tara nodded.

'I won't ask you if there's anything about me in there. But if there was, I hope you take it in context of what I've just shared with you.'

'Of course.'

Now alarm bells were ringing. She had to wonder if the reason David had been so keen to tell her about his personal problems with Carolyn was because he was anxious about something being exposed. Maybe he wanted to control the narrative by giving her his version of events first.

Tara's thoughts were interrupted as Mia and Tom had finally reached the place where she and David were standing.

'Doctor Black!' Mia seemed genuinely happy to see her. 'I'm so glad you're here.'

Tom was smiling too. 'Good to see you.'

It was the first time Tara had seen his face when it wasn't locked down with tension.

The couple stood close together and were holding hands and the main feeling was one of hope.

As a stream of guests came over to congratulate Tom and chat to the couple, Tara moved away, melting into the background. She checked her watch: she had been there almost forty-five minutes. She needed to have a reasonably early night because she would be leaving for the airport at three thirty the next morning. The thought of that trip was constantly with her, a quiet buzz in her belly.

Tom's voice rang out from across the room. 'Thank you everyone for joining us here tonight. I'll keep this brief. Thank you to all my amazing colleagues at Wembley Park Secondary who have come out in the cold to help me celebrate. And please, let's raise a toast to my amazing family. I am so lucky to have all of you in my life.'

A murmur rustled through the room. Julia and Mia were standing close together and Mia put her arm around her mother-in-law's waist. Julia was looking anxious; Tara guessed her mind was preoccupied with Freddie.

Tom raised his glass again, looking at Mia. 'And to many sleepless nights ahead!'

With Mia looking well, and the baby coming soon, it seemed that – for now at least – Tom was trying hard to put his concerns about Mia aside. Unless this was an act, in public.

'Now please everyone tuck into the mini salmon frittatas and goats cheese whirls, which are about to make an appearance.'

With the end of Tom's brief speech, the formalities seemed to be over. Despite Julia's conviction that Freddie would not miss his brother's celebrations, he still had not made an appearance.

As Tara scanned the room, thinking that she might give it another fifteen minutes before leaving, her eyes were drawn to the front window. Most of the cafés and shops were closed and there weren't many people around outdoors on such a cold winter's evening, but the alley was well lit.

Tara noticed a woman standing across from the gallery. She was alone, her shoulders hunched and her hands in the pockets of a baggy coat, with a large umbrella hooked over her arm. She looked ill at ease as she stared in at the party guests.

It took Tara a few moments to realise that she was looking at Carolyn Goring. The sight of her staring in at the gallery like that was disconcerting. Especially in view of what David had just told her.

And then to Tara's surprise, Carolyn Goring walked

through the gallery door. She hesitated as she stepped inside and looked around. Tara saw Carolyn's eyes settle on David Phillips, who had his arm around his son's shoulders as they laughed and chatted to a group of people around Tom's age. After a few moments, Carolyn tried unsuccessfully to smooth down her unruly hair and then propped her huge umbrella against the wall. She then went over to the drinks table and picked up a glass of champagne and took a deep drink.

Tara went over to stand beside her.

'Carolyn – hi.'

Carolyn didn't turn her head to look at her as she mumbled a hello.

'I'm surprised to see you here.'

'Tom called me, to let me know that Mia was out of hospital. He wanted me to know how grateful he is that I fitted her in and offered her reduced fees, given their circumstances, and that Mia was sorry for the abrupt way she walked out. He and Mia wanted me to come past tonight. Some sort of closure, I suppose.'

Or perhaps Carolyn simply couldn't resist the chance to be in the same room as David Phillips?

'I've finished my interviews with Mia,' Tara said, 'but there are still a few things that bother me.'

Carolyn stared stonily ahead. 'This is hardly the place to have a conversation about a patient.'

'Of course.' But that was exactly why Tara wanted to take this opportunity. She hadn't managed to crack Carolyn's veneer when they were alone together in a private office, but here, Carolyn was more vulnerable, surrounded by reminders of a painful time in her past.

If David's description was accurate, and Carolyn could lose control and be driven to violence, then she should not be working as a therapist with vulnerable people. That was partly why Tara was so concerned to get to the bottom of this. There were implications that went far beyond Mia's case.

'I was just chatting to David Phillips,' Tara said. 'The two of you have very different versions of why your relationship ended.'

'Is that so.' Carolyn bit down on her bottom lip.

Tara glanced across the room. David was still deep in conversation with three or four people she didn't recognise. She couldn't see where Tom and Mia had got to.

'According to David, you have a serious problem with jealousy.' Tara's voice was almost a whisper.

Carolyn turned to look at her for the first time, her eyes flashing. She remained stubbornly silent.

'Was taking on Mia as a patient a way for you to try to reconnect with David? Or were you trying to get back at him in some way, for leaving you?'

'My relationship with David Phillips was long over when I began treating Mia.' Carolyn was hissing at her. 'I have done nothing that is in any way unethical. If anyone has acted inappropriately, it's you. You are the one discussing sensitive client issues in a public place.'

When Tara looked up, David was staring at the two of them from across the room.

'Carolyn, do you have a problem with jealousy? Is that why you kept asking Mia about Alice Kelly? Because she was young and beautiful, and loved? Were you afraid that David was attracted to her?'

'The only problem I have is with David's lies.' Carolyn had raised her voice and a group of people next to them turned briefly to stare, then averted their eyes.

Her reaction confirmed what Tara already suspected: David Phillips was Carolyn's Achilles heel.

FIFTY-THREE

ONE WEEK BEFORE ALICE'S DEATH

Carolyn's last patient for the day has cancelled at short notice and so she's finished work early. She calls David a couple of times, thinking they might grab an early dinner together, but he isn't answering his phone. That happens a lot lately; he's been ignoring her calls.

She decides to take a chance and head over to his place in Paddington. When she arrives, she's pleasantly surprised to find his car is parked in one of the residents' bays outside the building. He's home early too. He'd been in surgery all night the evening before, so he'd probably come home, switched off his phone and passed out.

Carolyn takes the lift up to the seventh floor and lets herself in to the apartment. The first thing she notices is the large gift bag on the console table next to the door. A green, glossy bag from Harrods, the handles tied with a gold ribbon. She's never known David to go anywhere near that place.

'David? It's me.'

The package on the hallway table draws her in. She is tempted to look inside, like a child, hoping it might be for her. She pulls at the bow and it comes undone. Inside, there's a box wrapped in tissue paper and tucked down the side of that, a receipt. She reaches in and carefully lifts the piece of paper out. There are six items listed. An eye-wateringly expensive scarf, and then various lingerie pieces. Pieces she herself would never wear.

It's then she picks up the scent of a woman's perfume. Or she thinks she does; she's a little light-headed. Dread grows inside of her as she walks down the passageway. The door of the bedroom is ajar. Something makes her stop and look through the crack before calling out again. David is sitting on the bed. He has taken off his jacket and tie and the top button of his shirt is open. He's holding a glass of red wine.

That smell of perfume is stronger in there. Musky, over-bearing.

And the girl. Long blonde hair and a flash of red lace under-wear. Carolyn steps back, clamps a hand over her mouth.

Girl is the right word. She's so, so young.

She feels a rush of dizziness. She isn't sure she can trust her own eyes.

FIFTY-FOUR

Tara was left standing at the drinks table, as Carolyn moved off to the other side of the gallery to greet Julia.

Mia had appeared back at her side though, her eyes brighter than Tara had seen them before. 'There's something I need to show you.'

She was smiling, brimming with excitement, as she took Tara through a door, then down a short passageway to the office at the back of the gallery. The place was sparsely furnished, more of a storage space, with a desk and chair and not much else.

Tara realised she was standing in the office where Mia had walked in on Alice stealing Julia's data.

Tom was already in there, leaning against the desk, still in his relaxed mode, with the top button of his white shirt open.

Mia was pointing at the large, framed photograph that had been hung on the wall facing the door.

Alice. She was standing in a pool of sunshine, faced away from the camera, but she was looking back over her shoulder, laughing. She had a colourful scarf with a print of a tiger draped over her back and shoulders. With her sweep of black eyeliner and the diamond stud in her nose catching the light, there was a passion captured in the picture that was breathtaking.

'When I got back from the ponds yesterday,' Mia said, 'I had another look through those photographs on my camera, and I found this one, and others too, from the same set I took at the cottage. They're so different from the ones you saw at the hospital.'

'I had this one printed and framed,' Tom said, 'because we want to give it to Alice's mother. But we both wanted you to see it first.'

'It is an extraordinary photograph.' Tara could see why Julia believed that Mia had a special talent.

'It's so strange,' Mia said. 'I barely remember that afternoon. But when I looked through the memory card again I found so many like these. The ones that show how much I loved her.'

Tara hoped this gift to Alice's family would be Mia's final goodbye. She hoped that Mia could be freed from her burden of guilt.

'Knock knock.' David Phillips was in the doorway. 'Tom, Paul Walker has to leave, he's looking for you to say—'

David's eyes flitted past them, to the pictures of Alice on the wall. He stopped mid-sentence, looking as though he had seen a ghost.

FIFTY-FIVE

When the others had left the office, Tara stayed behind to have a closer look at the portrait of Alice. She had seen something on David's face. A look of fear.

The photograph of Alice was in colour and the pattern on the scarf was clearly visible and distinctive. The fabric was brightly coloured in pink, red and yellow, and in the centre there were two tigers. One was lying down, a female perhaps, and a larger tiger was standing over her. They were looking at each other, their mouths almost touching.

A picture was beginning to form in Tara's mind.

She turned to look at the blank screen of Julia's desktop computer. Were the contents of Julia's hard drive really something that Alice herself or her boss James Sharp would find so useful? In her research, Tara had found out that the Sharp Gallery was far larger and more successful than Julia's anyway.

It had always been a possibility that Alice went out on that walk to meet someone, but it seemed unlikely that Alice had gone out in the middle of the night in rural Oxfordshire to meet her new boss.

So maybe the theft of Julia's data had been more personal.

The more she thought about it, the more Tara saw David Phillips at the centre of everything. There was a deep and enduring animosity between David and Julia. If David was still seething from losing the house and other assets in the divorce, then the contents of Julia's hard drive might have been very useful to him. Julia herself had feared there was evidence of tax evasion and that would have given David tremendous power over his ex-wife. If only psychologically, to torment her.

David owned that cottage in Oxfordshire; he knew the area well.

Could Alice have stolen that data for David? Was it Tom's father she had planned to meet that night?

Tara walked back into the gallery in time to see Julia heading out of the front door. She scanned the room but could not see David or Carolyn anywhere. Mia and Tom were deep in conversation with a group of people she didn't recognise, their arms around each other's waists.

She reminded herself that her work on this case was over. Her report was complete and she had a flight to catch in a matter of hours. Mia was stable. The sensible thing to do was to stay out of this, or at most, make another phone call to DS Ayola.

Tara slipped out of the gallery, shrugging on her coat as she walked along the damp, chill alley along the uneven paving stones. She was glad she'd decided on the flat pumps instead of the one pair of heels she owned. She turned sharp left into another narrow lane leading off Flask Walk, which was a cut through to Heath Street where she could find a cab.

As she entered the alleyway, she picked up the scent of cigarette smoke mingled with a floral perfume. A few steps further on she saw Julia, leaning against the wall of the dimly lit space, inhaling from her cigarette. And next to her was Carolyn Goring.

The sight of the two women standing close together crystallised something else for Tara.

If David had been the one going out in the middle of the night to meet Alice, that would have triggered a furious response from both Julia and Carolyn, albeit for very different reasons.

They both turned to look at Tara as she approached them.

'Were you two talking about David, by any chance? He's hurt you both, in vicious ways.'

'I should get back to the gallery,' Julia said. 'They'll be cutting the cake soon.'

Tara did not budge. The alley was narrow and she was blocking Julia's exit. 'Julia, I know you blame David for a lot of Freddie's problems. And Carolyn, David is still attacking your reputation. He told me that you are pathologically jealous. He used those exact words.'

'I told you, David lies about a lot of things.' Carolyn spoke through gritted teeth as she and Julia exchanged a glance.

'Not only that,' Tara said, 'but David told me that you can't control your temper. He said you assaulted him. You're lucky that he was too embarrassed to go to the police.'

'Embarrassed? Oh my God.' Carolyn looked at Julia, as if for support. 'I would never—'

Julia said nothing. She was leaning back against the wall, inhaling deeply on her cigarette and looking straight ahead of her. But she was listening closely.

Tara took a step closer to the two women. 'David told me that he landed up in A and E because of you, Carolyn. He claims he had a serious burn on his hand and an injury to his cheekbone. Is that true? Because if it is, you should not be seeing vulnerable patients.'

Carolyn took a step forwards. 'Did David also tell you that at the time I assaulted him he had his hands around my throat?'

Tara was shocked into silence.

'I was trying to get him off me,' Carolyn said. 'I thought he was going to kill me.'

Julia was calmly inhaling; she was not surprised by what she had heard. She took out another cigarette, handed it to Carolyn and lit it for her.

After a while, Carolyn began speaking again. 'I'd been fooling myself, seeing what I wanted to see. A man who was mature, intelligent, kind and funny. A man who could share love. Then slowly, I began to see the real David: a sleazy, vicious monster. When I walked in on him with an escort, a girl barely out of her teens, we had a huge blow up. That was the day he put his hands around my throat. But you see, I had no bruises. He was the one with proof of injuries. There was no point taking it any further. I could have lost my practice.'

Tara turned to Julia. 'He did that to you too, didn't he?'

Julia nodded. She ground out her cigarette under her heel and reached into her coat for the rest of the pack.

'Freddie saw it. When he was a little boy. He always tried to protect me, to get in between us.' Julia's hand was shaking too much to get another cigarette out of the box. She gave up, shoving it back into her pocket.

Suddenly, Freddie's voice came back to Tara, loud and clear. *I make myself useful by keeping the garden looking pretty and driving Julia around at night, because she's blind as a bat in the dark.*

'Julia, you could not have driven out to the cottage on your own the night Alice died. Freddie told me you're night blind.'

Carolyn and Julia glanced at each other again, but this time they remained stubbornly silent.

'Who was driving the car?' Tara was right on the verge of uncovering the truth, she could feel it. 'Both Freddie and Mia have paid a high price for whatever went on that night. They deserve some relief. They need to know what really happened.'

Julia sighed. This time, she managed to get a cigarette out of the box and light it. 'I was out of my mind that night, I was petrified of what Freddie would do. I tried get hold of David. As much as I hate him, I have to ask for his help with Freddie sometimes. But David wasn't answering and his phone was turned off. In desperation, I called Carolyn to try to get hold of him.'

'And then you drove out to the cottage together. You were both there.'

Julia nodded. 'I begged Carolyn to help me. She drove and then she waited in the car, and I got out to confront Alice, just like I told you. When things got heated, Carolyn turned off the headlights, I guess to try to stop me doing any more damage. When she turned them on again, Alice was gone. That's all we know.'

'And you kept quiet because you didn't want to risk bringing attention to yourselves, or to Freddie.'

'The police were investigating,' Carolyn said. 'None of us were ever under suspicion.'

'Not all police investigations are as thorough as they should be. Clearly.' Tara took a step backwards.

Both women were looking at her now. She had their full attention.

'Carolyn, you were David's alibi, weren't you? You and David both claimed you'd been together all night. I can't figure out why you would want to protect him. Unless - you kept quiet because you lost control?'

Carolyn spoke up, calmly. 'Look, enough is enough. This is ridiculous. Neither of us were involved in Alice's death and neither of us arc obliged to answer any of your questions.'

Tara was losing them, losing momentum. Carolyn had found her equilibrium again so fast.

She didn't budge. 'Did you do more than swing at her with that torch, Julia? Are you really going to let Freddie take the blame for what you did?'

'No!' Julia looked horrified. 'But David would have destroyed Freddie if I'd opened my mouth. I'd left him a voice-mail, saying that Freddie had gone out to the cottage and that I was afraid he'd do something dangerous. And if Carolyn had spoken up, David would have said she's pathologically jealous and can't be trusted. He had evidence that she was violent. There was no point.'

'David has been violent to both of you. You must have suspected that he had something to do with Alice's death?'

Julia stumbled, struggling in her heels, her ankle twisting on an uneven paving stone. 'Dammit.'

'I need you to look at this.' Quickly, Tara took out her phone and opened the photograph she'd snapped of Alice's portrait before she'd left Julia's office.

Julia looked at it but there was no reaction. Carolyn was standing sideways on, refusing to look at the screen.

'What is this about?' Julia said.

'Look at it!' Tara held the phone up right in front of Carolyn's face.

Reluctantly, Carolyn focused on the image. The sight of the photograph unnerved her, just as the sight of it had unnerved David earlier. Her eyes widened for a split second. She swallowed, turning her head away so she didn't have to see the screen.

'David reacted to this photograph too,' Tara said. 'It scared him.'

Carolyn pursed her lips. 'You need to move out of my way.'

Tara could feel her own anger rising inside as the words burst out of her throat. 'You lied to Alice's family. And Mia's mind has been poisoned by not being able to say goodbye to Alice. You could help so many people by telling the truth.'

Carolyn began walking past Tara in the direction of the gallery without saying a word, her expression icy. Julia dropped her half-smoked cigarette and ground it out viciously with the heel of her shoe.

'Carolyn,' Tara called out. 'I'm not finished. You're a danger to your patients.'

Carolyn stopped and looked back. Tara imagined she heard a low growl come from her throat and she was about to say something, but then all three of them were distracted by the sound of slow, deliberate footsteps coming towards them.

FIFTY-SIX

David's smile was forced as he approached the three women. 'Tom said you'd be out here sneaking a smoke, Julia. He's been waiting for you to cut the cake.'

He ignored Carolyn, looking through her as though she did not exist.

Tara knew that the sensible thing to do would be to step away from this, but she could not resist. She held up the phone. 'I saw your reaction to this photograph of Alice. You were shocked.'

David's eyes flickered to Carolyn, who avoided his gaze. Then he composed himself, speaking to Julia with another stiff smile. 'Are you coming? Or shall I tell them to go ahead without you?'

Tara found herself biting her bottom lip in frustration. This pact of silence had endured for the past three years. Those fragments that would complete the picture were still missing. She looked down at that beautiful picture of Alice, wrapped up in the scarf as vibrant as her smile.

'Jungle Love by Hermès,' Carolyn said.

Tara turned to her in surprise.

'That's the name of the scarf Alice is wearing in that photo. David gave it to her.'

'Have you lost your mind?' David said.

'I have the receipt,' Carolyn turned to look squarely at David now. 'I found a gift bag from Harrods in your apartment and I couldn't resist a peek inside. I saw a scarf and some lingerie. All very expensive. I hoped you'd give it to me, but of course you didn't. It was a gift for Alice. Your son's girlfriend. Was she wearing that scarf for you, David, on the night she died?'

'If you have the receipt, Carolyn, then you have questions to answer.' David turned to Tara. 'This is what I was trying to tell you about. It's an illness.'

'Except it's all going to be on your credit card, isn't it?'

'For God's sake. Don't be ridiculous.' David spoke through gritted teeth.

Julia gave a shrill bitter laugh. 'That's what he does, Doctor Black, he tries to make you think you're crazy to cover up his lies. That's what I put up with for thirty-odd years.'

David took a few steps forward, backing Julia up against the wall of the alley. 'Did you put them up to this?'

'Get off me.' Julia shoved him backwards with both hands, forcefully.

The three women faced him, standing in a semi-circle around him. It was his turn to be backed up against the damp wall.

'They found fibres in Alice's throat,' Tara said. 'I wonder if they would match that scarf. It sounds very distinctive.'

Julia's eyes widened. Her hand went to her throat. Perhaps even she had not understood what David Phillips was capable of.

'David?' Julia choked out. 'Do you have any idea what this will do to Tom?'

'Calm down, Julia. Yes, I have a history of seeing other

women, due to being in a very unsatisfying marriage, but I can assure you that my son's girlfriend was not one of them. Now – are you coming to cut the cake or not? I'm not going to engage in this idiocy any longer.'

'Where were you that night, David?' Carolyn asked. 'I waited for you, but you never turned up.'

'And your phone was turned off all night,' Julia added

Tara felt the embers of satisfaction lighting up in her belly. The two women had finally decided to turn on him.

'You're both insane.' David laughed, but nervously.

'I have always suspected that you went out to the cottage to meet Alice Kelly that night,' Carolyn said.

Then it was Julia's turn. 'Alice let slip that you talked to her about me. You were badmouthing me and I know you would never have done that in front of Tom. So how many times was Alice alone with you?'

Tara took a step forwards. The three women were in a line, standing shoulder to shoulder. 'Did you persuade Alice to steal Julia's data for you?' Were you grooming your son's girlfriend?'

Aggression was flowing off David in waves. The civilised mask dropped away and the real David Phillips, the man Carolyn and Julia loathed, was standing in front of them, scowling and snarling as he spoke. 'Is it not enough that my bitch of an ex-wife stole my house, went after every penny I had, left me living in some new-build shoebox on the seventh fucking floor and alienated me from my younger son? And now I have to put up with this *bullshit* from a bunch of hysterical women!'

'What went wrong that night?' Tara asked him. 'Alice was on her way to meet you, so what happened? Did she change her mind about giving you that memory stick? Did you lose your temper? Did you try to seduce her and she rejected you? Did you rape her?'

'Another meddling, controlling bitch of a therapist, just what the world needs.'

David Phillips hated women.

'Did you hurt Alice?'

Tara turned at the sound of Mia's voice. She had no idea how long Mia had been standing and watching them.

David took a breath but he was off balance, lost for words.

'Did you hurt Alice? *Answer me!*'

'Of course I didn't hurt Alice.' David was attempting to speak in a more reasonable tone, trying to put the civilised mask back on. Only it didn't quite fit. 'Why don't we all calm down and not ruin Tom's birthday, all right?'

'Alice would never tell me who gave her that scarf. I knew there was something fishy about her having a Hermès piece.' Mia's voice was more determined than Tara had ever heard it; every shred of anxiety had vanished. 'What exactly was the nature of your relationship with my friend?'

'All right.' David put his hands in his trouser pockets, looking between the four of them now. 'You want to know about my relationship with Alice? I've always tried to protect you from this, Mia, but I suppose I have no choice now. Alice was very important to me because Tom was very much in love with her and I hoped that she would be my daughter-in-law. Alice was and always will be the love of Tom's life.'

Tara saw the flash of pain in Mia's eyes. David knew exactly where to insert the knife; his cruelty had a surgeon's precision. She moved towards Mia, putting a hand on her back, trying to guide her away before David could do any more damage. 'Let's go back inside—'

But Mia would not budge and David wasn't finished.

'It was obvious to me, and frankly to everyone who knew my son, that Tom was on the rebound after Alice's death. Most of all, I should think it was obvious to you, Mia. But you took full advantage, didn't you? And who could blame you? Tom is a good man. You only had one thing going for you, and you milked it for all it was worth. You were all that was left of Tom's connection to Alice.'

David was a master of gaslighting. He was desperately trying to divert attention away from what he'd done, and still refusing to take a shred of responsibility.

To Tara's relief, Mia stayed completely composed. She would not be provoked. 'You're so cruel, David. And you're a liar. I understand now why Julia and Freddie hate you so much.'

Tara tried to steer Mia away, but she was resisting. Her body felt like a coiled spring.

David was coming closer and closer. He was in full swing, out of control now. He wanted to destroy.

'You know Tom married you on the rebound, don't you? He married you out of pity.' David leered over them, barking at them, his spittle landing on their faces. 'Anyone could see from a mile away you were mentally unstable. But Tom felt sorry for you, that's all it was. I knew you'd make his life a living hell!'

'You bastard!' Mia lunged at him, slapping his face.

David laughed at her. 'Want to give that another go, crazy lady?'

'Mia, don't. Don't give him the satisfaction.' Tara pulled her away and this time Mia didn't put up a fight.

David was smirking as he straightened his coat. 'You'd better pull yourself together, Mia, or you won't keep custody of your daughter for very long. Clearly, despite all the therapy you've had, you're far from cured.'

Mia put a hand protectively across her belly.

Tara tried to shield Mia as she spoke, planting herself between the younger woman and David. 'I think you groomed Alice. I think you palpated until you found her weak spots, her longing and her feeling of deprivation. You used her and convinced her to steal for you so you could get leverage over your ex-wife. I think that Alice left the cottage that night to come and meet you because she was supposed to give you the memory stick. But something went wrong. Maybe Alice changed her mind. Maybe Mia had got through to her and convinced her that what she was doing was wrong. And that's when you lost control and you took all of your rage at Julia out on Alice.'

Tara had no way of knowing if what she was saying was anywhere close to the truth. Her gut told her it was, but there was no tangible proof, only strands of circumstantial evidence. Mia was listening to every word though, and maybe this narrative would at least give her an alternative ending to her trauma. A better memory.

David clapped, slowly. 'What a great story. That would suit all you bloodsucking vampires, wouldn't it? To pin this all on me and alienate me from my son and my granddaughter.'

'Don't you dare ever speak to my wife or my mother like that again.' Tom was walking towards them. He came to stand with Mia and Tara, who were huddled together, and he put his arm around Mia's shoulder, pulling her close.

Now Carolyn spoke up. 'Doctor Black is right, isn't she? You lost your temper, didn't you, David? You can't control yourself around women. You enjoy hurting us.'

Then it was Julia's turn. 'I never told anyone what you did to me,' she said. 'I blamed myself, just like you taught me to. I believed I provoked you, because that's what you told me. Every time you put your hands around my throat, I believed it was my fault. Is that what you did to Alice?'

Mia and Tom were looking at her in horror.

David turned to his son. 'I saved you, my boy. I saved you from that whore. Alice threw herself at me. Opened her legs every chance she got, betrayed you. She would have made your life a living hell.'

Tom's was holding tight to Mia's hand. 'You will never, ever get anywhere near your granddaughter. I'll make sure of that.'

Without another word, David put his hands in his jacket pockets and turned around and walked in the opposite direction, towards Heath Street. He disappeared around the bend in the alleyway without looking back.

Mia moved closer into Tom, her head sinking into his chest as Tom kissed the top of her head.

FIFTY-SEVEN

FIFTEEN MINUTES BEFORE ALICE'S DEATH

As Alice walks along the lane, she feels carefully around her temple to see if she's still bleeding. She doesn't think so. She'd hit her head on something on the ground when she'd fallen, when that brute Freddie had come for her. She's probably going to have a serious bump there tomorrow.

She wants to get this over with. All she wants is to go back to bed. David won't be thrilled when he finds out that he drove all the way out here for nothing, because she doesn't have that memory stick. Maybe he'll give her a lift back to the cottage because she really doesn't feel up to walking. She's not feeling too good; her head is pounding.

Alice pulls the scarf more tightly around her shoulders. She'll miss the feel of it. She loves the softness of it, the bright colours, the two tigers most of all. But Mia is right, it's time to give everything back, everything she has stolen. She should never have accepted the gift in the first place. She sees it for what it is now: a bribe.

Crack. Alice stops and looks behind her, anxious at the sound.

A strange, animal cry comes out of the darkness. A fox, maybe. Or a cat in heat.

She tries to walk faster, her temple throbbing as she lights the lane ahead with a torch. She can hardly see two feet in front of her. She's nearly reached the place where she and David arranged to meet. It's not far from where she and Mia were out taking photos that morning, a small space carved out of the lane where cars can pull over.

This was a stupid bloody idea, walking along country roads in the dark. It's barely five-hundred metres from the cottage, but it's starting to feel much longer.

She's so relieved when she sees the shape of David's Mercedes looming in the darkness. The headlights are turned off.

She's almost running now. She reaches the passenger door, fumbles around and finds the doorhandle. She pulls on it, but it's locked. She pulls again, feeling afraid, as though Freddie or Julia might jump out at her from the darkness. What a night. Serves her right, she has to admit. Talk about Karma.

The door opens. Alice slips inside, into the softness of the leather seat, into the crisp smell of David's aftershave. She lays her head back against the headrest and lets out a deep sigh.

'Poor baby. Were you afraid of the dark?'

Alice feels sick about this whole thing. It's all got out of hand.

'David, you know, I've been thinking. Maybe this isn't such a good idea.'

The feeling of guilt had started when Alice had looked into Mia's eyes as Mia begged her not to hurt Julia. Then it grew stronger. She'd had the strongest urge to take Tom's necklace off before she went out to meet his father and betray his mother. And now, even though nothing has ever happened between her and David – not like that – she feels disloyal and deceitful.

He holds out his hand. 'Come on, don't tease. Where is it?'

She shakes her head. 'I don't have the memory stick. I chucked it into the river. I felt bad, Julia's been good to me.'

'So what the hell am I doing out here?'

The shift in his mood unsettles her.

David had seemed so wise. So caring. And Alice had always had a thing for older men; she couldn't help it. He'd started by giving her his number, and making time to talk to her about her career. It was David who'd made the introduction to James Sharp at the Mayfair gallery. Afterwards, he'd taken her to an expensive restaurant and they'd drunk ridiculously expensive wine, and he'd told her all about his problems with Julia. She'd thought it was all harmless.

David had asked her not to tell Tom about their boozy lunch, because of what he'd confided in her about his ex-wife.

Alice pulls the scarf away from around her neck. Without it, she feels cold. 'I need to give this back to you.'

'What are you talking about?'

She leans across and drops it in his lap. 'I can't accept this.'

'Too late, you already did.' He picks up the scarf, drapes it around her neck again. 'If you don't have anything to give me, then why did you make me drive all the way out here to see you?'

His tone has shifted again. It's sleazy now as David grabs the ends of the scarf and pulls her towards him. 'I think I can guess what you really want.'

Alice pushes him away. 'Stop.'

He doesn't listen; he's crushing his mouth against hers. She shoves him back, hard this time, alarms bells screaming in her ears.

'Let me out.' Alice pulls on the doorhandle but it's locked.

'Little cocktease, aren't you?' His fingers grab at her, pulling her T-shirt lower, his hand pushing up between her legs. 'Tell me what you really want.'

'I said *stop*.' She's had enough of being pushed around for one night. 'Get off me or I'll tell Tom what a snake his father is.'

He slams her head back against the window glass. 'Well then you'll have to tell him what a whore his girlfriend is.'

Alice is in shock. She can't move or speak. She's crushed up against the car door and David is pulling the ends of the scarf tight around her throat and she's beginning to feel afraid.

She tries to fight back, scratching at his face, but he's too strong, and the scarf draws tighter and tighter around her throat. She's trying to dig her fingernails in to pull it away, to get some air. He won't let go, won't loosen the pressure.

'Please, stop.' She can barely get the words out. Her head is thudding and the scarf is squeezed so, so tight. 'Please, I'm sorry. I'm sorry.'

David's face is red, his eyes somewhere else; he is someone else.

Alice feels like she's about to pass out.

She doesn't want to die.

She has so little breath, so little energy, and he's pressing so tight around her throat and she can't breathe, her nails grasping at silk, and she's terrified, and all she sees are the stars exploding.

Please stop. I can't breathe.

She has no voice.

FIFTY-EIGHT

Tara was sitting alone at a café on a cobbled square in the heart of the old town. The tables around her, which had been empty when she had first arrived early that morning, were filling up. She didn't know a soul in this remote little town in southern Italy.

Except, maybe, Matthew. Only she might not know her brother anymore either.

She was staying in a modest bed and breakfast run by a kindly Italian lady who didn't speak any English but who hovered over Tara at breakfast trying to get her to eat more of the feast that could feed at least six people.

She had left London early on the morning after the party at the Leonard Gallery. It was obvious to all of them who had witnessed the scene in that alley that David Phillips was responsible for Alice Kelly's death. He had arranged to meet with Alice the night she died, and something had gone wrong. His hatred of women had erupted, and so had the violence inside of him.

Tara did not know whether any of the others would choose

to go to the police to report what they knew, but she had written everything up in detail.

It had been a relief to send her report over to DS Ayola, even though Tara did not know whether she would think there was enough new evidence to re-investigate. There was a chance the police may well take no further action. If anything, her report would potentially create extra work the officers did not need or want in a case that they were satisfied was already resolved. But that side of things was not her responsibility. At least, she told herself, even if there was no firm evidence, Mia and Tom now knew the real David Phillips.

There was still the question of how unethically Carolyn had acted, and whether she was safe to be seeing patients, but Tara would deal with that when she was back in London. And Freddie was still missing.

As the minutes ticked by, sitting at the table, with a double espresso and a bottle of water in front of her, she felt as though she was watching a foreign movie, detached from her own life. This could not be real. She may be about to face the last of her family demons. Closure was within touching distance.

There was a family at the table next to her. Tourists. Americans, from the sound of it. A little girl with long dark hair was playing cards with one of the adults, smiling and swaying to the music playing from the speakers overhead. The girl looked so happy, so loved and protected. Tara felt wistful for a sense of safety she would never know.

She rubbed her palms against the plastic arms of the chair and pushed the soles of her trainers down onto the cobblestones. She inhaled the fresh sea air.

She could see why someone would choose this place if they were running away. It was small, remote and beautiful. On her right, there was the Adriatic Sea and on her left were the walls of an ancient castle. Opposite her, across the square, was a magnificent villa set behind tall pines.

From where she sat, Tara had a view of the entire piazza and also of the two street entrances leading onto it. According to Ray Jameson's source, the man she was looking for, the one in the photograph, came here every morning, at the same time. Tara had his address too, but she wasn't brave enough – or reckless enough – to try to see him at home. Ray was right; she no longer knew who Matthew was. A public meeting would be better, at least in the first instance.

And then, at precisely eight thirty, there he was, walking across the square. Baseball cap, greying beard, rake thin, wearing a denim shirt and jeans. Frustratingly, he sat down at a table on the far side of the café with his back to her. He and the waitress seemed to share a casual familiarity, and from their body language, Tara could tell he was a regular. They were too far away for her to pick up any of their conversation.

The worst part was that she still did not know if the man she was looking at was her brother. It felt desperately wrong that she did not recognise him, but then it had been almost three decades. The brother she knew was in his early twenties, barely an adult. This man looked to be around fifty, which would be about the right age for Matthew now.

When the waitress had left his table, Tara pushed back her chair, got up and walked across the café, weaving between tables on unsteady legs.

'Matthew?' A sense of being on autopilot had kicked in, and it was as if Tara was watching herself from above as she stood beside his table.

He looked up. He had responded to that name. At first, there was no recognition at all when he saw her face. No reaction. But then, shock maybe? There was definitely... something. The first tiny bit of hope lit up in her core.

Tara needed to see his eyes to be absolutely sure. 'Please, would you take off your sunglasses?'

He did as she asked, laying them slowly down on the table-top. *So he speaks English.* Tara stared, examining every millimetre of his face, until she found the Matthew she knew – behind the sunburn and the lines around his eyes, in the shape of his nose and mouth. In those brown eyes, which were so like hers.

'Matthew?' she repeated.

'You must be mistaken.' He put his sunglasses back on.

It was too late; she had already seen the recognition in his eyes.

'I don't think so.' Tara pulled out a chair and sat down opposite him. Neither of them spoke.

Why do you not want to see me?

Then the waitress was back with his espresso and a glass of water and Matthew thanked her in Italian. '*Grazie.*'

The woman asked Tara if she wanted anything else. Tara shook her head. By the time she turned back to him, Matthew was pulling the cap down lower over his face. He refused to look at her as he got up and walked away, leaving his coffee untouched.

When she got back to the bed and breakfast, Tara tried to hide her red eyes behind sunglasses, but the owner, who seemed to hold herself personally responsible for Tara's wellbeing, was not fooled. Tara did her best to reassure her that nothing was wrong, though she was pretty sure that most of what she was saying was lost in translation. Then she took herself to bed, closing the shutters to block out the sun.

Her brother was alive. She was not mistaken about his identity.

On one level, that was a joy. On another, it was devastating. The reunion she had dared to fantasize about was never going to happen. After all these years he had not reached out to her. No hug. Not even a hello.

Tara had never wanted to believe that Matthew had left her willingly. Now, she had no choice but to face up to what she had been denying all these years: he did not want anything to do with her. Matthew had not wanted her to find him.

The sobbing came on suddenly and she gave in to it, lying on her side in her bed until she eventually fell asleep.

When she woke, it was after lunch and the small town had shut down for the afternoon. Tara sat down at the rickety desk in her room, tore a page out of the new, empty notebook she carried around out of habit, and wrote her brother a letter.

Dear Matthew,

Daniel helped me to find you. I have now taken over his bank account, and I will continue to make the transfers to you, no matter what happens.

 I came here because I miss you every single day.

 If you do not feel the same way, I can accept that. But if you would like to talk, even once, I will be on the piazza tonight, at nine. I hope you come.

I love you.

She left it unsigned. She would not have known whether to put her old name, or the new one. With Matthew, she wasn't sure who she was anymore.

FIFTY-NINE

The night was pleasantly mild, and when Tara arrived at the square it was busier than she had expected. The space was being set up for an open-air concert, with a stage and several rows of chairs. Musicians dressed all in black were arriving carrying their instruments.

Tara sat at the table Matthew had chosen that morning.

Earlier that afternoon, before the rest of the town had emerged from the afternoon nap, she had taken a walk through the silent streets to the address Ray had given her, where Matthew lived in an apartment above a *tabaccheria* in a small building on the main shopping street.

She had put her note through the letterbox, and then left. If Matthew did not respond to it, she would make her peace with that. In effect, he was a stranger to her now. The old Matthew had died the same night her parents did.

Five minutes to nine. Tara checked her phone and found nothing of interest. It was dark now. Snatches of string instruments and horns floated across to her table as the musicians prepared to play. Small children ran around and around in circles, weaving between the stalls selling pancakes, their shouts

and laughter puncturing the night. The smell of melted chocolate filled the air. For some reason, the joy in the children's
voices brought on an intense longing and her eyes teared up
again.

So it was through blurred vision that she saw a now familiar
bearded figure moving across the piazza towards her. When he
reached her table, he removed his cap, revealing tousled grey
hair underneath, which he pushed back with sunburned hands.

'I quite like the beard,' she said. 'And the tan.'

'I work outdoors. On an olive tree farm.'

His voice was just the same. And maybe it was the blurry
vision, but his face was starting to become more familiar too,
changing into the one she remembered.

'Let's walk,' he said.

Tara stood up, securing the strap of her bag across her chest
and leaving a few euro coins behind on the table, hoping it was
enough for the coffee she'd ordered. Matthew had already
started walking. She followed him through the narrow lanes of
the old town, until they reached a street with a steep incline,
and then they were heading down and down, towards the sea.

At first, they walked in silence, stopping often to flatten
themselves against the wall to let cars pass by. Tara's belly was
churning. She might be about to get the answers to questions
that had haunted her most of her life and now she wasn't sure
she was ready for the truth.

Why did you leave me?

Headlights loomed ahead and Tara shrank back. This road
was pretty dangerous.

After a while, she felt herself becoming warmer and looser.
She kept glancing at his face in the darkness, getting used to
him again. Being with Matthew was like having a part of her
childhood back; a missing piece of her heart returned. She
wondered if he felt the same way.

They had begun an even steeper descent, down several

flights of steps. Tara held on to the handrail. On either side
there were flower beds planted with large, vicious-looking cacti.

Since Matthew was saying nothing yet, Tara began. 'I don't
remember much about the night our parents were killed.'

Silence. This might be her one chance and she couldn't
waste time. She had to dive straight in. Matthew was so distant;
there was every chance he may choose to disappear again.

'I remember the party,' she said, 'the one you weren't
supposed to have while our parents were away for the weekend.
I remember all the alcohol you bought, and how you laid the
bottles out on the kitchen counters. I remember you and Sabine,
all over each other as usual. I remember the house being full of
people and dark and noisy. At some point, it all... fades away.
Everything else I know comes from witnesses and whatever was
in the police reports. Please, tell me what you know.'

At last, Matthew began to speak. 'They came home early.
Mum went straight up to their room, but Dad stayed downstairs, yelling at everyone to clear out. Once they'd all left, he let
me have it. *"You will clean up every single inch of this house, do
you understand me? Do you understand?"'* Matthew raised his
voice, in an almost perfect imitation of their father.

They'd reached the bottom of the steps. Matthew moved
confidently along another winding footpath; this one was
narrower than any of the others they'd walked down that night,
and enclosed between two high walls. Tara had to work to keep
up with his pace.

'I ignored him,' Matthew said, 'and then I threw up all over
rug in the living room. After that, I went to the kitchen and sat
on the floor with a bottle of vodka.'

'You always did know how to wind him up.' Tara remembered their conflict so well, and how Matthew would almost
goad their father into a deeper fury.

'He wanted to hit me so badly,' Matthew said. 'I could see it,
in his eyes and his fists. He was itching for it. He swore a lot and

grabbed me by the back of my T-shirt and threw me out of the house, down the back stairs. Luckily there were only three of them.'

He half-smiled. This was the old Matthew she recognised well, always making a joke out of his pain.

'I'm sorry,' she said.

'Don't be. You haven't heard the end of the story.'

Strains of a violin and high notes of an opera singer floated down from the square above. Tara wished they'd stayed up there, safe, surrounded by light and life and other people. This narrow path stank of damp and seemed to be endless.

'What happened next?' She had a horrible, sinking feeling as she asked that question.

What if Ray Jameson had read this situation right? Who was she with, exactly?

'After a while, he unlocked the back door and told me I'd better get back inside and clean up my own vomit. I grabbed a bunch of roller towel and some spray from the kitchen and went into the living room. I got down on my hands and knees, trying to get the muck out of the carpet.'

Matthew stopped. He leaned against the wall a moment. Even in the dark, Tara could see that large wet circles had formed under the arms of his T-shirt. He suddenly heaved, as though he might throw up.

GET DOWN.

She heard her father's voice. She remembered.

'He came up behind me and pushed my face into the mess on the carpet.' Matthew stopped. 'Are you sure you want to hear this?'

Tara nodded, feeling queasy at what was still to come.

SIXTY

To Tara's relief, they had reached the end of the claustrophobic passageway and suddenly the marina was spread out in front of them, with a wide promenade, lights everywhere and a smattering of people out walking. In the window of a café, the arm of a hot chocolate machine swirled thick, warm liquid around in a glass vat.

Matthew kept walking, heading down a wide set of winding stairs towards the sea. The bay was calm, with the sound of waves lapping against the pebbled shore and myriad small fishing boats bobbing gently on the water. Matthew sat down on a low concrete wall. Tara sat next to him; not too close but not too far. They were the only ones there.

She gathered herself. Now she'd started this, she had to finish. 'I want to know everything.'

Matthew was calm. Resigned. 'I was on my hands and knees, and he gripped the back of my neck and shoved me down, pushing my face into the carpet. I couldn't breathe. His knee was in my back, in my kidneys... I was scared and furious and I lost it. It was fast, but I remember most of it. I shoved him off me and I grabbed that stupid, heavy statue of a cat that

Mum kept next to the fireplace, and I smashed it into the side of his head and I kept pounding and pounding and I didn't stop.'

For a moment, Tara mentally checked out. She was an impartial observer, listening to a patient, to someone else's story. Then the cold wind coming off the sea brought her back to her own body. And it all came crashing down on her, like a wave hitting the shoreline. The bitter, painful truth.

'I didn't want to stop,' Matthew said, 'even when I knew... even when he wasn't moving.'

All of these years Tara had wished and pretended that her brother could not have done what everyone else believed he had. She'd clung to the hope that Matthew was innocent. That he had run because he was somehow traumatised. She had feared he was dead, and that the person who had murdered her parents had murdered her brother too. Because death was the only reason she could ever think of that her brother wouldn't come and find her.

She had clung to the memory of the Matthew she knew. The gentle boy who loved dogs and playing chess and would help her so patiently with her reading. The big brother who held her hand and took her to school and hugged her goodbye and even stayed to watch her walk into the classroom. She barely remembered the rest. The angry teenager. The hate-filled years.

And now, there was truth. Tara looked at his profile as he stared straight out to the ocean. She thought of what Julia had told her about David Phillips, and how he could not love his younger son. The emotional scarring caused by a parent's cruelty was a form of death. Death of a boy's love for his father, of his self-esteem, of his soul.

What did it say about her that she could not condemn her brother for being a killer?

Matthew had gone silent.

'Our father wasn't the only one killed that night. So what happened afterwards?'

'I'm not sure. After that it's all in short bursts. Flashes. After I... after he wasn't moving, I went outside and downed what was left of the vodka. I think I threw up again, in one of the flowerbeds. And then Daniel came back.'

'Daniel?'

'He said he had a bad feeling. He'd been walking down to the station after Dad had kicked everyone out, but then he turned around and came back to the house. There was no answer at the front door, so he came round the back. I was like a zombie. All I wanted was to lie down and pass out but he wouldn't let me. He didn't ask me anything, but I guess... I guess he saw the blood. He made me start walking, across the Heath. At some point, we got in a taxi back to his place. I took a shower, dressed in his clothes, took his passport, and then we both got on the Tube at West Hampstead. Daniel came with me as far as St Pancras and he bought me a ticket and I just kept going. It was crazy. I don't know what I was thinking exactly, but I do know I wanted to get as far away as I could from that house. I knew the police would come for me and I didn't want to go to jail. I ended up in France, then Switzerland, then I went south as far as I could go. Until the train line ended and I was here and I couldn't go anymore. And so I stayed.'

Connections were fizzing in Tara's mind.

So that was how Daniel knew where Matthew was. Daniel had helped him run. Maybe that sense of guilt was also what bound the two of them together all those years. Daniel had known about the killing.

It was hard to be furious with a dead person, but Tara was very, very close. The enormity of what Daniel had kept from her was too much.

There was something that seemed incongruous in Matthew's story, though. He said he'd felt like a zombie, that he'd consumed a huge amount of alcohol, and that his memory was patchy, but on the other hand, he'd been able to travel right across Europe with a passport that did not belong to him. So he must have had his wits about him more than he wanted to admit. He'd gone into self-preservation mode.

And he had not mentioned remorse, either. Not once.

This whole time he'd been talking, he hadn't looked at her; he'd been staring out at the water. He was telling her what she wanted to know, but he was also keeping her out. And there was still one crucial part of that night he'd left out.

'What happened to Mum?' she asked him.

'I don't know. I swear. When I left the house that night, I didn't know she'd died. I found out later.'

'From Daniel?'

He nodded.

'Do you think you could have done something to her that you don't remember?'

'It's possible. Like I said, I'd been drinking all night, I was completely off my head. But if I did hurt her, I don't remember it.'

The images Tara had been avoiding since that night on Wildway Close pushed their way into her mind. She had seen herself going into her parents' room; she had felt intense frustration and the impulse to act out her own pain. She had pictured herself holding that pillow.

But she was not a violent person. She could never have done what she'd imagined. All those nights, when she'd gone back to the old house on Wildway Close, she had tried so hard to remember that she had pictured many, many different scenes. None of them had ever felt true.

'Could there have been someone else in the house?' she asked, clinging on to a last little bit of hope.

'I don't remember seeing anyone else.'

'If it was me—' Tara paused. She had to ask the question

that had defined her life. 'If it was me... I mean, if you saw me doing something violent in the house that night, I want you to tell me.'

Finally, he turned to look at her. He didn't answer straight away. His eyes were dark, mirroring her own.

'I want to know.'

'I don't remember you being there. I don't remember seeing you do anything. But then, there are still blanks in my memory. Bits of time I don't see.'

Were she and Matthew the same? Had they both lost control that night when pushed too far by the people who were meant to love and protect them?

No. The simplest explanation was that if Matthew could kill their father, he was capable of killing their mother too, only perhaps his mind would not accept that second crime.

Maybe he had killed their mother so he did not have to see himself reflected in her eyes as a monster. Maybe that's why he'd run.

'Matthew, have you ever hurt anyone else since that night?'

'Never. I swear.'

Now, the question that lodged like a knife in her heart. 'Why did you never contact me after all these years?'

He shrugged. 'I wanted you to be safe.'

'From what?'

'I thought that you could have a life. A normal life. Without hiding. And...' Now he looked at her, really making eye contact for the first time. 'I was ashamed. I didn't want you to see me that way. What I'd done... I never wanted to look at you.'

So he did remember: how she'd adored him and looked up to him.

Matthew was not the same, though. Not her big brother, not her protector anymore. Not the person who loved her most in the world and would always keep her safe.

'I didn't want to go to prison for what I did,' he said. 'I was scared of living in a cell. So I chose to live like this. A nobody. Hiding. But I'm outside, I'm not in a cage.'

'If you had given yourself up, you'd probably be a free man by now.'

'I'll never be free. I killed my own father.'

Tara wanted to reach out and hold his hand, but she couldn't.

She looked at her brother, trying to understand how he felt. There was grief behind his words, but she couldn't tell if the grief was for their father, or for himself and what had become of his life.

What a waste.

Did Matthew deserve forgiveness? He had been young, and a victim of emotional abuse. None of that justified killing a man, but even the justice system – had he faced up to what he'd done – would have considered him eligible for parole by now. And she too may have found freedom long before.

'Daniel never told me where you were,' she said. 'All these years. And he knew how desperate I was to find you.'

'I made him promise. I threatened him. I said I'd disappear again if he dragged you into this.'

'But the two of you stayed in contact?'

'For a while. At first, he was my lifeline. Back then, I couldn't work. I had no papers and I had to destroy the passport because I knew it would be reported lost or stolen. He helped me with money to survive.'

'And he kept sending you money, all these years?'

'Always. Even when I said I didn't want it anymore. Even when I cut off all contact. I have plenty of work now. People know me around here, they trust me. I don't keep the money. I give it away.'

The fact that Matthew had cut off all communication in a way made Daniel's betrayal seem less brutal. Maybe Daniel thought there was no point in Tara knowing her brother was alive if Matthew didn't want anything to do with her. Maybe he didn't want Tara to know her brother was a killer.

Maybe Daniel's silence had been an act of mercy. She'd rather see it that way.

It struck Tara that Matthew might not even know that Daniel had died.

Daniel died last year. It was sudden, in a hit-and-run accident, and I was with him at the end. She could not say those words out loud. That was too much.

Tara shivered. The wind coming off the water was biting.

'Can you imagine what it was like for me, not knowing if you were dead or alive?' she said instead.

'I'm sorry.'

She wanted him to reach out and hold her hand. Put his arm around her shoulder. Instead, he moved slightly further away on that cold concrete wall and she knew they didn't have much more time.

'In the beginning,' she said, 'after you left, I felt like I was dying. Being separated from you hurt more than anything else.'

How could you leave me?

'We used to be so close.' She was trying, and failing, to reach him.

The worst thing, the salt in the wound, was her sense that Matthew regretted the fact that she had tracked him down. He wasn't happy to see her, and this conversation was a burden for him. It was finally sinking in that the reunion she had fantasized about was never going to be.

'So,' she said, 'what do we do now?'

'I can't offer you anything. I'm sorry. I'm broken.'

'You're my brother.'

Matthew left, again. He stood up and walked away from her without another word. The temperature had dropped sharply, and the wind snapped at her face and her bare hands as she sat on the low concrete wall in front of the bay by herself.

Their time together had not been what Tara had hoped for, but strangely, she felt relief. She had found him. Her brother was alive. In his own way, he was well.

Everything changes. There is still hope.

A group of young people had gathered next to her. They were laughing, drinking, making out. It was time to go home. Except that when she stood up, had dusted off her jeans, and was putting the strap of her bag across her chest, Tara realised she had no idea how to find her way back through those pathways and up the steep hill to the bed and breakfast.

She began walking anyway, to keep warm. She would start by making her way up the first, well-lit staircase to the café, where she'd seen that hot chocolate machine, and from there she'd ask directions or maybe she'd find a taxi.

Maybe she would go back to the piazza, catch the end of the concert, and drink a glass of wine. Maybe tomorrow, she'd take a day trip somewhere, to see more of this place that Matthew had made a home.

She became aware of footsteps coming up behind her. *Matthew.* She turned around, smiling, ready to—

'Gelato?' A cabochon emerald glinted in its gold bed, catching the glow of the streetlamp.

Ray Jameson held out an ice cream cone in one of his solid, steady hands. 'I wasn't sure which flavour to get you. I thought coffee would be a safe bet.'

SIXTY-ONE

Everything felt different when Tara walked into the mews house on her first day back in London one week later. She was different. Lighter.

She bent down to pick up the post that had stacked up inside the door while she was gone and then turned on the heating before going upstairs to put on some strong coffee. In the kitchen, she messaged Olivia, while brushing away some silvery dog hair that had somehow found its way onto her black trousers. Ray's jet was full of Ziggy's fur.

She sat down at her desk with her mug and dealt with a bunch of work emails she'd not responded to while she was away. New enquiries, mainly. Then she flipped through the envelopes. Bank statements and various utility bills, interspersed with colourful flyers advertising a bunch of new restaurants that had popped up in the area. One letter was more interesting than the rest. A rich cream-coloured envelope with Tara's name and address written in a neat blue cursive script. No name or return address on the back

Tara slid her letter opener under the flap and opened it with a sharp movement. There was one page inside on heavyweight paper in the same neat blue script. Her eyes ran down to the bottom of the page. It was from Carolyn Goring.

The note was concise and direct. Carolyn had gone to the police to make a full statement about the night Alice was killed. She also informed Tara that she was taking a sabbatical from her psychotherapy practice, and was enrolled in an intensive treatment programme herself. For the time being, she had suspended her professional registration.

Tara was relieved. This spared her from having to take any action herself. Carolyn could pose a danger to other patients; she had missed an important diagnosis and she had let her personal issues get in the way of treating Mia, whether she admitted it or not.

After she'd filed Carolyn's letter away with Mia's notes, Tara found a new message on her phone. She was pleasantly surprised to see that it was from Louis at the gym.

I've missed you at kettle bells. Hope to see you soon??

She had missed that class. Maybe she missed him too, a little.

Later, Tara would head to the gym, but first she had arranged to meet with Mia.

There was something familiar, reassuring even, about navigating the hospital corridors: the blue and white signs, the arrows directing you where to go, the linoleum floors, the fluorescent lighting. It was like slipping back into an old routine, or like going home. Tara still hadn't got used to the solitary nature of private practice, especially since Olivia had been on maternity leave. And it had been a wrench, leaving the place where she had found Matthew to return to her slightly lonely life.

When Tara entered Freddie's hospital room, Mia was at his

bedside with her new baby fast asleep in a sling on her chest. Freddie was on his back, intubated, with his eyes closed.

He had been found, his bike crashed into a tree near his father's cottage in Oxfordshire. Tara had no doubt that this was related to his guilt about what he had done to Alice. Freddie had not regained consciousness since the accident, and that was not a good sign in terms of his prognosis. She wished she had said something more to him, something that would have stopped him getting back on that bike with what she was sure was a death wish.

Mia patted the baby's back gently through the sling as she greeted Tara with a hushed but warm hello. The tiny girl was wearing a knitted green cap. Her little face was adorable with rosy cheeks and cupid's bow lips.

'She's perfect,' Tara said.

'She really is.' Mia gazed down at her daughter with a look of sheer love.

'What's her name?'

'Flora. Goddess of flowers and spring.' The baby's little forehead crinkled as she frowned in her sleep. 'Though our little goddess is not a big fan of sleep unless someone is wearing her. Julia's been helping with the night feeds so Tom and I can get some rest. She's been a lifesaver.'

'That's great.' Tara had pulled up a chair on the opposite side of Freddie's bed.

For a while, the only sound was the pulsing of the monitor.

'Tom and I went to see DS Ayola together,' Mia said. 'We told her everything about David.'

'Do you know if they're re-investigating?'

Mia shook her head. 'I'm not sure. They don't tell us everything, so there may be more going on behind the scenes. David's cut off all contact from the family.'

Freddie's chest rose and fell as the ventilator moved air in and out of his lungs.

'How have you been feeling?' Tara asked.

'Different.' Mia looked across at Tara with a tentative smile. 'Really good, actually. I've read your report so many times. It helps. I feel like it's all sinking in.'

'I'm so glad.'

'What I saw in Carolyn's office feels more and more unreal. That whole time feels like some kind of strange dream now. I'd be lying if I said I could let it go completely, or that I don't think about how and why Alice died most days, but I do feel better in myself, even after those terrible things I saw when we were at the ponds.'

Mia looked down at the floor, as if seeing her mother's body once again. 'I'm starting to separate out the things my mother used to tell me from who I really am.'

This was a hopeful beginning. Mia was coping really well given that she was taking care of a new baby, recovering from depression, and dealing with shocking new information about Alice Kelly's death.

Mia bent down and kissed her baby's head, breathing in her smell. 'I love being her mum.'

Tara could see from her expression that she meant it.

'I really can't thank you enough.' Mia looked up and it was the first time Tara had seen her really smile. Her whole face came to life.

Tara felt both deeply happy and awkward. Sometimes it was harder to accept a client's gratitude than anything else they might throw at you.

'You know where I am if you need me,' she said.

Mia nodded, both her arms wrapped tight around her daughter in the sling.

A LETTER FROM LUANA

I want to express my appreciation to every single person who has read *The Guilty Patient*. If you would like to keep up to date with my latest releases, please sign up at the following link. Your email address will never be shared, and you can unsubscribe at any time:

www.bookouture.com/luana-lewis

If you enjoyed *The Guilty Patient*, I would be very grateful if you could write a review. These make a real difference in helping new readers to discover my books.

Thanks,

Luana Lewis

ACKNOWLEDGEMENTS

Thank you to my brilliant editor, Helen Jenner, for her guidance in making this book so much better. I am grateful to the entire Bookouture team for their ongoing publishing support and author care.

As always, Emma Smith Barton has been there every step of the way. Sarah Fisher and Rachel Tucker have given me ongoing and unwavering encouragement. John Truby, Sam Simkin and Sophie Hannah have all helped in my development as a writer. Finally, thanks to my family for their patience and for putting up with being ignored while I wrote through nights and weekends alongside my day job. I am very grateful.

PUBLISHING TEAM

Turning a manuscript into a book requires the efforts of many people. The publishing team at Bookouture would like to acknowledge everyone who contributed to this publication.

Audio
Alba Proko
Sinead O'Connor
Melissa Tran

Commercial
Lauren Morrissette
Hannah Richmond
Imogen Allport

Cover design
The Brewster Project

Data and analysis
Mark Alder
Mohamed Bussuri

Editorial
Helen Jenner
Ria Clare

Copyeditor
Lusana Taylor-Khan

Proofreader
Jennifer Davies

Marketing
Alex Crow
Melanie Price
Occy Carr
Cíara Rosney
Martyna Młynarska

Operations and distribution
Marina Valles
Stephanie Straub

Production
Hannah Snetsinger
Mandy Kullar
Jen Shannon
Ria Clare

Publicity
Kim Nash
Noelle Holten
Jess Readett
Sarah Hardy

Rights and contracts
Peta Nightingale
Richard King
Saidah Graham

Printed in Great Britain
by Amazon